# Ordinary Joe

## JON TECKMAN

THE BOROUGH PRESS

The Borough Press
An imprint of HarperCollins*Publishers*
1 London Bridge Street
London SE1 9GF

www.harpercollins.co.uk

A Paperback Original 2015
1

Copyright © Jon Teckman 2015

Jon Teckman asserts the moral right to be identified as the author of this work

A catalogue record for this book is
available from the British Library

ISBN: 978–0–00–811877–8

This novel is entirely a work of fiction.
The names, characters and incidents portrayed in it are
the work of the author's imagination. Any resemblance to
actual persons, living or dead, events or localities is
entirely coincidental.

Set in Minion by Palimpsest Book Production Limited,
Falkirk, Stirlingshire

Printed and bound in Great Britain by
Clays Ltd, St Ives plc

# ORDINARY JOE

Jon Teckman was born in Northampton in 1963. He served as an advisor on film policy to both Conservative and Labour governments before becoming Chief Executive of the British Film Institute in 1999. He now lives in Aylesbury, Buckinghamshire with his wife Anne and sons Joseph and Matthew. *Ordinary Joe* is his first novel.

For Mum who so loved books
and
for Mike who so loved life

'[you are both] so much in my thoughts at all times especially when I am successful and have greatly prospered in anything, that the recollection of [you] is an essential part of my being'

*after* Charles Dickens

# QUEENS, NEW YORK

The first thing I noticed about Olivia Finch – that very first time I saw her in the flesh – wasn't her breasts bouncing like pale pink pomegranates as she worked herself into a frenzy on her lover's lap, nor even her 'billion-dollar backside' – an epithet conferred upon her in a recent article in *Variety*, which reported that 'Olivia Finch's rear end is now a bigger box office draw than the faces of most of her Hollywood rivals.' No – God's truth – the first thing I noticed was the small, amateurish tattoo scratched into her left bicep in blue ink. 'John 3:16' it read. I looked it up in the Gideon when I got back to my room that evening: *For God so loved the world, that he gave his only begotten Son, that whosoever believeth in him should not perish, but have everlasting life.* I asked her about it later – when all the madness was at its maddest – and she told me it was just a stupid thing she'd had done when she was a kid and off her face on cheap booze. But, she said, she still liked the message: the idea that one person

1

could love another so much that they would give up everything for them.

That first time, all I could think about was how come I'd never noticed the tattoo before. It certainly hadn't been apparent in her Oscar-nominated role as Cleopatra in the recent remake of *Antony and Cleopatra*. They must have CGI-ed it out in the edit. It's impossible to know what's real and what's faked in the movies these days. Olivia's breasts looked real enough, but who knows what work she'd had done to them. And what she was doing to her co-star Jack Reynolds – while a small group of us stood watching in spellbound silence, occasionally nodding our appreciation as the couple pulled off a particularly complex manoeuvre – looked real too, but, of course, was only acting.

I was standing in a makeshift studio in Queens, dressed in a set of ill-fitting blue overalls, watching top director Arch Wingate re-shoot scenes for his latest movie, *Nothing Happened*. Standing next to me, his huge frame squeezed uncomfortably into a similar outfit, stood the film's producer, Buddy Guttenberg, beaming like a spoiled child on Christmas morning. The overalls had been his idea. 'I've been in this business twenty-five years, Joey,' he'd told me as we put on our costumes in an empty trailer in the studio car park, 'and I still haven't been allowed on a closed set unless I've been togged up as a gaffer or fucking electrician.'

Wingate had a justified reputation for being a perfectionist. The joke in Hollywood was that he would still be re-editing the film while the posters were going up outside the cinema. His passion and attention to detail made him one of the best film-makers in the business but also one of the most expensive. As one of the people responsible for raising the money for this film and ensuring a return on our investment, I should have been concerned about how much he was spending on almost imperceptible improvements to his creation. As a film buff, though, I was delighted by the chance to watch the great man in action.

'Bit more passion, please, Olly,' Wingate shouted as the couple cavorted wildly on the oversized bed. 'Jack, move your left leg across to the right half a foot so I can get a better view of Olly's butt as she straddles you. That's it! And give it a bit more energy, guys, OK? You're supposed to be enjoying this!'

Somehow, it seemed the most natural thing in the world for this beautiful couple to be making mad, passionate love in a tandoori-hot building on a warm October afternoon while Buddy and I looked on like spectators at a lawn tennis championship.

'So what do you reckon, Joe? Happy with the way we're spending your money?' Buddy whispered from the corner of his mouth, elbowing me sharply in the ribs to make sure he had my full attention.

'It's amazing, Buddy,' I replied. 'The camera angles Mr Wingate is going for are incredible. No one else would dream of shooting it like that.'

'Camera angles?' Buddy laughed, 'Fuck the camera angles, Joey – have you ever seen tits like those? Jesus, Mary and Joseph! She's like the Venus de fucking Milo with arms! That girl is so hot she's melting the polar ice caps all by herself. Those UN Climate Conference guys are considering having her banned to save the fucking planet.'

After half an hour of repeated takes of the same scene

– each one, to my untrained eye, exactly the same as the last – Arch Wingate announced a break. The actors were handed robes and bottles of water and did a few warming-down exercises, Jack Reynolds flexing and admiring his biceps while Olivia laid the palms of her hands flat on the ground six inches in front of her feet, stretching her hamstrings.

'Hey Arch,' Buddy bawled, 'meet my good friend Joe West from Askett Brown in London. He's the guy who raised all the money you're now chucking away on this meshugganah movie. He was just admiring your camera angles!'

Wingate smiled and shook my hand. 'Glad to meet you, Joe, and thanks for all your work on this. I really appreciate it. Tell me, is there enough cash left in the budget to hire a hit man to get rid of this fat putz?'

I stammered back that I was pleased to meet him and how much I enjoyed his work, but stopped short of agreeing to his request for extra funding. I stood and listened to these Hollywood legends as they exchanged further insults, speaking only when spoken to like a well-behaved child. When the actors walked past on their way to their make-shift dressing rooms, Buddy called them over too.

'Hey folks, come and meet the guy who's paying your wages!' The actors smiled indulgently at me, enjoying the joke. They knew as well as Buddy that it was their names attached to the production that pulled the money in, not me. Everyone was, in effect, on their payroll.

Close up, Olivia Finch had an aura that transcended her physical beauty, lighting up the room more brightly than the thousands of kilowatts of energy pouring from the hot studio lights. Even her feet, peeping out from beneath her long robe, seemed perfect.

'Hi,' she purred in a soft Southern whisper, taking my hand momentarily in hers, 'nice to know ya.'

I tried to reply with an intelligent comment about her work, but all I could manage was an adolescent grunt. While I blushed and burbled, Olivia showed no sign of concern that I had just seen her knicker-naked, throwing herself around in mock ecstasy. There was no more reason for her to be embarrassed by me watching her work than if she'd caught me poring over a particularly complex set of accounts.

# MILL HILL, LONDON

'Are you sure you've packed everything?' my wife Natasha called up the stairs. 'Passport? Dollars? Socks?'

'Yes, yes, yes,' I called back, reaching into my underwear drawer to pull out a couple more pairs of socks and throwing them into my suitcase, then checking inside my jacket to confirm that my passport was, indeed, in my pocket. I travelled to the US – either to Los Angeles or, as in this case, New York – seven or eight times a year, but each time we would still go through this pantomime as if, for Natasha, two small children weren't enough and she was intent on treating me like a third.

I zipped and locked my suitcase, then wrapped a personalised red, white and blue luggage strap around it, ostensibly for extra security but also to help me identify it when it belly-flopped onto the baggage carousel at JFK. I stuffed a few final papers and the latest Stephen King novel into my briefcase and switched off the light as I headed out of the bedroom and down the stairs. Natasha was waiting for me at the bottom, ready to give me some further instructions, while also keeping an eye on Helen and Matthew as they wrestled on the ground nearby.

'You're sure you have your passport, love,' she asked, 'and your tickets. Remember what happened last time.'

'It wasn't last time, Nat, it was three years ago. And since then I've made loads of trips abroad and never forgotten anything.'

'What about a travel plug? We must have dozens of the bloody things upstairs because you have to buy a new one every time you get to Heathrow.'

Damn! She had me there – and she knew it. Without saying another word, she slipped back up the stairs, returning a few moments later with a plug to meet the needs of the New York electrical system.

'Thank you, love,' I said, then, 'my taxi's here. Better get going.' The children interrupted their version of *The Hunger Games* just long enough for me to give them each a hug and plant a kiss on their perfect wrinkle-free, unblemished foreheads.

I kissed Natasha on the lips, more dutiful than romantic now after so many departures. The runway scene from *Casablanca* this was not.

'Have fun,' she said as I turned to make my lonely way out of the house.

'What? With Bennett there? I can't imagine it being a barrel of laughs, can you?'

'Fair point,' said Natasha. 'Well, try not to let him annoy you too much. It's only a few days.'

The door clicked behind me and I took a couple of steps

down the path before I was stopped by a thought – an important thought – that ambled up from my fingers through my nervous system to my brain. I fumbled for my keys and turned again to face the house. Before I could insert the key in the door, though, it opened and there stood Natasha, a grin splitting her face from ear to ear.

'Travel safely, you schmuck!' she said, as she handed me my briefcase and closed the door.

# MANHATTAN, NEW YORK

I still loved New York. Every time I cleared the airport and drove into the city in the back of a yellow cab, I could hear the strains of Gershwin's *Rhapsody in Blue* and the opening lines of Woody Allen's *Manhattan* playing inside my head. I had been here many times since my first visit – not long before 9/11 changed the skyline forever but did nothing to dent the pugnacious, optimistic spirit of the natives. Even from that first visit, the city had been a curious mixture of the new and the familiar. So many of the sights and sounds, even, bizarrely, the smells, were already known to me from movies and TV programmes that I never felt like a stranger here. And yet, even after many visits, I could still be startled by something unforeseen: the hidden squares, an eagle soaring over Central Park, even the sight of a thief on a bicycle stealing rolls from a hotdog van and pedalling off down Broadway like an Olympic competitor while the vendor hurled Bronx-tinted insults at his departing form.

And I still loved the movie business. The whole crazy, over-the-top, passionate, extraordinary process of turning stories into frames of film (or, these days, pixels) with which to captivate millions of strangers sitting silently in the dark. I was one of the money men – one of the guys behind the scenes who helped to introduce the money to the story and hoped they'd enjoy a long and fruitful relationship. That was why I'd been invited by Buddy Guttenberg (the most over-the-top and passionate movie man of them all) to watch the final re-shoot of *Nothing Happened* and that was why I was back in New York for the film's world premiere. I had been to a lot of these fancy industry events – but I'd yet to grow tired of them. Whatever the films themselves were like, the parties were usually great, dripping with celebrities, money and Hollywood's trademark extravagance.

One thing threatened to spoil my enjoyment that night. My new boss, Joseph Bennett, was my 'date' for the evening. Bennett was living, walking proof that God could not possibly have created man in His own image. He was an over-ambitious, untrustworthy, supercilious, arrogant prick (Bennett, I mean, obviously), who had been identified early in his career as someone destined to climb to the very top at Askett Brown.

I had never been on anyone's list of those most likely to succeed, but I'd found my niche in the growing media sector and had done pretty well. It was only in the last few years that Bennett's superior confidence and connections had seen him rise above me. Now he had been promoted to head the Entertainment and Media Division – my division. Having spent his entire career in the mineral extraction sector, Bennett knew plenty about oil and gas, but less than zilch about the movie business.

This would be Bennett's first – and, as it turned out, last – film premiere. After all the build-up and hoop-la and the standing ovations as the talent arrived and took their seats, the film itself was disappointing. For all Arch Wingate's attention to detail, he seemed to have missed the most important element for any film – a decent script. When it was over, I left the cinema as quickly as possible to avoid having to tell anyone intimately involved in its conception and delivery what I thought of their efforts. Nobody wants to hear they've given birth to a disappointing baby. I didn't even wait in my seat long enough to see my name flash past at the end of the credits, or join in the over-enthusiastic applause. I grabbed Bennett and we made our way quickly up Broadway to the aftershow party at a glitzy restaurant near Central Park.

I had been there for lunch once before, but now, all done up for a top Hollywood event, the venue had been transformed. Multicoloured flashing lights bounced off the mirrors that adorned every possible surface, reflecting back on themselves, making it seem like we were in the middle of a newly discovered constellation. Beyond the elaborately decorated tables there was a small dance floor, beside which an aged six-piece band were playing gentle swing tunes, easing people into the evening.

I hate the opening moves of any formal social occasion – having to find someone to talk to who'll find me interesting too. Not easy for an accountant, I can assure you. Bennett shared none of my inhibitions. Within seconds of our arrival he had attached us to a group of bewildered studio employees, introduced us and, on discovering they were junior back-office staff, made our excuses and moved on. This process was repeated several times as he swept through the party desperate to find someone of suitable seniority to engage in meaningful conversation.

Eventually I spotted a couple of people I knew from Buddy's production company, Printing Press Productions, and persuaded Bennett they were worth talking to.

'Hi Len, Di,' I said as we approached, shaking his hand and giving her a hug. 'How's married life, then? Carl still treating you OK?'

'Fantastic, thanks,' Len laughed, 'but don't they say the first year is always the easiest? Besides, I only got married so I can treat myself to a *fabulous* divorce when I get bored with him!'

Bennett coughed loudly, inviting me to make the introductions. 'I'm sorry,' I said. 'This is Joseph Bennett, the new Head of Entertainment and Media at Askett Brown. Joseph, this is Len Palmer, Buddy Guttenburg's Executive Assistant, and Diana Lee who works with Len. These two guys are Buddy's eyes and ears. Between them they—'

'Hi, guys. How're you doing?' Bennett cut in. 'I guess West's already given you the low-down on his new boss.' He emphasised the word 'boss' like a plantation owner addressing his slaves. 'I was a bit miffed when they told me I was moving to film. Thought it might be a bit of a backwater if I'm honest with you. But, you know what, I'm starting to think it could actually be pretty cool.' He looked around the room loftily, like an owl perched high in a tree's upper branches, then nudged Len, spilling some of his champagne. 'A lot better-looking crumpet here than out on the rigs, I can tell you,

Les! Only one kind of woman tends to go into the oil business and they're the ones who aren't much interested in men, if you know what I mean!' He gave a short blast of his dreadful braying laugh, like a donkey that's seen a cow sit on a thistle. 'But seriously, I'm really looking forward to working with your Mr Goldberg and the other top guys at the office. Bring you a little of the old Bennett magic. Do you know, when I was in oil, I achieved 300 per cent growth in net billings in four years? Three hundred per cent! I mean, I know this is a completely different ball game but it's got to be a damn sight easier than oil. There, you're lucky if every fifth or sixth project makes you any money.'

Had Bennett paused for breath, any one of us could have pointed out to him the similarities between making movies and drilling for oil. In both businesses you have to throw truckloads of money into highly risky ventures without knowing if you'll see any return at all. Every film is, in effect, a prototype – the exploration of a virgin field. Filmmakers try to mitigate their risk by reusing elements that have been successful in the past– top stars, top directors, proven storylines. That's why they make so many sequels.

Diana had developed models and spreadsheets that could help translate Buddy's more instinctive approach to filmmaking into something closer to a science. They couldn't guarantee the success of a film any more than a man with a geological survey map and a big drill could guarantee striking oil. But they could ensure that the studio maximised its returns if it did strike screen gold. She could have told Bennett all this, if he'd stopped talking long enough to let her. And if he hadn't already written her off as the secretary's secretary.

'So you're both assistants, are you? That must be fun! Are you invited to a lot of these parties or is this a special treat? I think it's great that companies on this side of The Pond have such an open policy on who they'll employ as secretaries. At our place, we mainly get pretty young things like you, Diana. It might be a laugh if we had a few blokes as well, don't you think, West?'

'Actually, we're not—' Di began, but Bennett wasn't looking for answers.

'That's not to say I don't like having the pretty ones around, mind you. I'm not saying I'd like some old poofter sitting on the edge of my desk taking dictation, or firtling around under it looking for a bonus, if you catch my drift! But it would be a bit different, wouldn't it, West? Blokes as PAs? Might even be an opportunity for you!' He let out another rattle of his machine-gun guffaw, entirely oblivious to the fact that, as usual, he was laughing alone.

Di flashed Len a glance that could only be interpreted as asking the silent question: 'Who is this jerk?' Len passed the look onto me as if it were the parcel in a child's party game. I could only shrug apologetically. When a waiter penguined past with a bottle of champagne, I stopped him and invited my three companions to replenish their glasses. This caused Bennett to pause long enough to allow Len to spot an imaginary acquaintance somewhere over my left shoulder. 'Oh, Di, look – there's um . . . Frank and, er . . . someone else we know. Shall we go and say hello?'

Diana needed no second invitation. Waiting only to flash me a sympathetic smile, she prepared her escape. Bennett looked confused for a second but then remembered his professional training. 'It's been lovely to meet you both,' he said, pouring out the charm he usually kept buried under thick layers of crassness like his beloved oil beneath the strata of the earth. 'Do keep in touch.' He handed them each a pristine new business card as if it were a communion wafer blessed by the Holy Father himself. 'And here's one for you too, Mr West,' he said with a barely suppressed snarl as he stuffed the sliver of stiff white paper into the breast pocket of my dinner jacket. 'Joseph Bennett, Head of Entertainment and Media Division. Try not to forget it!'

As soon as I could, I made my own excuses and put as much distance between myself and Bennett as was physically possible without actually leaving the party. I found myself walking past the VIP area, roped off to provide a sanctuary inside which the top talent could enjoy their evening unmolested by the rest of the guests.

'Hey, Joey,' I heard someone call from inside the rope, 'over here.' Turning, I saw Buddy Guttenberg beckoning to me to join him at his table. With the casual flick of one eyebrow, he alerted the bouncers to let me through, and with the other he indicated an empty chair next to him and invited me to sit down. I didn't realise until I pulled back the chair that sitting with Buddy were Arch Wingate, his partner, the multi-Oscar-winning actress Melinda Curtis, and the two people I had recently watched feigning fornication: Jack Reynolds and, peering shyly out of the shadows, the impeccable Olivia Finch.

'Arch, you remember Joey West,' Buddy said, brooking no argument as to whether or not that bold statement was correct. 'I brought him over to Queens last year to watch you burning my money on all those unnecessary fucking pick-up shots. Joey, you remember Arch, of course, and this is Melinda Curtis who I don't believe you've met.' Judging by his expression, Arch Wingate was pretty sure he'd never clapped eyes on me before either. He managed a disinterested half-smile while his wife raised a limp hand in unconscious impersonation of a royal wave, then returned to haranguing a waiter who had put a little too little ice in her mineral water. She looked thoroughly miserable. It was bad enough having to turn up to these events to support her own movies – sheer hell for a film she wasn't even in. Undaunted by their lukewarm reaction, Buddy clapped one of his enormous paws on my shoulder and continued: 'And I'm sure you remember our wonderful stars Jack and Olivia. Guys, this is Joe, my pal from London.' Jack Reynolds looked right through me with dead eyes as if my very existence was an affront to his celebrity. Olivia, though, looked up and smiled in my direction.

'Hi, Joe,' she said before returning to inspecting her nails, an operation which seemed to require all her attention.

I blushed and told the table I was pleased to meet it. Buddy laughed at my shyness but did his best to make me feel part of the group, keeping my glass filled and pitching me time and again as *the* man who had got the film made – repeated references which did not go down well with the *auteur* Arch Wingate. 'Hey, Joe,' Buddy said, when the conversation lulled, 'why don't you tell the guys about that Irish tax deal you did? I love this story. I tell you, this guy is a fucking genius!'

'It really wasn't that complicated,' I began modestly. 'All I did was tap into a bit of the tax write-off money that's sloshing around over there, leveraged it up by linking it into a corporation tax offset, and then underpinned it against their enhanced capital allowances to maximise the cash flow impact and net bottom line benefit . . .'

Jack Reynolds couldn't contain himself. 'Jesus Christ, Buddy, where did you find this guy? Fuck's sake, if I wanted to be bored shitless, I'd have stayed home and watched one of Olivia's old movies on cable.'

I felt myself reddening to the very tips of my ears. To my even greater embarrassment, while Buddy laughed heartily at my discomfort, Olivia Finch sprang to my rescue. 'Leave him alone, Jack,' she insisted, before fixing me with her angelic gaze. 'You must be so clever to do all that stuff. I am just so dumb with numbers. I bet I'm getting ripped off from here to Christmas with all my money stuff.'

'Not just numbers, sweetheart,' Reynolds mumbled, grabbing a half-empty bottle of champagne and struggling to his feet. 'Not just fucking numbers.'

'Oh, go screw yourself,' Olivia shouted after him as he lurched off towards the dance floor. 'Asshole!' She turned to me, the anger instantly drained from her face, one expression replaced by another like the swapping of masks. 'Hey, Mr Money Man, why don't you shift over here so we can talk properly. I bet it's real exciting dealing with all that high finance, isn't it?'

I did as I was told, then sat there dumbly, wondering whether my next comment should be about European tax harmonisation or her film.

'I loved the movie, Ms Finch,' I told her, an exaggeration that teetered close to being a lie, 'and,' steering closer to the truth, 'you were sensational.'

'Oh, do you really think so?' she said, playing down her

acting talents which were almost on a par with her beauty. 'Thank you so much. And please, call me Olivia.'

The waiter returned with another bottle of champagne and refilled the glasses of everyone at the table. 'So, tell me,' Olivia continued after taking a small, delicate sip from her glass, 'what did you really think of the movie? It kinda sucks, doesn't it? Go on, you can be honest with me, English.'

'No, I wouldn't say that,' I replied as evenly as I could. 'OK, I'll admit, it's not the best film I've ever seen but it's far from the worst.'

'So what is the best film you've ever seen? You must have seen hundreds in your time.'

'Oh, you know,' I said, 'I like a lot of the old classics. Stuff from before you were born. From before I was born, even.'

'Like what?' she persisted. 'Go on, try me. I might not be quite as dumb as I look.'

'No, I didn't mean that,' I replied, a little too quickly. 'I'm just trying to think of something that you might have seen as well. They made some great films in the nineties, you know.'

Olivia shifted to a more upright, more rigid, position. 'Just answer the goddamn question, English – what is your favourite movie?' She spelled the words out slowly as if talking to a child. Or an idiot.

'OK, then, if you must know, it's *Sullivan's Travels*. It's an old—'

'Preston Sturges movie!' Olivia almost screamed, 'Joel McCrea and Veronica Lake. Oh God, I love that film! It didn't do as well at the box office as Paramount hoped but that might possibly have been because they released it right about the time of Pearl Harbor! I guess that's what's known in the business as bad timing! And I absolutely adore Veronica Lake. When I was a kid, I grew my hair real long and tried to get it to flick like hers, you know? Sturges made some great movies, didn't he? *The Great McGinty*, *The Lady Eve*. But you hardly ever hear about him these days, do you? These kids today coming out of UCLA and NYU think cinema began with Quentin Tarantino. They don't know anything about Sturges or Hawks or Frank Capra. And that's just the Americans. Try talking to them about Fellini or Pasolini and they'll think you're trying to sell them a foreign car.'

'Better not mention Ford, then,' I said with a smile. Olivia looked at me blankly before she got the joke and laughed with far more gusto than my witticism deserved.

'Yeah, you're right there, Joe. John Ford would definitely be off their radar.' Olivia paused for a moment and took another sip of her drink. A broad grin spread slowly across her face as if she'd just had a really naughty notion. 'Do you know who my real all-time favourite actress is? The one I would have loved to have been? Go on, have a guess, Joe. You'll never guess.'

I had no idea. A few minutes earlier I'd have gone for a banker like Marilyn Monroe or perhaps Elizabeth Taylor, but Olivia's knowledge and enthusiasm had floored me. 'Tell me. Who?'

'Hedy Lamarr!' Olivia announced, then looked at me, her eyes alive with anticipation, eager to gauge my reaction as if she had just revealed the ultimate secret to the meaning of life. 'She had it all. She was beautiful. She was a really talented actress and she was so clever. She actually invented the gizmo that makes wi-fi work – did you know that? Isn't that amazing? When this is all over, I would love to be remembered for something more than having a great body and being able to read out lines that someone else has written for me.'

'How do you know all this?' I asked, without fully thinking through the implications of my question.

'What?' Olivia blazed back. Her moods, I was discovering, could change like traffic lights at a busy junction. 'You think I can't appreciate great movies because they're in black and white? I was born poor English, not stupid! But I'm one of the download generation. When I was a kid, my dad got hold of a knocked-off laptop and I used to carry it around with me wherever I went, like it was my favourite doll. Any chance I got to hook up to the Internet, I'd see what movies I could find. There wasn't much point watching *Die Hard* or *Mission Impossible* or big-budget wham-bam shit like that because the connections were so bad you couldn't see what the hell was going on. So I'd watch all the old classics. At least then I could hear what the actors were saying even if I couldn't see what they were doing. I could probably give you the whole of *The Apartment* or *All About Eve* by heart.'

Before she had a chance to deliver on this promise, we were distracted by a commotion and the staggering figure of Jack Reynolds hoving back into view, pursued by one of the doormen who was controlling access to the VIP enclosure.

'Come on, Olly, we're going,' he slurred, grabbing Olivia by the arm and attempting to pull her from her seat.

'Get your hands off of me, you ape!' Olivia snapped back, digging her fingers into her co-star's hand.

'Hey, hey! Come on, guys,' said Buddy rising quickly from his seat at the other end of the table and hurrying to get the situation under control. 'It is kind of late, Olivia. Perhaps you should be going.'

'I'll go when I'm ready,' she replied, staring directly at me for support. 'And, as it happens, I'm ready now. It's been lovely talking with you, English. We must do this again some time.' She rose and air-kissed everyone at the table, her scent lingering in the space she vacated like a jet's vapour trail, then wafted off into the bright party lights, followed closely by Jack Reynolds. I'd met a few stars in my time but never before been so close for so long to such insouciant, commanding elegance. I felt completely intoxicated by the experience. That and the four or five glasses of champagne I'd already consumed.

My head was starting to spin and I knew I'd overdone it but, what the hell! The drink was free, I was celebrating a successful trip and I'd had to babysit Bennett all week. And I was suddenly feeling very alone in the busiest city on the planet. It was almost one o'clock which made it six back home in London. Natasha would, without knowing it, be enjoying her last few moments of sleep. Soon she would receive our standard early-morning call – assaulted by a hyperactive three–year-old who greeted the dawn of each new day as if it had to be the best one ever. I missed them – even the rude awakenings – and was glad I'd be seeing them again soon. It was time to go back to the hotel.

I should have looked for Bennett to see whether he was ready to leave too. It would have saved a lot of trouble if

21

we'd stuck together – would have saved his life, now I come to think about it. Frankly, though, I reasoned at the time, he was a grown man and could find his own way back to the hotel. I tottered to the exit, slightly unsteady on my feet but not so drunk that I couldn't hail myself a cab.

Exactly drunk enough, it turned out, to make the biggest mistake of my life.

I've always liked to think that, essentially, I'm a nice bloke. In fact, until that night, I would have settled for that on my gravestone: HERE LIES JOSEPH EDWARD GEORGE WEST. ESSENTIALLY A NICE BLOKE. So what happened next – and most of what's happened since – has to be seen as being out of character.

As I reached the exit, my nostrils picked up a familiar perfume. I looked around and saw Olivia locked in animated conversation with Jack Reynolds. They didn't notice me and I was almost past them when I heard Olivia yelp and saw that Reynolds had grabbed hold of one of her arms. It wasn't clear whether he was trying to stop her from hitting him or from getting away. But there was no doubt she was not enjoying the experience and was struggling to free herself from his grasp.

I still don't know what possessed me. Instead of continuing out into the cold night air, I stopped, stared for a few moments, then heard a voice that sounded like mine but couldn't possibly have been, say: 'Hey, Ms Finch, is everything OK?'

They both looked at me in stunned silence. Reynolds, the archetypal tough guy in so many movies, dropped Olivia's arm and seemed to shrink as I walked towards them, shuffling a couple of paces to his left to position Olivia between us. She, still a little shocked at this turn of events, could only mutter, 'Er, thank you, um . . . English, we're fine. I was just leaving actually,' then turned and made her way out of the bright lights into the lobby area beyond.

I followed after her, making sure that Reynolds stayed where he was, skulking in a dimly lit corner of the room. Three liveried cloakroom attendants spotted Olivia approaching and raced to find her coat, fighting for the right to be the man to present it to her. I fumbled for my cloakroom ticket, checking every pocket of my jacket and trousers two or three times before I remembered that I didn't have a ticket because I didn't have a coat. It had been a warm April evening when I'd left the hotel with Bennett. Now, looking through the glass doors into the darkness outside, I could see it was raining hard. I contemplated a long, wet wait for a taxi along with every other hapless maggot drawn into the Big Apple.

Olivia pointedly ignored me as she slipped on her designer raincoat and peered out into the rain. She stepped towards the door, then sprang back as if she'd received an electric shock. 'Oh crap!' she said, 'there's a whole load of paps out there. I hate being snapped when it's late and raining and I look such a goddamn mess – they'll have me on my way to rehab by breakfast time. Don't these guys have homes to go to?' There was no malice in her voice, only the sad resignation that the huddled masses outside had their job to do photographing her, just as it was part of her job description to be photographed by them. 'Hey you,' she called to the doorman, who was standing smartly to attention by the exit. 'Can you see if my car's out there?'

The doorman scuttled out only to reappear thirty

seconds later, rain dripping off his hat and down his shoulders from even that brief encounter with the elements. 'Your car is right at the end of the path, Ms Finch, and your driver is waiting to open the door for you as soon as you reach him.'

'How many of them out there, do you reckon?'

'I'd say around twenty-five to thirty,' he replied. 'A few more down the right-hand side than the left. I couldn't see any long lenses across the street or in any of the apartments.' He was starting to sound like he might be in Special Forces or the CIA.

'I really do not want to get papped tonight,' Olivia mumbled under her breath. 'Listen,' she said to the doorman, 'can you walk with me to the car and cover me from the guys on the right and' – to me now as if I was also part of the team dedicated to preserving Olivia Finch's pride and dignity – 'English, can you take the guys on the left?'

Before I could even think about an answer, she grabbed my arm and pressed herself into my chest. She was slightly taller than me in her heels and had to stoop to bury her head into the crook of my neck. While the doorman strode out ahead, expertly blocking every flash-fuelled photograph as if it were a sniper's well-aimed bullet, I struggled along, trying not to trip over her feet, blinded by the bright lights and deafened by the shouts of 'Over here, Olivia!' 'Hey, Miss Finch, look this way!' and, hurtfully, 'Oi – Blubber Boy, get out the goddamn way!'

The driver opened the door of the black Lexus, then moved alongside me and the doorman to create a human barrier between Olivia and the photographers who had crowded around the car, snapping away feverishly like piranha attacking a fresh carcass. Just as I was wondering how I was going to work my way back out of this scrum, I felt a hand pull me down into the car. I stumbled and half-fell onto the long back seat. Without a word, Olivia buried herself under my tuxedo, sticking her head up into my left armpit. I turned my face away from the window and ducked down out of view, muttering a silent prayer that the deodorant I'd applied all those hours earlier was still working.

I heard the driver's door open and close, the click of the key in the ignition and the purr of the engine as we pulled away from the kerb. With the smooth motion of the car, it was a few seconds before I realised that part of the gentle vibration I could feel was Olivia giggling under my jacket. When she was sure we were safely away from the mob, she looked up, her hair splattered across her face like a pair of blonde curtains, make-up smeared around her eyes. 'That was fun,' she laughed, the Southern girl cutting through her mask of Hollywood sophistication, 'and you sure do smell nice under there. So, can I drop you back at your hotel?'

'Really, you don't have to. Actually, I wouldn't mind a walk – clear the head a bit, you know.'

'Nonsense, it's – what do you Limeys say? – raining cats and dogs. Please, I owe you for helping me out back there.'

'Well, OK, if you insist. I'm staying at the Hotel du Paris on Fifth.'

'Travis,' Olivia called out to the driver, 'can we drop my friend here at the Hotel du Paris on Fifth? Thank you. His name's not really Travis,' she added, turning to me with a huge smile illuminating her face, 'I just call him that after that psycho in *Taxi Driver*. Drives him nuts!'

25

We drove on in silence while Olivia repaired the damage to her face and hair, squinting into a small compact mirror. When she was restored more or less to her former glory, she folded the mirror away and replaced it in a pocket at the back of the seat in front of her. Then she turned and stared at me for what seemed like an eternity. 'Who exactly are you, English?' she said. 'What the hell am I doing letting some guy I hardly know into my car? Please promise me you're not some kind of a stalker. I've already got quite enough of those.'

'I'm not, I promise,' I said, watching the raindrops racing across the window as the car sped through the Manhattan streets. 'And I'm sorry that I stuck my nose in like that back at the party. That really wasn't like me at all.'

'You don't have to apologise, English,' she said, posting her right arm through the crook of my left, until her hand rested awkwardly on my thigh just below my lap. 'That jerk was really busting my ass. Buddy likes us to be pally off set – you know, to get the media sniffing around for a story, "are they, aren't they?" and all that crap. But he wanted to carry on the act right through to home plate, if you know what I mean. The guy is old enough to be my father – did you know that? They keep these poor bastards hanging on, still believing they're God's gift to women when some of them can hardly stand up in the morning, let alone get it up. With us women – bang! As soon as your tits start heading south, it's all over. Then twenty years in the wilderness off Broadway before you can come back playing the Next Big Thing's mom and try to grab yourself a Best Supporting Actress nod.'

The driver interrupted her to tell us we'd arrived at my hotel. 'That's a shame,' said Olivia, 'I was enjoying our little chat. I know, why don't I let you buy me a drink to say thank you for rescuing me earlier? I'd love to buy you one but, you know, they don't let me carry any money.'

Before I could say 'no', Olivia had unclipped her seatbelt and the driver had opened her door and was helping her from the car. I would have one drink with her, I told myself, and then go straight to bed. Alone. I was even looking forward to telling Natasha all about it – 'Hey, you'll never guess who I ended up with in the back of a limo after the party.' I couldn't wait to see the look on my wife's face.

The hotel bar was still open and I guided Olivia to a table in the corner. It was almost dark, as if Prohibition had never been repealed in this part of the state and drinking alcohol was still illegal. A few hardy, late-night souls chatted quietly in twos and threes or sat silently alone in the dimness. One over-dressed and under-sober woman looked twice at Olivia to make sure it wasn't her before concluding, loudly, to her companion that the broad in the corner looked a little like 'that actress, Whatsername?' But apart from that, and the surly attention of a waiter who was clearly more interested in ending his shift than serving his customers, we were left alone – the middle-aged, middle-class, middle-income Englishman and the brightest star in the Hollywood firmament. What on earth would we talk about?

We talked about her, mostly. With little prompting, Olivia was happy to tell me all about her life so far. How she had grown up in a small southern town straight out of a Dolly Parton song without two nickels to rub together and a father who was a perfect gentleman when he was sober but was never sober. She had discovered at an early age that she had a talent for acting and, as she became a teenager, for turning boys' heads. At sixteen she had hitch-hiked to Los Angeles and waited on tables while waiting for an acting job. She'd been engaged twice – first to her high school sweetheart and then to the guy who directed her first film (the one she didn't like to talk about) – but right now she was between engagements.

Olivia enjoyed telling her stories as much as I enjoyed listening to them. She played all the roles in each anecdote, switching between accents and characters with the consummate ease you would expect of such an accomplished actress, turning each one into a mini-screenplay any of which would have made a better film than the one we had sat through earlier in the evening. Before I knew it, I had finished my drink and, despite my earlier resolution, found myself calling the waiter over and asking him to refill our glasses.

'So, Mr Money Man,' Olivia said as the waiter returned with our fresh drinks and set them down clumsily on the table in front of us, 'that is quite enough about me for one night. Now I want to hear all about you. I bet you have some fascinating stories to tell. Tell me, did you always want to be an accountant?'

I looked at her closely, trying to find any signs of mockery in her eyes, but there were none. 'Good God, no!' I replied. 'Who would? A career in accountancy isn't something boys dream of alongside space travel or driving trains. It's something you fall into – like a hole.'

Olivia laughed out loud, breaking the silence of the room and causing the other bar-dwellers to turn and look at us. 'You are so funny, Joe. That's one of the things I really like about you. You know, I've always preferred a funny man to a good-looking one . . .'

'Gee, thanks,' I replied, only slightly pretending to be hurt.

'Oh God, I'm sorry. I didn't mean to imply that . . . you know. In fact, I think you are a very attractive man, Joe. I've always had a bit of a thing for older men. Apart from my dad. I hated that sonofabitch. You have gorgeous eyes, you know – deep and soulful. Has anyone ever told you that?'

I smiled and blushed. No, no one ever had, least of all one of the most beautiful women in the world.

'So what did you want to do?' Olivia continued.

'I'm sorry?'

'When you were a kid. We've established that you didn't lie awake at night fantasising about a life as a bean counter – so what was your dream?'

'Do you promise not to laugh if I tell you?'

'Try me,' Olivia replied edging a little closer along the bench seat, intrigued to learn my deepest, darkest secret.

'OK. I wanted to write. To be a novelist – or perhaps a screenwriter. I remember when I was about nine we drove past a bookmaker's – you know, a betting shop – and I asked my mum if they would make my book when I was older. I thought it was the same thing as a publisher!'

'Aw, that's so sweet,' said Olivia, edging closer still. 'So what happened?'

'To what?'

'To your dream, Joe. Why did you end up counting things instead of writing about them. I'm glad you did in one way, because otherwise we might never have met. But it seems like a real waste. You have a creative soul – I can see it in your eyes. Why don't you write? All you need is some paper and a pencil.'

I took a sip of my drink. The intensity of the memory surprised and upset me. 'When I was fifteen,' I began, 'and had to choose which subjects I was going to study at school, I told my parents that I wanted to be an author and so I needed to study English. My dad said "No, son, you mean an auditor," and told me to do maths. And so, like the good Jewish boy I am, that's what I did – what my parents told me to do.'

'But it's never too late, Joe. You're nobody's prisoner now. You can do whatever you want.'

'Olivia,' I said, with a mirthless laugh, 'I have a wife and two kids and a bloody great mortgage, so I'm afraid the writing's going to have to wait. God, look at the time. I really should be getting to bed.'

Olivia shuffled closer to me still, placed a hand on one of my thighs and kissed me, lightly, on the cheek.

'I think you're right, English,' she said.

She took my hand and led me out of the gloomy bar and to the lift lobby, pressed the call button and asked me my room number. Somewhere, arrested by the alcohol, the tiredness and those extraordinary eyes that fixed mine and pulled me into the depths of her beauty, was a part of me that wanted to tell her to leave me alone, to let me sleep – but it was as if monochrome pictures of my wife and children were being ripped from the walls of my brain and fed into a neurological shredder, while images of Olivia, in glorious, vibrant Technicolor, were put up in their place. And all I actually said as we stepped into the lift and started the slow ascent to paradise and madness were the three little words: 'Six Twenty-Five'.

The film begins on the screen inside my head. I see a man in early middle age and a much younger woman, walking down a long hotel corridor. They are making a lot of noise in their attempts to stay as quiet as possible. She is incredibly beautiful. He is extraordinarily ordinary. Her skin is smooth and pale; her shoulder-length hair deep blonde; her blue eyes alive with a heady mixture of alcohol, lust and devilment. His face is lined and creased beneath his thinning hair, his grey eyes reflecting only the alcohol and the lust.

He pushes a white plastic card into a slot on the door and presses down on the handle, takes the card out and turns it over and tries the handle again, then takes it out, swears, turns it around and tries a third time. A green light comes on, reflected in his glasses and they tumble into the room through the half-opened door. He presses a switch on the wall and lights on each side of the large double bed – wider than it is long – snap into life. There is a short canopy at one end of the bed beneath which a single wrapped chocolate rests on an ivory pillow. She pushes him up against the wall and presses her lips to his, giving him no option but to kiss her back. Her dress is bright blue with silver flecks and she sparkles like a diving kingfisher as she glides across the room, kicks off her shoes and pours herself onto the bed. His dinner suit is off-the-peg and baggy, the trousers an inch too long. He fumbles with his unfamiliar bow tie, then hops inelegantly on one leg then the other as he tries to disengage his feet from stiff black brogues.

31

I fast-forward to the next significant action. The couple are now in the no-holds barred wrestling match of fornication. They are naked, apart from the man's socks: black with a picture of Mr Silly above the words 'Have a Silly Saturday' picked out in red letters, a birthday present from his children which, in his indecent haste, he has failed to remove. I am surprised to see how much of a lead the man is taking – orchestrating their movements, calling the shots.

This is hard to watch. I fast-forward again and come back in when it is all over. She is lying to one side of him, an arm wrapped around his chest, a leg interlocked with his. She sleeps blissfully, while he lies awake staring at the ceiling. He looks as if he has just received the worst possible news.

I open my eyes and the film ends. No stirring John Williams score. No endless credits. No pathetic little mentions of pathetic little accountants just above the line that says that no animals were harmed in the making of this movie. No escape. It wasn't a bizarre erotic dream. It happened. I was there and she was there. The Hollywood superstar and her man: the frightened, treacherous, adulterous, stupid little bastard.

Me.

I must have drifted off because I became suddenly aware of strange noises in the bedroom and sensed the absence of Olivia from the bed. I peered through the darkness at the source of the noise and saw her carefully picking something up and placing it on a chair. A few seconds later, there was a flash of light as the bedroom door opened, followed by the solid thud of it closing again. Then I heard the diminishing click-clack of her heels on the parquet corridor floor as she stilettoed away from my room and, I devoutly but erroneously hoped, out of my life forever.

When I was sure she had gone, I dragged myself out of bed and took a long, hot shower, leaving the plug in the bath so that the water accumulated at my feet. When it was ankle deep, I lay down in the second-hand suds and closed my eyes, letting the stream of water from the still-running shower drip irritatingly on my head and splash down into the bath. It was a form of torture designed to make me pay for my sins but all it did was drive out all other thoughts and bring to my mind, with a remarkable clarity, the events of the past twelve hours: the chatting, the drinking, the laughing and joking, the creeping along the hotel corridor, the falling into bed – the making love. No, not making love – that was too nice, too husband and wifey. Not *making* love like you *make* a promise or make a vow or *make* a baby. This was *committing* adultery, like *committing* a crime or *committing* perjury – or *committing* matrimonial suicide. I banged my head with increasing ferocity against the tiled wall of the bathroom, trying to dislodge these thoughts, but they were stuck fast in my mind just as I was now stuck with the reality of what I had done: something awful and despicable and completely un-undoable.

I lay there for what seemed like hours until the water had gone completely cold and my body was as ridged and wrinkled as an elderly bull elephant's scrotum. I dressed and packed and then went down to the restaurant to meet Bennett for breakfast. We sat mostly in silence, our conversation limited to requests for condiments and butter to be passed and, in my case, occasional offers to fetch more coffee. Bennett seemed keen to sample as many as possible of the myriad items displayed in the gargantuan buffet selection, which included everything from traditional cereals through to corned beef hash and doughnuts. This suited me fine – as long as he was eating, he wasn't talking.

'Good do last night, I thought, West,' he said eventually, as he used his final fragment of French toast to mop up the remaining puddle of maple syrup and drained his glass of cranberry juice. 'Some very interesting birdlife there, if you know what I mean! Where did you get to at the end? I looked all over for you but you were nowhere to be seen. You didn't cop off, did you?'

He concluded this remark with a noise situated approximately halfway between a laugh and a snort, leaving me in little doubt that he considered this to the most ridiculous proposition he had ever constructed. Either this or tell-tale signs of my infidelity were etched so clearly across my face that even Bennett could spot them. Or perhaps Olivia had left a physical souvenir for me. Perhaps my neck was covered in love bites or she'd carved her initials into my forehead with a sharpened emery board. *Keep calm, you idiot,* I told myself, *that snort was clearly derisory. Just stay composed and say as little as possible.*

'Yeah, it was good,' I replied, doing my best to sound nonchalant and avoiding eye contact. 'And I'm sorry about missing you at the end. I looked for you but couldn't see you anywhere. And I left pretty early anyway. So, I mean, I wasn't actually still there at the end when you were looking for me because I'd already left some time earlier. On my own. Newspaper?'

I handed him a *USA Today* and took one for myself and we flicked through them in a fruitless search for anything of interest to read before both noticing at the same time that this was, in fact, yesterday's paper, telling the day before yesterday's news. News from the day before the night I turned into a monster.

The New York streets were quiet as we drove to the airport. Just over the Brooklyn Bridge, I saw a huge billboard outside a large, modern church proclaiming: 'The Ten Commandments are not a Cafeteria Menu!!' Another day, I'd have smiled at these evangelistic ravings, but now the sign made me shudder. Until the previous night, I'd been doing pretty well against this exacting 5,000-year-old standard. I'd done a little coveting in my time and worshipped the odd false idol – who hadn't? – but otherwise I'd stuck to the rules. Now I'd blown it – thrown away the no-claims bonus I'd accrued over the years to be redeemed against eternal salvation – and for what? A night of drunken sex which already I could hardly remember and which I couldn't mention to another soul for as long as I lived.

When we arrived at JFK, we checked in and headed straight for the Business Lounge. I poured myself a coffee while Bennett helped himself to a Virgin Mary and we sat in silence reading papers and nibbling on crisps and nuts. Just as our flight was being called, I heard a sharp 'beep' and saw Bennett reach into his jacket pocket. He took out his phone, tapped a couple of buttons and stared at the screen, looking bemused as he read and re-read the message. Then he thrust the phone into my face. 'Here, West, look at this.'

Hey there, English. That was some night! I really enjoyed our chat – and the rest of course!! Thx for looking after me. You were grrrreat!

xxx☺

Now it was my turn to look confused. If this message was – as it seemed – from Olivia Finch, how had it found its way onto Bennett's phone? Had she slept with him as well? Perhaps she had a thing for accountants. In which case, where was my message? I checked my phone. Nothing. Not even a 'thank you for having me'.

'What's that about, then?' I stammered.

'I have no idea,' Bennett said. 'Must be a wrong number.' He pressed another couple of buttons, deleting the message and turning off the phone. 'Come on, West, we'd better get boarding.'

# SOMEWHERE OVER THE
# ATLANTIC

As soon as we were airborne, Bennett settled down to watch an unfunny American comedy and for the next two hours proceeded to laugh like the stand-up's wife at a talent contest. I reclined my seat and tried to get some sleep, adjusting and readjusting my position for maximum comfort and turning up the music in my headset to smother the cackling of my neighbour. Feeling sick with a potent combination of tiredness, guilt, confusion and coffee, I closed my eyes and tried hard to embrace oblivion, but every time I was on the point of dropping off, those indelible images of my crime would reappear inside my head, screaming at me and dragging me back to the new reality I had so casually created.

Nothing made sense to me. How had I ended up in bed with one of the most beautiful women in the world? How could I have allowed it to happen? And how could she? I imagined the look on my friends' faces if I turned up for the quiz night at the King's Head next Thursday evening with Olivia Finch on my arm – specialist subject: 'The Lives and Loves of the Rich and Famous'. The thought made me smile for a split second but then I remembered: this wasn't a game. This wasn't a movie or some crappy television sitcom. This was my life and Natasha's life and the kids' lives. And I'd just fucked them all up.

I ordered a beer from the stewardess, hoping that a drink or two might help me sleep. But, of course, it didn't. All it did was send my mind hurtling off in a load of other directions, trying to make sense of all that had happened. Why was Olivia now texting Bennett of all people? Or had he hooked up with someone else and was just playing dumb? Perhaps it really was a wrong number and had nothing to do with me or what had happened last night. Coincidences do happen.

When his film finished, Bennett turned off the screen and fell instantly into a deep, apparently guilt-free slumber. After several more drinks I was finally able to close my eyes and drift off into a fitful sleep myself.

*I am woken up by a rough hand grabbing my shoulder, almost pulling me from my chair – I must have undone my seat belt to go to the toilet whilst still half asleep. Wordlessly, the figure leads me to the back of the Business Class section which opens out into a large, splendidly furnished lounge with a bar and pretty stewardesses serving drinks for thirsty, drunken passengers. To my surprise, I spot myself sitting in one corner chatting to Olivia Finch. We are laughing and she is running one of her hands up and down one of my thighs as if it is a piano keyboard. We finish our drinks and stand up and she leads* me by the hand past where I am still standing with my mysterious friend, although now I realise that he is no longer there and my hand has been taken by another spirit, who leads me back to my seat and forces me to sit down. The TV screen flickers into life and I see a woman and two children sitting down to tea around a kitchen table – fish fingers, sweet corn and chips. They all look happy. 'One more sleep until Daddy gets home,' my wife tells my children and they both cheer and Matthew throws a spoonful of sweet corn at his sister.

The screen goes blank and another hand, skeletal and sharp, digs into my shoulder, forcing me to rise again. I float above Bennett's prostrate form and my face is forced up against the window, staring into the bright light of the late spring sky outside. Droplets of moisture appear on the window, then form themselves into recognisable shapes. It is the same scene as before – Natasha and the kids again but all a little older now. They seem sadder; they've lost their sparkle – not through age but because something bad has happened. Something has ripped the life they knew away from them and left them with a shell. From this single vignette, I can tell that I am no longer around. No longer there to hug them and kiss them goodnight and tell them how much I love them and how proud I am of them. Edited out of their lives. The Director's unkindest cut.

'But tell me kind spirit,' I imagine myself saying as self-pitying tears start to run down my face, reflecting the water droplets on the window, 'are these the things that will be or just the things that might come to pass?'

The spirit replies in my voice: 'You'll have to work that out for yourself, arsehole.'

# HEATHROW AIRPORT, LONDON

The next thing I knew, a stewardess was tapping my shoulder and asking me to put my seat in its upright position for landing. The instant the plane touched down there was the usual rush to gather bags and coats from the overhead lockers and to get from the plane to the front of the queue for Immigration as quickly as possible. As we hurried down the gangway and into the terminal, Bennett switched on his phone, which immediately started to warble like a dyspeptic baby crow. I turned mine on, too, but it stayed embarrassingly silent. Not even a 'welcome home, one of the kids has escaped' from Natasha.

Bennett stared intently at his screen as we made our way through Passport Control and out to the baggage carousels, occasionally pressing buttons and making curious clucking noises. Eventually he let out one of his appalling grunt-laughs, like a vixen on heat caught in a combine harvester, and passed me his mobile. 'Here look at these, West,' he said appreciatively. 'It's more messages from that same number, but this time, they're clearly addressed to me. Bizarre!'

There were four new messages highlighted on the screen, all from the same unidentified number:

So Mr Joseph A Bennett. Gone all quiet on me, eh? I didn't wanna be too bold before but I like REALLY enjoyed last night. You were incredible!!! Cant wait to see u some more.

Olivia xxx☺☺☺

Hi, me again! Forgot to say Im gonna be in London soon with the movie so we can meet then. How cool is that??? Would be great to hook up again real soon.

Olly x☺

What? Still not talking to me? Hope ur not one of those love em and leave em guys, English!!! What's up, Babe? Text me pleeese! I miss you!

O ☹

Hey – ur NOT one of those love em and leave em guys are u? You had better fucking not be. I dont give what I gave u last night lightly. Please don't be mean to me, English.

Bennett looked at me in eager anticipation, waiting for my response. 'You know what this is, don't you, West?' He

41

sounded wistful but amused. 'Someone's having a pop at me. Isn't Olivia the name of that bird in the film we saw last night? The rather tasty one? I bet it's those bloody studio guys trying to make it look like she's after me. The bastards!' He smiled as he tapped the phone absentmindedly on his chin, his expression full of fondly remembered laddish high jinks. He was enjoying this – it meant they'd recognised him as one of the boys. It had taken him a while to crack this crazy business but now he'd done it. Now they appreciated that beneath the highly professional, executioner's mask he was a regular guy. Someone who got things done but could have a laugh as well; a chap who worked hard and played even harder. 'Classic, isn't it? They've really made her sound like some crazy neurotic actress. What a gas! How do you reckon I should reply?'

I hadn't a clue. Something didn't stack up. No one in Hollywood knew Bennett well enough to joke with him like this and, even if they did, no one would dare impugn the reputation of a star like Olivia Finch.

'Come on, man,' Bennett harried me, 'I haven't got all day.'

I could have stopped the whole thing right there but something was compelling me to go on, like when you pass a car crash on the motorway hard shoulder and implore yourself not to look but look anyway. I could have said: 'Hey, Joseph, you'll never believe this but, guess what? It was me who slept with Olivia Finch last night! Yup! Gave her a good seeing to and, for some reason, she thinks it was you. What a hoot! I say, old man, would you mind terribly not mentioning it to anyone at work? Or to Sandra in case she sees Natasha at their book group and spills the beans. You know how the ladies love to gossip! Thanks, awfully, mate. I owe you one.'

If I had said that then none of the rest of what happened would have happened. Bennett would still be alive. Olivia might have won an Oscar or two by now. And I might still be working at Askett Brown. Living on my own, no doubt, as Bennett would have gone straight home and told his wife, who would have lost no time making sure Natasha knew and my feet wouldn't have touched the floor. Natasha was not the forgiving kind when it came to infidelity. She had always made it quite clear that there would be no three strikes and you're out for me. One slip of the libido and it would be 'hit the road, Jack, and take your dick with you in this bag I've knitted out of your scrotum.'

Perhaps it was this thought that stopped me from breaking the chain. The moment passed as quickly as it arrived and I found myself taking the coward's way, encouraging events forward with my silent acquiescence. Instead of shouting: 'Cut! Let's take it again from the top but this time the little fat guy will own up,' I adopted the role of someone who enjoyed a laugh as much as the next bloke but occasionally had to be the damp squib.

'Why don't you text back something like: "Just got off a long flight. Can't talk now. Catch you later"?' I said. 'They'll think you're still playing along but soon realise that you can't be bothered to get down to their level. What do you think?'

'I see where you're coming from, Westy,' Bennett replied, mulling over his options, trying to think at least two moves ahead. 'Slow-play it a bit. See what they do next. Yeah, I can see how that might work for someone like you, West, but it's not really for me, is it? If these guys know anything about me, they'll be expecting me to hit back at them hard. I've got to show them who's in charge here – who's the prankster supremo – otherwise they'll think they can walk all over me.' He paused to tap retardedly on his phone. 'Hey West, what do you call one of those films that's almost the same as another film but different? You know – same story, same actors but different title. Comes out after the first one.'

'A sequel?' I suggested, after my brain had assessed and dismissed all other options.

'That's it!' he said, 'that's the feller!' He tapped at his phone again, then passed it to me. 'Here, what do you think?'

> Glad you liked it, babe. I had a cracking night too – deffo up there in my all-time top ten. Let's hook up again when you're over in old London Town and go for a sequel. JB

I felt a knot tightening in my stomach and my toes curling up in anticipatory horror. 'Don't you think that's a little, well, provocative, Joseph?' I said, knowing that the more I protested the more likely he was to persist in his course. 'The old slow-play sounded pretty good to me.'

'Yeah, you may be right, mate,' he replied, looking off into the middle distance as I finally spotted my suitcase sliding down the chute and onto the carousel. Then he pressed the Send button anyway.

It was past ten o'clock by the time we had collected our luggage and walked out into the arrivals hall. Bennett tossed me a clipped 'G'bye, West!' as his driver stowed his

'Joseph Bennett' sign and picked up my boss's enormous suitcase while I sloped off to queue for a taxi. Every trip Bennett ever went on was, essentially, an ego trip and he wasted no opportunity to make sure I knew where the power lay in our new working relationship. Although we both lived in North London, it would never have occurred to him to offer me a lift and I was glad not to feel obliged to accept.

# MILL HILL, NORTH LONDON

The taxi journey home seemed to last an eternity which was nowhere near long enough for me. I felt an oppressive, suffocating guilt about everything that had happened. I was dreading seeing Natasha again and also worried about how Olivia would feel when she read Bennett's latest text. It was totally irrational of me to blame him for any part of what had happened – yet still I did blame him. Why had he had to make the terrible situation I'd created so much worse? Why, when faced with competing options of what to do, could he not have done the right thing? Why did he have to be such an arse? Was it, as the scorpion said to the frog, simply his nature?

The house was almost completely dark when I walked in. Looking up the stairs, I could see a faint light peeping out from behind the three quarters-closed door of our bedroom. Natasha was probably sitting up in bed reading, looking forward to hearing all my news. And I still had absolutely no idea what I would say to her when I saw her.

I rifled through the post on the table, annoyed at the staggering ordinariness of it all, reminding me I was back in the real world of bills and junk mail and putting out the dustbins on a Sunday night.

I took off my shoes, picked my way through the dark living room into the kitchen and ran a glass of water from the cold tap. I gulped it down in one draught, then decided I needed a pee, so I popped into the downstairs toilet and took my time emptying my bladder as quietly as I could before washing my hands as if I was scrubbing up for a delicate operation. Then, bereft of further reasons for delay, I climbed the stairs with all the perky enthusiasm of a condemned man walking to the execution chamber, opened the bedroom door and prepared to meet my fate.

Natasha was propped up on her pillow, fast asleep. The book she was reading – this month's book-group selection – hung limply in her right hand, a thumb wedged uncomfortably in the crease where it had tried to close, saving her place. She was still wearing her glasses and her soft brown hair had fallen forwards, half-covering her eyes. She looked at peace – as if she had gone to bed without a care in the world.

I made no attempt to wake her, grateful to put off even longer the shattering of her delusions. Carefully, I prised the book from her sleeping hand and placed it on her side table. Then I turned off the light directly above her head, and replaced it with the weaker glow from my bedside lamp. I tiptoed into the children's bedrooms just to look at them as they slept. Helen was lying exactly as I imagined Natasha had left her. Not a hair out of place, her duvet perfectly even and tucked up crisply under her chin like a floral pie crust. By her head lay her favourite teddy – a souvenir from a previous trip to New York – now worn in places from too much loving. I wanted to hug her and plant a kiss on her perfectly smooth forehead but didn't feel I had the right. How could I use the lips that the previous night had wandered all over Olivia Finch's illicit body for such a precious assignment? I watched her breathing for a while, then muttered a quiet 'goodnight' and left.

Entering Matthew's room, I was greeted by a totally different scene. He was spread-eagled across his bed, his limbs arranged in a casual swastika. All his bedclothes were on the floor – his duvet, pillow and even his under-sheet. Perhaps he had woken in the night in the throes of a terrible nightmare and thrashed around wildly waiting to be rescued, or perhaps he'd gone to bed still pretending to be a spaceman or a dinosaur hunter and somehow managed to strip his bed in the midst of the action. Matthew was a deeper sleeper than his sister so I risked stroking his hair as I lifted his head to replace his pillow. I re-covered him with his Thunderbirds duvet and left the room. He would have to make do without his sheet tonight.

Finally, I went into the bathroom, stripped off my well-travelled clothes and ran a bath. After I'd brushed and flossed my teeth and scraped my face with an expensive exfoliating cream (the legacy of some long-forgotten Father's Day or anniversary), I poured a generous helping of bubble bath into the running water, stirred it to create a thick foam and climbed in. I lay there without moving a muscle for some minutes, enjoying the sensation of the hot water on my skin. Then I scrubbed myself vigorously with a harsh abrasive scrunchy thing of Natasha's (the legacy of a long-forgotten

Mother's Day or anniversary) like a religious pilgrim purging himself, desperate to obliterate every molecule of my sin.

By the time I hauled myself out of the bath, towelled myself down and walked back into the bedroom, it was after midnight and Natasha was snoring contentedly. After a week of looking after the kids on her own, she would be at least as shattered as I was after my almost sleepless night and long journey home. I turned off my light and slipped into bed. As I closed my eyes, I remembered that I'd left Natasha propped up with her glasses still perched on her nose. I turned my lamp back on and tried to remove them without disturbing her, but as I lifted them, one of the arms caught her in the eye and she woke with a start. For a moment she was completely disoriented as if she didn't recognise this strange man in her bed and I feared she would scream, but once her vision had cleared and the fuzzy shape resolved itself into the familiar figure of her husband, her look of alarm broadened into the most welcoming of smiles.

'Ah, honey, you're home,' she whispered, 'am I glad to see you!' Then a pause as a look of concern spread across her face. Had I already given away something in mine? 'Is something wrong?'

'No,' I replied, hiding the truth with casual ease. 'I'm just really tired. Go back to sleep and I'll tell you all about it in the morning.'

'You're on earlies,' she said so quietly that I could barely hear her, her eyes already closed. She was asleep again before my head hit the pillow.

Despite the feeling of almost numbing exhaustion, it took me ages to fall asleep. I was still on New York time and my mind was buzzing. Should I tell Natasha what had happened? She'd never believe it – she'd laugh in my face at the thought of me, plain old Joey West, schtupping Olivia Finch. She'd laugh even more if I told her that not only had I slept with this lustrous, illustrous woman, but, it appeared, she seemed to think I was Bennett.

I can't have been asleep very long when I was woken by a bouncing bomb of a small boy erupting into the room, jumping up and down and shouting at full volume in his delirium at seeing his daddy after so long. A week is a long time for a three-year-old and quarter past five was as long as Matthew could wait before coming in to check that I really was back.

'You're on earlies,' Natasha reminded me from behind locked eyelids. 'All week.'

Matthew threw himself on me, forcing me awake. He had some exciting news that couldn't wait. 'Daddy, daddy,' he shouted, 'we've got a new fucking fish! Mummy bought us a fucking fish!'

I was half dragged out of bed and out of the room, pausing only to grab my dressing gown from the back of the door to protect me from the early-morning cold. Matthew swept down the stairs before me and into the living room. He wasn't tall enough to reach the light switch, but was unperturbed by the darkness, negotiating his way through the cluttered room and skipping over discarded toys as if fitted with radar. When he reached the small, octagonal fish tank in the corner, he felt around on the lid to activate the switch that threw light into the watery casket.

'Where is it?' he said to himself as he pressed his nose up against the glass to get a better view inside, 'where is the fucking fish? Daddy,' he called, remembering I was there but not bothering to look back, 'can you fee the fucking fish?' I shook my head silently to indicate that I could not, in fact, see the fucker, while Matthew remained deep in concentration, searching for this elusive aquatic phenomenon.

'Ah, there it is!' he said eventually, a note of triumph in his sweet little voice as he located his prey. He pointed to a louche leopard loach, partially hidden behind the ceramic pirate galleon, busily sucking algae off the inside of the tank as nature intended. 'There's the fucking fish, daddy! Can you fee him? Can you fee the fucker?'

I crouched down to look into the tank, but my view was obscured by my own reflection in the glass, so clear in the darkness of the room around it that I could see the tears making their pathetic, self-pitying journey down my cheeks. 'Yes, I can see him,' I said then, quietly to myself, 'I can see the stupid fucker.'

We studied the sucking fish for a while until I felt it was reasonable to turn on the TV and tune into one of the several dozen all but identical children's channels we had acquired. Matthew sat down next to me and I hugged him like a favourite toy as he stared at the screen. The repetitive squeaky voices drilled into my brain, crowding out the more important stuff I should have been contemplating at that time – like what the hell was I going to say to Natasha when she emerged from her well-earned lie-in. In some circumstances this could probably be used as torture, but for me, at that moment, the cartoonish cacophony delivered blessed relief.

At half past six, Helen glided into the room and perched on my lap. She put both arms around my neck and hugged me tightly, kissing me on my forehead, nose and lips. I realised how much I loved the smell of my daughter in the morning – she smelled of perfection. Not manufactured, thousand-dollar-cosmetic, perfumed Hollywood perfection – just pure, unquestioning beauty, innocence and love. With her face nestled alongside mine, her breath tickling my neck, I risked a couple more tears, hoping she wouldn't notice them trickling into her hair. My fists were clenched so hard that my fingernails dug into my palms. I wanted to scream – to rail like Lear against my own stupidity. If I loved my children as much as I knew I most definitely did, then how the hell had I let what had happened happen? How could I have risked all of this for all of nothing?

When the programme ended, Helen leapt up from my lap and announced she had something for me. She went out into the hall, returning immediately holding a piece of paper carefully in front of her, the blank side towards me to enhance the surprise. She poured herself back into my lap and turned the paper around to reveal an intricate drawing of four people – two big and two little – standing in front of two buildings – one large, one small. Half the picture was in daylight, the other half in darkness. In the lighter half stood a big person in a dress with brown hair and bright red lips, in front of whom stood a little person in a blue dress and an even littler person in some kind of trouser arrangement. All of them wore sad expressions despite the sunshine. Shrouded in darkness, a large person in blue trousers and a red shirt stood before a very tall building. He was almost perfectly round, like Father Christmas on dress-down Friday in Lapland. His expression was enigmatic – on closer inspection I saw that he had two mouths: one turned up in a smile, the other downcast and gloomy. One eye was bright and twinkling; the other looked sad and lonely.

'This is me and Mummy and Matthew,' Helen explained, pointing to the lady with the two dwarves on one side of the page, 'and we're all sad because you're not here. And this,' she said, pointing to casual Santa, 'is you in New York and it's dark because you said that sometimes it's night-time over there when it's daytime here and you're sad because you're missing me and Mummy and Matthew, but you're happy too because you're having a nice time and going to films and parties and stuff.'

'That's beautiful,' I said, huskily and I meant it. Then I noticed a small red figure in the top right corner of the piece of paper. 'What's that "6" for?'

'Oh, that's the mark Mrs Hodges gave it,' Helen replied. 'She told me it was wrong because it couldn't be light and dark at the same time and you couldn't be happy and sad. But she liked the drawing of the house and said that I'd coloured within the lines nicely, so she gave it a six and said it wouldn't be going up for parents' evening.'

'I shall be taking that up with Mrs Hodges,' I heard Natasha say, and looked up to see her standing in the doorway, looking tired but strangely elegant in her white bathrobe and leopard print slippers. I was surprised to see her up so early – usually whoever was on 'lates' eked out every possible second of peace and quiet before joining the chaos downstairs. I'd been counting on waking her up with a nice cup of tea in my own time, fully prepared for our first proper conversation.

'You're up early,' I said. She walked across the room to

me and draped her arms across my shoulders, kissing me on the top of my head as I lowered my face away from her. My eyes, I feared, would be red and it was too early in the year for hay fever.

'I've got some presents for you,' I announced, creating a reason to get up and out of the room so I could compose myself properly. 'I'll make Mummy her tea and then I'll get them.' I heard the chorus of disapproval from the children as I left the room, leaving Natasha to deal with their appeals for the satisfaction of their fundamental human right to receive their gifts immediately. I used the time it took to boil the kettle and brew the tea to make sure I had every angle covered.

Handing out the presents bought me a little more time. Matthew, as usual, received a model plane bearing the livery of the airline that had delivered me safely home, adding it to his collection of twenty or more – one for every time I'd chosen work overseas over time with him and his sister. For Helen, I had found a watch with a selection of different coloured wristbands and Natasha looked pleased with a bottle of her usual perfume and a pair of inexpensive earrings. Everything came from the in-flight catalogue. Everything had to be as normal as possible and even the children knew that I hated souvenir shopping, preferring to spend every possible moment in the Business Lounge rather than joining the fight for last minute gifts at the airport. While Mattie settled down with his new plane, and Helen played happily with her watch, checking the coloured straps against her hair, pyjamas and skin, Natasha and I finally had time to catch up on all that had happened while we'd been apart.

'Not much to tell, really,' I lied when she asked me about my trip. 'Usual stuff. A few meetings with Buddy and the guys at the studio. They're really expanding fast over there. Buddy reckons they might make twelve movies next year which could mean a lot more work for us. We went to the premiere of the movie, of course – pretty lousy film but it should do OK at the box office. Bennett was a complete and utter prat throughout, as expected. Then I thought I'd come home and catch up on all the broken nights I've been missing. I really don't recommend getting eight hours sleep every night, hon. It's very over-rated.' I was aware I was speaking slightly faster than usual but otherwise thought I pulled it off pretty well.

'Same old, same old, then?' Natasha said, her tone gently mocking my casual account but otherwise carrying no obvious threat. 'So while I've been back here enjoying myself with the early mornings and breakfasts and packed lunches and school runs and cleaning and tidying and all the other exciting things that define my existence, you were having to go to meetings and film premieres. Poor baby.' She yawned and hugged her tea a little closer. 'Go on,' she said after a short pause, 'amaze me. How was the party? Did you get to see the divine Olivia Finch again? Or has she taken out a restraining order on you after you watched her doing it last time you were in New York? And did you manage to slip my phone number to George Clooney, by any chance?'

'Erm . . .' I began, hoping that my face hadn't turned as red as it felt from the inside. 'Er . . .' I continued with a little more conviction. 'I can't really remember now. Um. Yes, of course, I did see her at the party. You know, after the film. Just to say "hotel, Olivia" – I mean "hello, Olivia," you know?'

'Ooh,' said Natasha, 'so it's "Olivia" now, is it? May I assume we'll be exchanging Christmas cards this year? If I didn't know you better, I'd think you fancied her. Can't imagine why when you have this waiting for you at home.' She struck a pose, trying to look as glamorous as possible in her ancient, threadbare robe.

I could have said, 'Yes, actually, it is "Olivia" and I didn't just speak to her but spent a good part of Saturday night making mad passionate love to her.' If I had said that, I know exactly how Natasha would have reacted: she'd have given a long, loud laugh. Not directed *at* me in an unkind, belittling way but *with* me in a conspiratorial, in-on-the-joke, pull-the-other-one-it's-got-bells-on,we're-not-the-sort-of-people-who-get-down-and-dirty-with-Hollywood-superstars kind of a way.

But of course I didn't say that. I wasn't ready to tell such a bare-faced truth. Instead, I said, 'Yes, Olivia Finch. And, er, what's his name. The guy who was in, erm, that film . . .' I tailed off, aware that every film star reference would provoke another dozen enquiries from Natasha who was far more interested in the celebrity scene than in my role at its margins.

Fortunately, she was already off on a different tack. 'So what do you say to someone who you've actually watched shagging? Isn't it embarrassing? You're like one of those awful doggy blokes who stand around looking at people doing it through their car windows!'

'I didn't actually watch her doing it' I protested. 'She was acting. It's her job.' I was digging myself a hole and was relieved when stereo cries of 'Daddy!' announced that the uneasy peace that had existed between the children had broken down. They launched themselves at me, both desperate to tell me their version of whatever had happened before the other on the cleverly observed basis that whoever made their case first and loudest usually won my support.

I put on a DVD of one of their favourite animated films and settled them down either side of me on the sofa, glad of the diversion from any further questioning about New York. I closed my eyes and felt myself drifting off to sleep, my arms full of happiness, my head jumbled and confused.

'You just rest here, my love,' Olivia Finch whispered in my ear, 'I'm here to look after you now. You don't have to worry about a thing.'

I jolted upright, not knowing whether I was at home in London, still in New York, or had died and was languishing in purgatory. As my eyes focused on the TV screen, I saw a white rabbit tending to a bruised and bloodied badger, tenderly placing a damp spotted handkerchief across its brow.

'That's right,' said the rabbit in Olivia Finch's unmistakeable soft Southern drawl, 'I'll look after you now, my brave, brave fellow.'

# CITY OF LONDON

I was late into work that morning, using the excuse that, after my arduous journey, I needed a little longer to wake up and get myself ready. My desk in those days was in the open-plan part of the office, right next to the small refreshments area with its coffee machine and kettle and brightly coloured tables and chairs where we were supposed to go to be creative but which were rarely used. Although I was entitled to my own small office I had chosen to stay out in the open. I enjoyed the buzz of other people's conversations, feeling part of the crowd rather than separated off like a manager. It could be distracting at times, especially when a gang assembled for a chat over their cappuccinos, but that was preferable to the oppressive solitude of four glass walls and a standard-issue pot plant.

Bennett, of course, had the Full Executive Monty: large oak desk with leather swivel chair and two designer armchairs for visitors. An enormous TV dominated one corner of the room, on which he was supposed to keep an eye on the world's stock markets but which was usually tuned to wherever in the world cricket was being played that day. I looked through the open door as I walked past on the way to my own desk. The office was empty but it was clear from the mess of papers and the Styrofoam coffee cup on his desk that he was already in and hard at work. A high flyer like Bennett would never let a little jetlag disrupt his busy schedule.

I took off my jacket and hung it over the back of my chair as I looked at my almost completely empty desk, girding myself for the challenges of the day ahead. My assistant, Polly, had a habit of tidying my desk whenever I went away, meaning that for several days after my return I had no idea where anything was. I heard the click-clack of her shoes on the wooden floor as she approached and, at that precise moment, realised that, distracted as I'd been, I'd forgotten to bring her anything back from New York. It was an unwritten rule that we always bought our assistants a little something to thank them for organising the trip. I shared Polly with two other guys and we competed to outdo each other with our presents – a box of Statue of Liberty-shaped chocolates just wouldn't cut it anymore, though none of us had yet reached the levels of excess that Bennett displayed when buying presents for his assistant, Amanda. Then again, none of us claimed our gifts back on expenses either.

'Hiya, Polly,' I said cheerily, 'how's things? Wait till you see what I've brought you back from the States.' I was pretty excited myself about what it was and where the hell it was going to come from. 'You'll love it,' I hoped.

'Oh, you shouldn't have, Joe,' Polly replied in that curious accent that meant she could have grown up anywhere south of a line drawn across the M1 at Newport Pagnell, and east of Swindon. 'Did you see what Bennett bought Amanda? Latest fuck-off DKNY watch – she's been flashing it around to everyone. Looks very expensive. I hope you haven't gone to that much trouble for me.' Polly smiled. She, along with almost everyone else in the company, knew that Bennett's relationship with Amanda was more than purely secretarial. 'So, how was the trip?'

'Oh, you know,' I replied. 'Same old, same old.'

'And how was the film? And the party? Meet any stars?'

'Oh, you know, the party was pretty good – a lot better than the movie – but mainly it was just, you know, boring meetings.' Whenever I spoke to Polly, I seemed to take on the personality and speech patterns of a Second Division football manager.

'And how was Benny Boy?' Polly asked.

'That's Mr Bennett to you, Ms Nash,' I said in mock indignation, 'and, you know, he was the same old, same old . . .' I left her to fill in the blanks as she saw fit.

Polly placed a small pile of neatly ordered paperwork in my empty in-tray and walked back to her desk. I switched on my computer and waited for it to splutter into life, drumming my fingers impatiently as it ate up eight, nine or even ten seconds of my precious time before springing into life, and then I checked my e-mails.

I had dealt with most of my electronic correspondence while I was away, so my virtual in-tray wasn't much fuller than its physical cousin. Most of the backlog of messages was rubbish I hadn't bothered to open while I was in New

York which could now be deleted without another look. I'd just finished wading through all this junk when I heard the familiar ping of incoming mail and scrolled back up to the top of my in-tray to greet the welcome intrusion.

The message was from Bennett. He was one of those modern managers who rarely bothered to make the short journey from his office to my desk, opting instead for the convenience of the impersonal e-mail. The title caught my attention:

From: Joseph Bennett
To: Joseph West

FW: WHAT THE HELL'S GOING ON?

Hey, West, take a look at this. Even madder than before! It's not from her e-mail address, so I'm pretty sure it must be one of the studio guys having a pop at me.

What do you reckon I should do? I think they've gone a bit far now, don't you? Isn't there a law against pretending to be someone you're not? Drop in and see me when you get a chance. I'll be here all morning catching up on all the crap.

Joseph A. Bennett
Head of Entertainment and Media Division

Then came the apparently deranged ramblings of a Hollywood superstar:

From: CaddyMac@wannabe.com
To: JosephABennett@askettbrown.co.uk

## WHAT THE HELL'S GOING ON?

Please tell me what's going on. We had such an amazing time in New York – I swear I have never laughed as much as I did that night doing what we were doing! Seeing you stripped down to just those crazy socks set me off and after that I just couldn't stop giggling! Believe me, English, when you act all day for a living it is such a treat not to have to do any pretending on your night off! You were truly magnificent!

I know you like me too, so how come you're treating me so mean? Like I was just some cheap pick-up for you to enjoy and then toss aside like a piece of trash. Well, let me tell you, Mister Joseph A. Bennett – I know all about trash. Most people would say my family were trash, but I always wanted something better than that. I've tasted dirt and I never want to taste it again and I've worked damn hard to make sure I don't have to.

Please don't be mean to me, English. Send me something nice and friendly real soon, sweetie-pie. I'd hate to have to take this to Buddy. He gets really pissed if people upset me.

Olivia xxx ☹☹☹

'Christ!' I thought after I'd read Olivia's message a second time. She really did appear to be barking! What had I done to her?

Still not having a clue what I would say to Bennett when I reached his office, I typed 'on my way' into a reply e-mail, grabbed my jacket and got on my way.

Amanda was nowhere to be seen when I arrived, so I knocked and let myself in. Bennett was hunched over his desk, staring intently at his computer. He turned around when he heard me enter, then, without a word, returned to his vigil, focussing intently on the screen. He looked like a scholar analysing a newly discovered Dead Sea Scroll, searching between the lines of Olivia's message for hidden meanings.

'Hi, West,' he said, finally registering my presence. 'Bloody daft, isn't it? But it's really starting to annoy me now. Some bugger's having a go at me, and I want to know who it is. You know what I've been wondering?'

I was used to Bennett's autocratic conversational style and assumed he wasn't expecting an answer. True to form, he continued without waiting for a reply.

'The only people I can think of who might have done this are those two we met at the party the other night – you know the chaps who work for Buddy. What're their names?'

'Len and Diana?' I suggested

'Yes, that's them. I wonder whether I might have annoyed them somehow and now they're trying to get back at me. Maybe even trying to blackmail me. What do you think? I have to admit, it is starting to get to me a bit. And Amanda went off in a right old strop when I showed her this one.'

'You showed her?' I said, although it might have come out more like a shriek. 'What on earth did you do that for?'

'Because I thought she'd find it funny,' he replied without emotion, 'especially the bit about me standing bollock naked in just a pair of stupid socks. I've never worn a pair of funny bloody socks in my life, so whoever is doing this has got that wrong for a start. Take a seat, West. Sorry I can't offer you a coffee.'

I sat down in one of the pair of leather armchairs arranged in front of the television. I crossed my legs, but immediately uncrossed them again and tucked them away beneath me before Bennett had a chance to spot the image of Mr Messy and the legend 'Have a Messy Monday' emblazoned on my otherwise black socks.

'Anyway,' he continued, 'I've asked Amanda to see if she can find out who this CaddyMac might be. See if there's anyone by that name on Buddy's payroll. Do you think this could be down to Dan and Wotserface? I gave them both my card at the party so they've got my details. Do you think I could have annoyed them?'

'Len and Diana? Well, it's possible,' I replied. 'I mean it's possible you might have annoyed them. But neither of them would do anything like this. They're both professional people. It would be suicide in Hollywood to get caught passing yourself off as a major star.'

'Yeah, you're probably right,' Bennett conceded, after staring at the screen a while longer. 'I can't see anything, you know, Chinesey in the way it's written and I don't think that the old feller . . .'

'Len.'

' . . . yeah, Len, would have the balls for something like this. Not at his age. As you say, it would be curtains for them if they got caught upsetting an important business partner like me. Any other ideas?'

I shook my head, then shook it again more vigorously

when Bennett turned round to enquire, wordlessly, into my silence. He turned back to his screen and I could almost feel him thinking – hear the cogs whirring around, trying to knock his brain into the right gear. After an uncomfortable pause, he stood up and walked to the back of his office. He peered out through the Velux blinds that were integrated between the two panes of the glass wall: Wellington surveying his troops before the battle of Waterloo. Make that Napoleon.

'You know me, West, I like a joke as much as the next man. Remember that corker I played on you on our first day here?' I did. It hadn't been funny then and it still wasn't funny now. Bennett ignored the fact that I didn't join in his chuckling at the memory and carried on. 'But I really don't think this is funny anymore. I don't want to look like Mr Bloody Misery Guts by going in all heavy on whoever's behind this, but I will have to take it upstairs to Bill Davis if this carries on. What do you think I should do?'

I waited to see if he really was expecting an answer this time. I didn't have a clue how he should reply to Olivia – and I didn't really care. All that mattered to me at that moment was that my role in this confusion should remain hidden for as long as possible. For the rest of my life, would be a good start.

'Well?' Bennett's hectoring voice interrupted my thoughts. 'Come on – you know these people better than I do. What will it take to make them stop this bloody nonsense?'

'I don't know, Joseph,' I said. It wasn't yet ten o'clock on a Monday morning and already I was tired and wanted to go home. To crawl under my duvet until the world had woken from this hysteria and returned to dull normality.

'I really can't think of anyone who would do a thing like this, so I can't help you. Sorry.'

Bennett's usual composure deserted him for a moment as he realised that, despite his best efforts to involve me, he was on his own. 'You are fucking useless, West! I have no idea what those fat bastards in LA see in you. You've been a useless turd since the day we both started here. I'll sort this out for myself and then I'll tell Bill Davis about the whole bloody thing. And I'll make sure he knows exactly how much help you've been. Now bugger off back to your cubicle while I deal with it.'

I sloped off, leaving Bennett as I'd found him, hunched over his desk staring at his computer, like a heron at the water's edge following a fish. I went back to my desk and pushed papers around as I watched the minutes tick slowly by towards lunchtime. After about an hour of minimal activity, I heard another ping. I had mail.

From: JosephABennett@Askettbrown.co.uk
To: CaddyMac@wannabe.com
Bcc: Joseph West

RE: WHAT THE HELL'S GOING ON?

OK. We've had our bit of fun and it was a good laugh and all that but it really has to stop now. We are profes-sional people and this kind of thing can easily get out of hand. So let's put an end to it now before anyone says or does anything they'll regret. I really don't think either of us wants to see anyone getting into trouble over this nonsense so I suggest we cool it before things go too far.

I sincerely hope that we can continue our relationship

on a purely professional basis in the future and I trust
that this will be acceptable to you too.

Yours,
Joseph A. Bennett
Head of Entertainment and Media Division

Although it was still some way off anyone's definition of
lunchtime, I left the office as soon as possible and went
for a walk, ostensibly to buy that present for Polly but also
because I needed to clear my head. Clearly it *was* Olivia
who was pestering Bennett – nobody else would know
about my stupid socks unless she'd posted an account of
our illicit tryst on Facebook or put a photo of the offending
items on Instagram – but why? And how would she react
to his latest awful reply. She was a sweet girl and she didn't
deserve to be mistreated by that oaf. And could I really
stand by and let it happen when the whole thing was my
fault in the first place, just to save my own skin?

When I got back to the office it was alive with rumours
and not much work was being done. Polly seemed pleased
with the designer sunglasses I'd managed to find her, but
was far more interested in quizzing me about what had
happened on my trip.

'Have you heard about Benny?' she warbled as she put
the glasses down on my desk with barely a second glance.
I prayed I hadn't left any labels anywhere that could identify their source as London EC1 rather than downtown
Manhattan. 'Course, you have – you were with him, weren't
you?'

'I only know what he's told me,' I lied. 'He denies anything went on out there. He reckons it's a couple of his mates at Buddy's place winding him up.'

'I didn't think he had any mates over there,' Polly replied, 'and you were there. Surely you'd know if he'd shagged Olivia Finch.'

'I wasn't with him every second, Poll. And I certainly didn't spend the nights with him. Askett Brown can still run to a separate room for each for us, you know.'

Polly smiled. 'Yeah, but you must have seen if he was talking to her or anything. Did you speak to her again? You didn't set them up, did you?'

I was probably blushing as I conceded that I had indeed spoken to Olivia at the party but had definitely not introduced her to Bennett. It felt like a police interrogation as Polly probed me for more inside gen she could feed to her colleagues. If information was power in the City, good gossip was like the uranium at the generator's core. God forgive me, but I couldn't resist adding: 'But we didn't leave the party together so I suppose anything could have happened after I left.'

Polly shook her head thoughtfully. 'In some ways I can believe it – you know, given what a bastard he is – but for the life of me I can't see her going for him, can you? She seems such a beautiful person and he's a complete and utter tosser. And if he had done it, wouldn't he be bragging about it rather than trying to cover it up? He's not usually so coy about his out-of-office activities, is he?'

'I see your point,' I replied, wondering if she had stumbled upon a fatal flaw in my hastily constructed plan, 'but, remember, at the end of the day he is a married man. And I don't think Buddy – or Bill Davis – would be too pleased if they found out what's happened. I mean, what's alleged to have happened.'

'Well,' said Polly as she scooped up her new sunglasses and made to walk away, 'whether it's true or not, Amanda has gone completely fucking ape shit. God knows what Mrs B. will say when she finds out.'

# MILL HILL, NORTH LONDON

I left the office before five that evening, citing jet lag as the reason I couldn't put in the usual twelve-hour day. I'd like to say I left early because I was keen to get home to spend some quality time with my family after being away for a whole week. That may even have been partly true. But the main reason was that I wanted to be well out of sight before Olivia woke up in LA and went online to see if her lover had replied to her latest e-mail. I was trying to outrun the Internet.

I also had an important mission to attend to. After kissing Natasha and the kids 'hello', I sprinted up the stairs to our bedroom, pulled open the top drawer of my chest (we had matching 'his' and 'hers' furniture throughout our bedroom – identical cherry-wood chests of drawers, wardrobes, bookshelves and bedside cabinets all arranged in perfect symmetry) and started searching frantically for the smoking gun – the comedy socks that could pin the crime of my adultery on my weak, sloping shoulders. After a few minutes of fruitless excavation, an untidy pile of balled socks, odd socks, boxer shorts and briefs had spread across the floor by my feet.

'What on earth are you doing?' I heard Natasha say and looked round to see her standing in the doorway, leaning against one side like a drunken sailor against a lamp post. 'What are you looking for?'

'What?' I replied as if my wife had been addressing me in Serbo-Croat. 'Looking for? I'm not looking for anything. I just thought it was high time I gave my underwear drawer a bit of a clear-out. There's stuff in here I haven't worn for years. Look!' With some reluctance, I picked up a couple of pairs of perfectly good socks and a few of their unmatched cousins and threw them without ceremony into the waste-paper bin. Then I bent down and picked up the rest of my collection of undergarments and stuffed them back into the drawer. 'That's better,' I said, straining to push it shut, and still wondering where the hell the incriminating items might be.

'Are you feeling OK, love?' Natasha said, a look of genuine concern spreading across her face. 'Touch of jet lag? You do remember that I'm supposed to be going out this evening, don't you? I've got my book group. Would you rather I cancelled? I haven't actually managed to finish the book so I'm not too bothered about going.'

'No, you go,' I said, 'I'll be fine. It's about time you had a good night out.'

'I'm not sure I'd call sitting with a bunch of pseudo-intellectuals discussing the latest Booker Prize-winner a good night out, but thank you. I could do with getting away from this place for a bit. Are you OK to get the kids' tea sorted while I get ready?'

'Of course,' I said, kissing her on the cheek as I brushed past her in the doorway. 'No problem.'

Following Natasha's instructions, I went down to the kitchen and started to prepare the children's tea, mixing up an off-white, glutinous, cheesy sauce which I then threw over some quick-cook pasta and doled out into their favourite bowls. As I sat down to watch them spooning the goo in the approximate direction of their hungry mouths, the realisation suddenly struck me: the evidence I was looking for would still be in amongst the dirty washing I'd brought back from New York. Leaving the children to eat, I sidled into the utility room to continue my search. It didn't take me long to sift through the pile of laundry stacked up by the machine and find the guilty parties – my pair of black socks with the brightly coloured cartoon and the slogan picked out in red letters: 'Have a Silly Saturday'. I rammed them into my trouser pockets – one to the left; one to the right – then raced back into the kitchen just as the first spoonful of cheesy pasta hit the wedding picture of my parents-in-law that hung above the breakfast bar, the product of Matthew's poor aim or, to be fair, Helen's quick reactions in dodging the projectile he had aimed at her. His second salvo caught his sister square in the middle of the forehead.

'Matthew! Stop that!' I shouted, and heard my words echoed as Natasha arrived in the room, making exactly the same demand. She looked at me as if it was somehow my fault that our daughter was in floods of tears and thick, cheesy gloop was now sliding down her mother's stern, unsmiling, monochrome face.

'What is going on in here?' Natasha shouted, directing

the question at me, even though Matthew was still holding his spoon and reloading it with more of his dinner like a medieval soldier rearming his trebuchet. 'Where exactly were you while your son was redecorating the room?'

'I was here the whole time,' I replied, then corrected myself, 'almost the whole time. But I haven't got eyes in the back of my head and—'

Natasha cut me off. 'What's that?' she asked, pointing towards my groin.

I looked down. A Mr Silly sock hung down from each of my pockets like the drooping ears of a basset hound, as if the unfortunate beast had charged me from behind and this was all that remained visible. Gingerly, I removed the socks from my pockets as if I was as surprised to see them there as she was. 'Oh these,' I said. 'Well, um, I was just looking at how much washing I brought back from New York and thought I'd pull out anything that might live to fight another day. And these socks really aren't too bad, so—'

'Pass them over here,' Natasha ordered, holding out a hand like a Gestapo officer wanting to check my papers. I did as I was told and she held each of the socks up to her nose in turn, then extended her arm to create a safer distance between the offending item and her nostrils. 'Phew! If this is what not too bad smells like, I really don't want to test the rest of it. Put them back in the pile, then clear up this mess. I'll see you later. And Matthew, put that spoon down right now or I swear I will tip the rest of the plate over your head and see how you like it.'

With that, she turned and marched out of the kitchen, leaving Matthew laughing, Helen crying, and me digging myself ever deeper into a situation which smelled a whole lot worse than my silly socks.

By the time I'd finished cleaning up the kitchen and dragged the children upstairs for an unwanted bath and then bed, I was too tired even to think about eating, so I plonked myself in my favourite chair in front of the TV. When Natasha arrived home, I was fast asleep next to a half-finished glass of wine which itself was next to a half-empty bottle. She woke me with a brusque knee to my left shoulder. The football I'd been watching had long since finished, replaced by some obscure activity involving men in Lycra body stockings locked in a cage beating each other senseless.

Natasha turned it off and turned on me. 'So why didn't you tell me about Olivia Finch?' she asked without any preamble or welcome home pleasantries. I didn't have to feign confusion. I'd been rudely awakened from a dream in which I'd been rushing up and down Fifth Avenue searching for presents. I'd already bought more fake scarves and handbags than I could carry but was desperate to buy more, as if I had a whole harem of wives and mistresses to cater for. 'Let me put it another way.' Natasha continued, 'when were you planning to tell me about what happened in New York?'

'I . . . I . . . I . . .' I was trapped. A kaleidoscope of fear whirled inside my head, forcing out rational thought. That image of the future appeared again, projected onto the screen behind my eyes. My children daddlylessly living out their lives, while I lurched familylessly through mine. I didn't have a clue what the next word of my reply was going to be – but I knew that my whole life depended on it. I gulped in air like a diver with the bends, scouring my brain for the right words to use – words that might yet save my marriage.

Fortunately, just as I was going down a third time, Natasha filled in the blanks for me. 'I have just had the embarrassment of sitting at my bloody book group while everyone talked about what happened in New York and I – whose husband was actually there – knew nothing about it. Poor Sandra Bennett just sat in the corner completely distraught. I mean, she knows her toe-rag husband has had the odd fling in the past but never anything like this. This could get into the papers and everything. And you – Mr See No Evil, Hear No Evil, and definitely Speak No Bloody Evil – didn't even bother to tell me about it. Bennett and Olivia Finch – it's unbelievable! Does everyone at work know?'

I fought to gather my composure, taking a large swig of wine to steady my hands and nerves. 'Oh that! Um, yes, I think so. Pretty well everyone. Amanda, his PA, went up the bloody wall! Polly and the rest of the girls were full of it, loving it. But, you know, it is only a rumour. He completely denies anything happened.'

'But you were with him, Joe! You must know what happened. You're not telling me that Joseph Bennett slept with the world's most gorgeous woman and forgot to mention it to you. He isn't capable of keeping something like that secret. And what do you mean "Amanda went up the wall" – what's it got to do with her?'

Reasoning that this was probably not a good time to offer up another juicy snippet I'd failed to mention for the past few months, I ventured onto a different track. 'Well, I wasn't with him the whole time, was I? And he swears blind he didn't do it. He reckons it's one of Buddy's guys having a laugh at his expense – or maybe even attempting to blackmail him. I guess that's why he told Sandra. Surely he wouldn't have told her if he really had done something, would he?'

That stopped Natasha in her tracks and, after pouring herself a glass of wine, she allowed me to tell her the whole story – the sanitised version of the story at least. Looking back on it now, that was the time when I should have told her everything – and taken the consequences – but the truth is that I didn't have the guts. So, instead, I told her what I understood had happened from Bennett's perspective, right up to the latest e-mail exchange. And once that moment had passed, it was too late. I was like a downhill skier who'd started his descent and then changed his mind –there was no going back now. All that lay ahead was a long and bumpy ride to the finishing gate.

'And what do you think?' Natasha asked when I had finished spinning my yarn. 'Do you think he did it?'

'There's really no telling with Bennett,' I said, 'but I'd have thought she had better taste.'

The wine had a thawing effect on Natasha and she quickly forgave me for leaving her in the dark. She sat down beside me on the couch, almost on top of me in fact, and snuggled up. She hadn't had a chance to welcome me home properly yet and it seemed that she was keen to put that right.

'Well he's welcome to her, if you ask me,' she said, speaking into my neck as she moved even closer. 'By all accounts she's a Grade-A Bunnyboiler. I've read about her in my magazines: once she gets her talons into a guy she never lets go. You know, there are times when I am really glad I married a steady, reliable bloke like you, Joe, who would never dream of sleeping with someone like Olivia Finch. We might not have as much money as the Bennetts – you should have seen the watch he brought Sandra back from New York! – but at least I know I can trust you. You wouldn't want to sleep with Olivia Finch, would you, love?'

How the hell do you answer a question like that? The whole point of people like Olivia Finch is that people like me want to sleep with them. That's why she's paid millions of dollars a movie. Sure, they have to be able to act a bit but the film industry is built on the idea that ordinary people will pay to watch beautiful people do extraordinary things, then go back to their humdrum lives to pretend to be them or be with them. Of course I wanted to sleep with Olivia Finch. I just wish to God I hadn't.

'Well,' I began, and allowed the pause to linger long enough for Natasha to readjust her position away from the cat-like comfort into which she had poured herself in the expectation of an easy conversation. There's a world of worry in a well-delivered 'well'. 'Yes, at one level obviously I find Olivia Finch attractive. I mean, she is very beautiful. Aren't we supposed to lust after people like her and dream we could have them one day?'

'But it's different for you,' Natasha said her tone quite different from a few moments earlier. 'You do get to meet people like her, don't you? You have met her.'

'You could hardly call what we did meeting each other,' I replied, trying not to sound too defensive. 'We said "Hi" once as she was pulling her dressing gown back on after a shoot and again at the party. That doesn't exactly make us best buddies, does it?'

'Oh yes, I forgot. Not only do you get to meet Olivia Finch, you get to meet her naked. Doesn't that give you some advantage over the sad old bloke fondling himself in the back row of the Odeon?'

'But it's not like that, Nat. It's part of my job, isn't it? I'm not likely to start playing with myself in the middle of a meeting or if I'm at the studio on official business, am I?'

'I don't know – are you? I don't have a clue what goes on at your work or inside your head these days, Joe. All I know is that you've now told me that you dream about shagging someone other than me. Is that why you didn't tell me about Bennett? Because you didn't think you'd be able to tell me without showing how cut up you are that he got to fulfil one of your fantasies?'

'So, are you telling me that you've never lusted after anyone on the telly?' I countered. 'Never fancied jumping into bed with George Clooney or Brad Pitt? It's funny how you suddenly discovered an interest in soccer whenever David Beckham was playing. Remember how you were when you saw Colin Firth in *Pride and Prejudice*? Dripping wet. And you were even worse when you saw him coming out of that pond. Come on,' I said, 'I'm a professional accountant who just happens to work in film. Looking at an attractive young actress means no more to me than looking at a well-put-together fixed asset register. It's just part of my job. You know I only have eyes for you and a complex consolidated balance sheet.'

'You're a bloody liar, West,' Natasha said, more accurately

than she knew. 'Just make sure you keep your hands on the books and off the talent. And,' she added gathering up the empty wine glasses – 'if George or Brad or Becks ever do pop round offering to re-pave our driveway or stick in a bit of double glazing, you make yourself scarce. OK?'

# CITY OF LONDON

I made sure I was in early the next morning, only to find those who had arrived even earlier rapt in conversation about the only story that mattered: had he or hadn't he? As the nearest thing to an eyewitness, I was in great demand for my observations and it took me a while to reach my desk. When I got there, I was surprised to see Bennett perched on the edge, absent-mindedly flicking through the papers in my in-tray.

He looked at his watch as I arrived and hung my coat on a hook on the wall. 'Ah, Mr West, I've been expecting you,' he said in unwitting parody of a Bond villain. 'For about half an hour, actually. Still, never mind that. Come with me to my office. I've had another bloody e-mail from that mad woman. '

I did as instructed and stood behind him as he opened his latest electronic billet-doux. He twisted in his chair so I could see the screen over his shoulder:

From: CaddyMac@wannabe.com
To: JosephABennett@Askettbrown.co.uk

RE: RE: WHAT THE HELL'S GOING ON?

Oh, so that was just a bit of fun, was it? Well, I'm glad you enjoyed yourself asshole because I've done nothing but cry since I got back to LA. Perhaps you should have thought about staying cool before you went too far in the first place. And what the hell do you mean we should keep this professional in future? Do you want to pay me? What the hell do you take me for? Or maybe you think I should be paying you.

I am just so confused, English. I really thought we made a serious connection that night but now it seems I was just another conquest for you. Bet you've been getting big kudos from all your homeys for screwing Olivia Finch, haven't you? Well, I've kept it a secret so far but I'm warning you if I don't start getting some answers from you real soon, I'm going to tell Buddy exactly how you've treated me.

Please write and tell me this is all just some kind of misunderstanding. What was it your guy Churchill said about the Limeys and the Yanks being separated by a common language? I'm really hoping he might be right. Listen, English, I'll be in London soon for the European premiere. Why don't we meet up and talk it over? I don't want to fall out with you, and I'd hate to see you get hurt like you're hurting me.

Olly xxx ☺☹

'*Wow!*' I thought to myself, not clear now whether Olivia wanted to marry Bennett or have him kneecapped.

'So, what do you make of it, West?' Bennett asked without looking away from the screen.

'Shaw,' I replied.

'Sure what?' said Bennett. 'What the fuck are you on about?'

'It was George Bernard Shaw who said that about the British and Americans being two peoples separated by a common language. Not Churchill. Common mistake . . .'

'I hardly think that is the most pressing or pertinent issue right now, is it, you moron? The pertinent question is what the fuck am I going to do about all this nonsense. Well, West?'

I was all out of answers, so I tried a question instead. 'Are you going to reply?'

'Nah,' Bennett replied. 'I'm going to let this one pass and see what happens. Give it the old slow-play. If it is someone messing me around, then hopefully they'll get bored and pack up. If they are out to get me, they'll have to show themselves at some point – and then I'll tear them a new arsehole. As far as Amanda can make out, there isn't anyone at the studio with a name anything like CaddyMac and it's not from their server, so it could be coming from anywhere. And if it really is this Finch woman, then she's got more problems than I have because I most definitely did not bonk her that night. That's one thing I'm absolutely sure about. I may have been a bit wasted but I would not have forgotten that!'

For the next few days Bennett received a series of e-mails from CaddyMac, each sadder, more confused and more vitriolic than the last. And then it went quiet. Perhaps his strategy had worked. We would find out soon enough. Buddy and his team were flying into London the following week for an important meeting and we were all invited to the London premiere of the film.

# BRENT CROSS, NORTH LONDON

That weekend I spent as much time as possible with the children, taking on double daddy duty both to make up for the time I had missed but also in an attempt to expiate my guilt – to banish the images of that separate future that had haunted me on the plane. I took them swimming on the Saturday morning, then, on the Sunday, we went to the Brent Cross shopping centre. I gave them some money to buy themselves a small toy each and bought them comics – flimsy publications they never actually read but wanted only for the cheap plastic toys stuck to the front cover – and myself a copy of the *Sunday Times*. Thus equipped, we went to one of the myriad coffee bars that had sprung up all over the centre, displacing the small retailers and meaning that the weary shopper was never more than a few yards from a cappuccino and a croissant or triple chocolate muffin.

I took Helen's and Matthew's drinks and snacks orders then found a table where I could keep an eye on them from my place in the slow-moving queue. I smiled pleasantly towards the three baristas as they collectively served the customer ahead of me – one to take the order, one to make the coffee and one to take the money and work out, after much umming and erring, something approximating to the correct change. Then I waited as they held a brief conference to discuss their previous adventure in the world of beverage-dispensing – perhaps it was company policy to review each transaction and identify what had gone well, what could be improved upon and what might be learned that they could apply to their next encounter with a customer. This particular review was focussing on an assessment of the poor choice of clothing of the previous customer, not least because of her 'enormous arse'. I waved a ten-pound note casually in the air in the hope that I might catch one of their six eyes. When this proved fruitless, I smiled again – the smile that had so recently melted the heart of a Hollywood superstar – and coughed a small, throat-clearing cough.

'What?' barked one of the girls behind the counter.

'One regular cappuccino, one hot chocolate with cream and marshmallows, this orange juice and two pain au raisins, please,' I asked.

'In a minute,' replied the girl. 'Can't you see we're busy?'

Rather than lose my temper, I tried the winning smile again, turning it up a few megawatts and lacing it with a drop of my newly discovered irresistible charm.

'And stop looking at me like that, you creep, or I'll call the fuckin' manager.' She turned to resume her conversation with her colleagues and I distinctly heard the word 'perv' above the babble of voices and screeching laughter. After several more minutes, during which the queue behind me grew ever longer, she turned around again, looked at me as though she had never seen me before in her life and asked me what I wanted. I placed my order and handed over the exact amount of cash for the transaction together with the correct loyalty card for this particular establishment, carefully selected from the half dozen or more I always carried with me.

I took the drinks and pastries back to the table and sat down. When I looked around I noticed that each table was almost exactly the same as my own: a hassled dad sitting with one, two or three children – toys and comics strewn across the table, an unopened newspaper silently mocking the parent from a spare chair or a stationer's carrier bag on the floor, the coveted sports section tantalisingly out of reach as spilled drinks were cleared up, chocolate wiped from faces, broken free gifts mended or spirited away with promises of replacements, arguments settled and fights broken up. There was a chance that, like me, these men might have been holding the fort while their other halves shopped or relaxed at home, but I didn't think so. There was an air of desperation about many of them, too much effort being put into making sure that their charges wanted for nothing, that every moment was as good as it could possibly be, that the memories of this morning would sustain them – all of them, father and child alike – until they met again the following weekend. Same time, same place, same things said and left unsaid. This, I reflected, was what divorce looked like. This was what happened to men who couldn't sustain their loyalty to one woman any more than they could manage it for their favourite coffee-seller.

# CITY OF LONDON

The gang from Los Angeles arrived right on time, their black Mercedes pulling up outside our building exactly five minutes before the meeting was due to start. It took great precision – and teams of well-paid assistants – to arrange their lives so they could board a flight on the other side of the world, walk off it into the waiting seats of a plush hire car and into the coffee-and-Danish land of the meeting room just as the clock announced the appointed hour.

This visit was vital to our continued good relationship with Printing Press Productions and we had pulled out all the stops to make Buddy and his team feel welcome and important. They were shown into the very plushest of our executive suites, with its antique oak table inlaid with mahogany marquetry and soft burgundy leather chairs that moulded themselves around every contour of the incumbent. While sipping hot drinks served in our best china and nibbling on their pastries, they could enjoy unrestricted views out over the City of London, taking in St Paul's Cathedral and the Tower of London and, away in the distance, the sketchy outline of the London Eye.

After the usual pleasantries had been exchanged, we took our seats – Americans on one side of the table; Brits on the other. Both teams arranged themselves in a predetermined order: Head Honcho in the middle and the rest of the group fanned out on either side in order of importance, like the top table at a society wedding. For them this meant that Buddy took the alpha male seat in the middle, with his Finance Director Mike Abrahams on his left and Len Palmer to his right, followed by Diana Lee next to Len. On our side, our senior partner Bill Davis was the silverback, with Bennett on his right and me on his left, opposite Len. Next to me was a young guy called Andrew Johnson who I was training up to take more responsibility for my film portfolio. He looked stricken with nerves despite Di's best efforts to relax him with a friendly smile from the seat opposite. Bennett stared at Len and Di as if peering into their souls, searching for signs of guilt.

Bill introduced his team and there were grunts of acknowledgement as Bennett offered his hand to each of them and then smiles and hand clasps when my name was mentioned. Buddy invited each of his team to introduce themselves and then it was down to business. Bill explained how important the PPP account was to Askett Brown and that he had brought Joseph Bennett across from our Oil and Minerals Division to strengthen the entertainment team. Then he invited Bennett to begin his presentation setting out how he saw the relationship between the two companies developing over the next few years.

Bennett rose to his feet and clicked a button on the small remote control unit hidden in his palm. A screen inched its way down the wall behind our heads and we swivelled in our chairs to achieve the best possible view. Bennett cleared his throat and took a long sip of water before clicking the remote again to bring up the first slide. With some surprise, I realised he was nervous.

This was the first big presentation Bennett had made since joining my division. Fortunately, he had swallowed a little of his monumental pride and asked me to help him with some background material. I'd given him data on the performance of recent PPP releases, their share of the UK and European markets, future growth potential, etc., working hard to make sure that the analysis was bang up to date, the forecasts realistic and defensible. Buddy's team would see through any inflated or overly optimistic figures in a heartbeat. I'd sent the data through to Bennett a week before the meeting, knowing that he would want to add his own style and interpretation. He hadn't so much as acknowledged my efforts, let alone asked any questions about the material. His one comment that morning – as we'd made our way to the meeting room – had been: 'Thanks for all that guff you sent me, West. Interesting – but a bit tame for this lot, so I've spiced it up a notch. Watch and learn, my boy. Watch and learn.'

He spoke briefly over the title slide, introducing himself again and explaining what he was going to talk about, then trundled headlong into the main presentation. From the moment the next slide appeared, I knew we were in for a long and painful morning. Under the title 'Oil Magnet' was a picture of a group of self-satisfied men in business suits and hard hats standing on an oil platform. On their shoulders sat an insufferably smug Bennett holding a huge fan of high-denomination banknotes.

He paused to let the image sink in, then intoned in a low stage whisper, like the commentary at a Planetarium, 'The Alpha Seven oil platform, the North Sea, 150 miles from land. That man being held aloft by a group of grateful shareholders is, of course, Yours Truly. In my hand is just a small part of the profit I'd delivered to them from that one small platform.' His voice rose as his nerves receded. 'The guys seemed to think these incredible results were all down to me. But, of course, that's not true. I reckon only about 90 per cent of that success could be pinned on my slender shoulders.' He laughed to indicate that this was an attempt at self-deprecating humour but, as was often the case with Bennett, he laughed alone. 'My aim, gentlemen, is to put you in the same position as these guys on the screen.'

'What?' Buddy interjected. 'You want to take us 150 miles from civilisation to kiss someone's ass? Have you never been to LA?'

Bennett ignored the laughter from both sides of the table and pressed on. 'No, sir! I mean, I am going to put you on top of your world. Let me explain.'

For the next forty-five minutes, Bennett ran through a series of highly complex, extraordinarily dull and generally irrelevant slides based on a complete misunderstanding of the information I'd sent him. His first twenty slides were all about the wonderful world of mineral extraction and the crucial part he had played in it. By the time he turned his attention to the film industry, he had all but lost his audience. A couple of the Americans were checking e-mails or playing Angry Birds on their iPhones. Buddy was clearly and loudly asleep.

Unable to understand the information I'd given him and too proud to ask for an explanation, Bennett had simply ignored my stuff and pressed incoherently on with his own. Every slide displayed his ignorance in glorious Technicolor. He presented a plethora of statistics showing how Printing Press Productions was failing compared to the other Hollywood studios, ignoring the fact that most of their competitors had at least a seventy-five-year head-start on them. Everyone – except Bennett – knew that PPP's performance in the three years they'd been operating had been sensational – but, as long as they were only able to distribute only six to eight films a year, they struggled to compete on equal terms with the major studios who were distributing twice as many. What they were looking for now was an injection of capital to help them move to the next level of operation. What they were getting was a lecture on how they needed to rethink their film-making strategy and concentrate on making more films that people like Bennett and his mother wanted to watch.

After Bennett's final slide, there was a brief silence while people came to terms with the fact their ordeal was over – like hostages released from a long siege. Len nudged Buddy to wake him, making no attempt to conceal what he was doing. Bennett clapped his hands together enthusiastically and said: 'Right gentlemen – and lady – any questions?'

All eyes fell on Buddy as he lifted himself slowly in his chair. He drew out the dramatic pause by leaning forward to pluck an orange-flavoured boiled sweet from a bowl in the middle of the table, unwrap it and pop it into his mouth.

'Yeah,' he said eventually, 'I have a question for you, Mr Bennett.' He pushed the sweet into one of his cheeks with his tongue. 'My question is: what's it like to fuck Olivia Finch?'

The collective intake of breath threatened to suck all the air out of the room. All eyes switched to Bennett, who sat tight-lipped, his face reddening, his usual sangfroid blown to smithereens, his hoped-for triumph derailed. 'I . . .' he began, but Buddy's question had not been intended for an answer.

'You fucking jerk!' he bellowed. 'You have the audacity to sit here wasting our time with this crap when the only one of our assets you seem to have any handle on is Olivia Finch's ass. We've travelled over 5,000 miles to listen to this horseshit and we'd have gotten a better idea about our future prospects if we'd stayed at home and cracked open a fortune cookie. I suggest you go back to your pals in the oil business, Mr Bennett, ask them to dig you a nice big hole and bury you in it.'

He turned to me, his face stroke-red with rage. 'Joey, I want you to rework these figures into something that makes sense and bring them to my hotel room by five o'clock this afternoon. If they add up, Askett Brown keeps our business and you'll get a drink before we go to the movie tonight. If they don't, I'll be looking for new advisers in the morning.' Then he turned to Bill Davis, jerking his thumb in Bennett's direction. 'And Bill, I don't ever want to see this moron near me, or my business or, most of all, my talent again. OK?'

It was another question that didn't need an answer, but

Davis nodded, dumbstruck, anyway. Buddy stood up and gathered his papers from the table – making a point of leaving his copy of Bennett's PowerPoint slides untouched. The rest of his team followed suit. There were no handshakes or goodbyes – just an uncomfortable silence that hung heavily in the room as if our guests had brought a sample of high-grade LA smog with them.

Eager to regain control over events, Bill Davis rose to his feet. 'Andrew, would you show our guests out, please? Joseph, Joe – my office in five minutes.' Then he turned and followed the Americans out of the room.

I made a hasty exit and found the nearest bathroom. I stood at the sink and splashed cold water on my face, hoping I could wake myself from this nightmare. Suddenly I felt a sharp push in my back. I lurched forward, almost banging my head on the mirror. Looking up, I saw the incandescent reflection of the angriest face I had ever seen.

'It was you, wasn't it, West, you little cunt!' Bennett spat out the expletive with such hostility that a shower of saliva rained down on the back of my neck. 'I've been totally fucking humiliated in there and it's all your fault, isn't it? You did it and then made sure I carried the can.'

He grabbed me by the shoulders and turned me around, pulling me towards him until I could feel the hot breath from his nostrils on my forehead. His upper lip was curled and flecked with spittle, his eyes shining with rage. I was sure he was going to hit me – and damn sure it would hurt – but I tried to front up to him as best I could.

'Wh— what do you mean?' I asked, my voice cracking like a frightened child's. For the life of me, I couldn't understand how he'd worked the whole thing out so quickly.

'You know exactly what I mean, arsehole,' Bennett raged, tightening his grip on my collar and starting to bring his hands together, squeezing my windpipe.

'I . . . I . . . I don't . . .' I tried to articulate something but had no idea what. My throat hurt and I was beginning to fear for my life.

'You set me up, didn't you, West? You gave me all that shit information and made me look a bloody idiot in there so your fat friend would have me taken off the job. I'm going straight up to see Bill Davis now and I'm going to tell him that you're behind this. You hated it that I got promoted above you, didn't you? And now you're trying to undermine me with your bloody Jew mates. Well, you're not going to get away with it. Come on, you little bastard,' he said, finally relaxing his grip, 'let's see what Bill has to say.'

Like most of his colleagues at the top of Askett Brown, Bill Davis didn't like confrontation. If he had, he would have gone to Sandhurst straight from school rather than seeking out a more lucrative living in the financial sector. Companies like this tended to manage themselves. If a chap (because invariably they were chaps) performed well, he got promoted until such time as he ceased to perform well, at which point he would be advised to seek an alternative career path. Disciplinary issues rarely arose, and that suited Bill Davis down to the ground.

When Bennett and I arrived in his office, he was standing behind his large desk looking out of the window, staring at the distant landmarks of Westminster and the South Bank of the Thames.

Without turning to face us, he forced out his opening words as calmly as he could. 'Well, that was bloody embarrassing,' he said. After he had delivered this salvo, he turned around but found it too much of a strain and addressed his next remarks to the surface of his desk, his fingers gripping the bevelled edge so hard that his knuckles turned white. 'I don't know exactly what happened in there and I'm not entirely sure I want to know. But the two of you had better sort it out – and quickly. Have you got that? Joseph,' he said to Bennett, 'I want you to lay low for a while. Give the premiere tonight a miss and keep as far away from Guttenberg and his crew as you can, especially that bloody Finch woman. Is that clear?'

Bennett started to answer, but Bill was having none of it. He had planned what he was going to say and wasn't going to be distracted. 'I said, "Is that clear?"'

Bennett nodded. He was clenching his fists and opening them again like a boxer receiving his final instructions before a bout, his face still impregnated with anger, his ears such a deep shade of vermilion that I feared they might spontaneously ignite.

'West,' Bill said to me, 'you have four hours to sort those numbers out and get them over to Guttenberg. Got it?'

I nodded. Bennett's rage boiled over. 'But it was all West's fault!' he yelled, unable to control himself, desperate to clear his name. 'He gave me all that crap information in the first place. He set me up. I wouldn't be surprised if he's behind the whole bloody thing with the girl as well.'

Davis came down on him firmly. 'I said I don't want an inquest into what did or did not happen in New York. We don't have the time for that right now. All I want is for the

95

two of you to sort this out as quickly as possible and keep our client happy. Joe,' he said to me, 'you go and prepare the stuff for Guttenberg. Joseph, you and I need to have a little word over a coffee. Sit down and I'll have Sarah bring us one in.'

I couldn't get out of there fast enough. I hurtled down the four flights of stairs back to my floor and set to work unpicking the figures for Buddy. It wouldn't take long – all I had to do was go back to my original data and jazz it up a bit.

Soon after I got back to my desk, Polly came over with an Americano. A good assistant always knows when strong coffee is required. And, of course, she wanted to know about the latest developments in the 'Bennett Affair'. I fobbed her off by telling her I had to concentrate on the presentation, even though I was well ahead of my deadline. I didn't want to talk about what was going on right then – or face up to the fact that I might be enjoying the sight of Bennett being hung out to dry and pecked at by all comers.

Bennett appeared a little while later. He had calmed down a bit – his ears would only have registered a couple of hundred on a Geiger counter now – but he was still seething. Striding to my desk, he managed to be both quiet and aggressive at the same time. 'Thanks a bunch, pal,' he said from between clenched teeth. 'I've spent forty-five minutes being read the riot act by Bill Davis, and it's all your fucking fault. Just remember, West, you may be the big "I am" with these guys at the moment, but you're not untouchable. The whole ruddy business is only worth a fraction of what we get from one player in oil, so don't think we rely on keeping cosy with your pal Guttenberg. If he, or any of the rest of them, ever talks to me like that again, I'll punch his bloody lights out. And then yours.'

I couldn't imagine that this had been the conclusion of his conversation with Bill Davis, but I thought it best to let the matter lie. However unlikely it was that Bennett would resort to physical violence in the office, it wasn't a chance I wanted to take. He was bigger than me and had developed his fighting skills in the toughest environment there was outside of the military or the penal system – an English public school. The last fight I'd had had been when I was twelve and, if I remember correctly, she'd given me a bloody good hiding.

I nodded silently, never taking my eyes off his. I hoped I wasn't showing my fear but feared I almost certainly was. My mouth had gone dry – too dry for me to speak without squeaking like a cartoon mouse – and I felt redness spreading from my neck up across my face and beyond the distant frontier of my hairline. He held my gaze for some moments, before, satisfied he had made his point, he turned and stormed away, scattering Polly and an assortment of other assistants who had gathered to see what was happening. As the rest of them raced to their phones to spread the latest news, Polly asked if I was all right and offered me a fresh cup of coffee. I said yes to both, not because I felt all right or wanted another coffee but because I needed the few minutes it would take her to fetch one to regain my composure. When she returned, my hands were just about steady enough to take the cup from her without spilling the hot, black contents.

'You should have stuck one on him, Joe,' she said

supportively. 'He may be bigger than you, but I reckon he's just a big bully. You'd murder him in a fight.'

'Thanks, Polly,' I said, 'but let's hope it doesn't come to that. Now, if you wouldn't mind, I'd better get these figures done for Buddy. I've only got a couple more hours.'

# WEST END, LONDON

By half past four I was all tuxed up and in a cab on my way to the Dorchester. Buddy greeted me at the door of his palatial suite like a long-lost son. As he led me along the short corridor to the lounge, he enlightened me about exactly what size of an arsehole he considered Bennett to be. I didn't encourage him, but nor did I challenge his analysis, nodding and smiling politely as he unleashed a tirade of invective. It helped that Bennett really *was* an arsehole of Nobel Prize-winning proportions, but I still felt guilty at revelling in his humiliation.

I went through the figures with Buddy and he roared an appreciative 'That's more like it!' He was already half into his dinner suit and as soon as my presentation was over, he rose from his seat to finish the job. His large, round belly looked ready to explode out of his straight-out-of-the-packet, white dress shirt which looked at least a size too small to contain it. He desperately needed a cummerbund – ideally one reinforced with steel – if he was to avoid a sartorial calamity.

'Let me get your slides over to the guys in LA so they can start working on them while we're out enjoying ourselves,' he said, pressing a couple of buttons on his laptop, then rising with some difficulty from his comfortable armchair. He took the memory stick out of the computer and went to hand it to me. Then he remembered something. 'Oh, by the way, Olivia's meeting us here too. That cocksucker Reynolds has bailed on us at the last minute, so I'm her date for the night. Lucky girl! Listen, she's really sensitive about the situation with your dickhead pal and I don't want her thinking everyone in the whole of London's talking about it? So could you do me a big personal favour and play dumb about the whole thing? I've told her that I spoke to Bennett and sorted everything out, so she can just relax and enjoy the evening. If she finds out what I really said to that jerk-off in the meeting today, she'll hit the fucking roof!'

I nodded again – I'd have been more gainfully employed mounted on someone's dashboard with my tongue hanging out – but inside I could feel the panic rising. I needed to get out of there and fast.

'Listen, Buddy,' I said, 'I really should pop back to the office before we go. Drop this data stick back and check a few e-mails, you know. I'll meet you at the cinema later.'

'Nonsense,' said Buddy, 'I'm not the best tech guy in the world, but I do believe it is now possible to check e-mails on one of these things.' He paused to pick my smartphone up from the table and wave it in my face. 'And this,' he added, pushing my memory stick into the top pocket of my dinner jacket, 'you can take back into the office tomorrow. So open that bottle of champagne and pour us out a couple of glasses and let's get this party started.'

Buddy sauntered out of the lounge, tucking his shirt into his commodious trousers as he walked. Trapped in this luxurious prison cell with the sound of the joiners constructing the gallows hammering away inside my head, I forced the cork out of the bottle of Dom Perignon and poured two glasses. I knocked one of them back in one desperate swallow and was contemplating downing the other as well when I remembered that it was too much of this stuff that had got me into this mess in the first place.

'For the life of me, I don't see how a beautiful, talented girl like Olivia could jump in the sack with that schmuck,' Buddy shouted from the bedroom, raising his voice but otherwise continuing our conversation as if we were still in the same room. 'You I could understand, Joey – you're a lovely boy. But her type just don't go for regular guys like you, do they? Why can't they ever see beyond the money or the looks? They just make the same freaking mistake over and over again. Beats me. She's a sweet kid as well. Deserves better than to be dicked about by that prick . . .'

He was interrupted by a gentle knock on the door.

'Great, that must be her now. Can you get that for me, Joey?'

I prayed that it was room service, but knew not too deep down that if there *was* someone up there, He had stopped answering my prayers a long time ago.

Olivia stood in the corridor looking like every school-boy's favourite fantasy. She was wearing a simple but stylish red dress, set off by a small jewellery shop's worth of hired diamonds and rubies, with matching red stilettos that gave her a couple of inches' height advantage over me.

She looked surprised to see me – and not too happy

about it, either. 'Well, if it isn't Joseph A. Bennett, noted English asshole!' she said as she pushed past me and walked into the lounge. 'Buddy said he had a surprise for me, but he didn't tell me exactly what size piece of shit he'd dragged out to see me.'

'Please, Olivia,' I said trying to placate her. The last thing I needed was for Buddy to hear what was going on.

'Aw, that's nice! You remember my name. That's something, I guess.'

'I can explain,' I said, not totally sure that I could. 'About the emails and the texts and everything, I mean. But not here, not now. Buddy will be out in a minute.'

Olivia covered her face with her hands and drew her fingers slowly from her hairline to her chin where they slipped off and stuck together, pointing upwards, as if in prayer. There were tears in her eyes. I know actors are trained to be able to turn on the waterworks at will, but I had no reason to doubt that these were genuine – tears born of anger and confusion as much as sadness. 'How could you treat me like that, English? I really thought something special had happened that night in New York, you know? Like we'd really connected. And then it was like you didn't want to know me. Like you couldn't wait to get shot of me. I deserved better than that, Joe. How could you do that to me?'

'I'm sorry, Olivia,' I said, and I meant it. 'I didn't mean for any of this to happen. That time we spent together in New York was unbelievable – literally, I could not believe it had happened to me. But when I got home, I couldn't handle it. I just assumed that with you being a Hollywood superstar and me being an ordinary North London accountant we'd both forget about it and get on with our lives. I didn't think for a moment you'd want to see me again – I mean, I'm not in your league. Then, suddenly, you were texting me and e-mailing me and I panicked. I couldn't understand what was going on, especially as I didn't know you even had my phone number or e-mail address or anything. I'm sorry, Olivia, truly I am.'

I was throwing myself at her feet. It was for her to decide whether to stamp me into the thick pile carpet or show me some undeserved mercy.

'I guess I stole them,' she said, a trace of a smile appearing on her lips for the first time, as she thought back to that night in the hotel. 'I knocked your jacket off the chair as I was leaving and your card fell out of the pocket and I kind of took it. I'm sorry. It was a dumb thing to do, but I'd had such a great evening and I didn't want it to end.'

I poured her a glass of champagne, topping up my own at the same time. 'Can we talk about this properly later?' I said. 'We don't want a scene in front of Buddy, do we? He's trying to keep the lid on all of this for your sake, so can we pretend that nothing's happened and talk about it later, when we're on our own? Can we act like we're just friends – acquaintances, actually – for now? Can you do that?'

Olivia stepped closer to me, so close that I could feel the luxurious scent of her expensive perfume marching up my nostrils, attempting to encircle my brain and take it hostage – again. 'I am a Golden Globe-winning, Academy Award-nominated actress,' she said, her passion and pride etched into every syllable. 'I can pretend to be anything you fucking want me to be.'

'Hi Olivia, angel!' Buddy boomed, storming back into

the room trussed up like a Thanksgiving turkey. 'You look fantastic. Great to see you kids getting along so well. I told you I had a surprise for you, didn't I? You know, honey, I still reckon this guy's the real star of the movie. The things he did with those finances – beautiful! There should be a new category at the Oscars – Best Original Tax Deal!'

'Oh yeah, Buddy, very funny,' Olivia said, snatching her glass from my hand. Somehow she had managed to arrange her features into an expression that could be interpreted by Buddy as a friendly grin but simultaneously displayed to me the depth of her anger and hurt.

'Are we ready to go?' Buddy asked, knocking back his glass of champagne in one slug. Olivia and I took one last small sip from our glasses and placed them back, still half full, onto the table. Buddy helped Olivia on with a small, entirely decorative jacket that barely covered her shoulders and we made our way out of his suite. From the lobby, we were ushered by a doorman into a black Jaguar limousine, the three of us squashed into the back seat – half for Buddy, half for Olivia and me. Olivia placed her right hand on my left thigh and gave it a squeeze. I gripped the edge of the seat and looked out of the window at the passing light show. It was going to be a long evening.

We emerged from our short journey to the cinema to face the flashing of bulbs and yells of photographers, journalists and fans. Most were for Olivia whose name could be heard echoing around every side of Leicester Square. A few photographers recognised Buddy and satisfied themselves with grabbing easier shots of the larger, slower moving target. I was painfully aware of the sensation of having a crowd of people assessing me down their lenses, instantly identifying my lack of celebrity and lowering their weapons, like Quakers on a firing squad. I lived to face another day as Olivia made her way serenely along the red carpet, pinned in the photographers' gaze like a rare butterfly, while Buddy simultaneously tried to protect her and grab any spare attention for himself.

We were hustled through the cinema and shown into a small private green room where trays of delicious canapés sat untouched on a side table while waiters scurried around making sure that our glasses were never empty. I was struck by how bizarre the celebrity lifestyle must be – constantly flip-flopping between being gazed at and pointed out by crowds and then locked away in hiding. They were like mating giant pandas, wanting to be left alone to get on with their lives, but forced to perform to the galleries whenever their public demanded. It was a Faustian pact: you can have the money and the glamour and everything that goes with it, but in return you will forfeit your freedom. Why would anyone take that deal?

Buddy set to work clearing the buffet of food and entertaining the small ensemble of invited guests – ordinary people like me with some connection to the film or its distribution in the UK or the cinema where the screening was taking place – with his lurid tales of Hollywood excesses, all of which were preceded with a knowing 'Now, don't tell anyone else this, but . . .' before divulging some intimate and probably untrue secret about a household name or fellow producer. I was glad that Olivia and I were standing right with him or he might have included his take on 'The Bennett Affair' within his repertoire.

Eventually we were called through to the auditorium and shown to our seats at the front of the circle as the rest of the cinema stood to applaud us. Well, Olivia and Buddy at least. Olivia sat between Buddy and me and, as the lights went down and the opening credits began to roll, I felt the now familiar sensation of her hand – her left one this time – resting on my right thigh and staying there as if it was settling in for the night. Her little finger was dangerously close to my groin and I had to keep pushing myself back in my seat to avoid any accidental contact being made – accidental on my part that is.

'I've already seen this goddamn movie like a dozen times,' Olivia whispered in my ear as the action started. 'And it ain't no *Sullivan's Travels*! Why don't we sneak out and find some more champagne. Somewhere we can talk properly.'

I shook my head. I would have been happy to avoid having to watch the film again but I was determined to avoid being alone with Olivia if I could possibly help it. Besides which, the chances of sneaking out of there were next to zero. We were pinned in the middle of the row and any movement Olivia made would be closely watched by a small army of attendants hired to look after her every need. I turned my head and fixed my gaze on the screen. After a few moments, I felt a final, slightly huffy breath in my ear and Olivia turned her face as well.

When the film ended, the audience rose as one to offer the makers and stars the obligatory spontaneous standing ovation. Buddy, Olivia and I were ushered out of our seats ahead of the throng, protected by a phalanx of PR and security men. I was desperate to get away from there – from her – but I was trapped both physically by our entourage and also by the fear that if I did slip away now, I would leave Olivia alone with Buddy and her confusion over my identity would almost certainly be cleared up.

So, once again, I silently acquiesced, marching out through the cinema to the waiting car and taking my place alongside Buddy and Olivia with the only uncertainty now being around which of her hands would find contact with which of my thighs. For this journey I sat in the middle of our little gang, with Olivia's left hand back on my right thigh and Buddy's enormous ham-like right fist slapped down painfully on my left.

Once inside the Café Royal, Buddy led us past the bouncers into the sealed-off inner sanctum reserved for the most important guests. We sat down at a crescent-shaped banquette arranged around three sides of a table and Buddy whistled up some champagne. A couple of guys I recognised as working for Printing Press Productions in Europe approached our table and Buddy invited them to join us, ordering more champagne to make sure that no one would go thirsty.

One of the men sat down on my right while the other sat on the far side of Buddy, with Olivia beautifully framed in the middle of the group like a solitary rose in a field of thorn bushes. 'Good evening,' the man next to me said in impeccable English, offering me his hand, 'I am Georges Lafitte, Head of Legal, Europe, for PPP.' His statement carried an implied question, backed up by a raised eyebrow, silently asking 'And you are?'

My first thought was to wonder whether PPP also had a Head of Illegal Europe, but then I realised I had a bigger problem: how to introduce myself without Olivia, who was pressed up next to me as close as it was possible to be without being officially engaged, hearing who I wasn't.

'Very nice to meet you,' I said, ignoring his inquisitive eyebrow. 'Du champagne?' I added, using up pretty well all the French I knew.

'Merci,' Georges said, correctly assuming that I understood at least one more word. 'And you are?'

'I'm sorry?' I said, wincing and cupping my ear to suggest there was something about the noisy room or his accent that made it difficult to understand him from a range of three feet.

'I didn't catch your name,' Georges replied with more than a hint of exasperation.

'Oh, I am sorry about that,' I said.

'What is your name?' he persisted, sounding like Maurice Chevalier playing a Gestapo officer. He looked quizzically towards Buddy, perhaps wondering why he had brought the village idiot with him, but fortunately Buddy was deep in conversation with his other colleague. Unfortunately, this left Olivia in the middle of the group with no one to talk to, trying to listen in to both conversations at the same time.

I leaned a little closer to Georges and mumbled 'I'm Joe Mumble, from Askett Brown here in London. I was involved in pulling together the finance for the picture. What did you think of the film, by the way, Georges? Isn't it excellent?'

'I'm sorry,' it was Lafitte's turn to apologise. 'Joe . . .?'

'Oh, that's OK,' I replied, sounding more like an imbecile with every utterance, 'no problem.'

'No,' he said, his voice rising in irritation, 'I didn't hear your surname.'

'That's a shame,' I said, turning away from him. 'Why don't we talk to Olivia? I'm sure she's far more interesting than me.' As I turned, I became aware that, rather than creating a smokescreen to hide behind, my attempts at obfuscation had drawn everyone's attention to our conversation. Olivia and Buddy were both staring at us, trying to see what had caused the raised voices at our end of the table.

'What's the problem, guys?' said Buddy.

'Oh nothing,' I replied, smiling weakly. 'We've just been doing the introductions. I take it you know Georges, Buddy, seeing how you work together? And this, of course, is Olivia Finch and I'm Joe from Askett Brown here in London. So that's all sorted. Now, let me see if I can find a bloody waiter and get us all another drink. Don't know about you lot, but I'm parched.'

I rose quickly and edged my way around in front of Georges, desperate to get away for a few moments. As I passed in front of him, I heard Buddy explaining that my name was, in fact, Joe West and that yes, I had been a bit over-worked lately. I looked around and was relieved to see Olivia already in conversation with the other Frenchman.

I found a waiter who delivered another couple of bottles of champagne and then we sat chatting for some time, involving Olivia in the conversation as much as possible, while Georges Lafitte still eyed me as one might an escaped lunatic and Buddy held forth to his colleague. Olivia seemed diffident and shy – very different to the sparky, intelligent, interested girl I'd met in New York. Her responses to Georges' questions were monosyllabic and childlike, often preceded by a girlish giggle as if whatever he had just said had displayed wit and insight of Wildean proportions. It took me a while to understand that she was back to playing a role – that even off-screen she had to pretend to be someone she was not. The straightforward, uncomplicated Hollywood starlet paid large sums of money for her beauty and style but nothing for her brain. For the second or third time that evening, I found myself feeling sorry for her. All that success, all that acclaim. And all that misery.

Just after midnight, Buddy called across to me. 'Hey, Joey, these guys reckon they can get me into the casino next door. Would you mind seeing Olivia back to the hotel? You can take my car if you like.'

'Actually . . .' I started to protest but Buddy had no time to hear what I had to say.

'Excellent!' he confirmed over the hubbub of the party crowd. 'Look after my girl.' He gave Olivia a peck on the cheek and disappeared as unobtrusively as a man of his size and volume ever could, one arm slung over a shoulder of each of his French friends.

We collected Olivia's jacket from the cloakroom and stood at the threshold of the club, waiting for Buddy's driver, feeling just the faintest of breezes on our faces. The usual media scrum was in position on the street outside waiting for Olivia to come out and give them a few poses. 'Hey,' Olivia said, smiling, 'why don't we walk back to the hotel? It's only a few blocks, isn't it? There must be some kind of service entrance to this place we can sneak out of to avoid those guys. A walk through London at night – wouldn't that be romantic!'

Also bloody dangerous, I thought, but before I could point out all the obvious objections to this course of action,

Olivia grabbed my hand and started to drag me away from the main entrance. We found a fire exit next to the lifts and went down a flight of concrete steps into the basement. There were a few cardboard boxes lying around, but otherwise the exit was clear – we pushed our way through the fire door and out into the service bay. The ragged collection of various coloured dustbins and empty linen cages was in spectacular contrast to Olivia's casual glamour, but she seemed to enjoy picking her way through the rubbish, taking off her stilettos and tiptoeing carefully around any obstacles like a child let loose in an adventure playground.

'Are you OK?' I asked at one point as she stumbled and almost fell.

She replied with a carefree chuckle. 'I'm fine, English, this is fun! I wasn't always Olivia Finch, Hollywood superstar, you know.'

We strolled through the cold night air, Olivia's arm threaded through mine, carefully stepping over or around the human detritus that littered the damp pavements. Olivia knew London from the movies where double-decker buses and black cabs driven by cheery Cockneys made their way up and down uncluttered roads, past famous landmarks all arranged within thirty feet of each other. This was different. All around us, wild-eyed escapees from Dante's Inferno leered out from dark doorways, reeking of fags and filth, posturing for trouble. For the second time that day, I felt the bile of my cowardice rising as I hurried Olivia along, cursing myself for exposing her to such danger. She was made of sterner stuff, though. When one young thug of indeterminate gender lunged in front of us, spilling their cider so that it splashed perilously close to

Olivia's $1,000 shoes, she neatly pushed them back from whence they came, answering their vitriolic complaints with some choice obscenities of her own.

'I'm sorry,' I said, when I was sure we were clear of danger, 'London's changed a bit since Mary Poppins' day.'

She turned to me and smiled. 'Don't worry, English, I saw a hell of a lot worse than these punks in Carolina. Even your drunks are polite compared to ours! And thanks for not making a scene. If you'd whacked that guy there might have been all kinds of trouble.'

'No problem,' I said, 'although I'm not entirely sure it was a guy,' which just made Olivia smile even wider.

When we reached the safe haven of the Dorchester's foyer, I felt a strong sense of déjà vu: the beautiful actress, the happily married man, the hotel. What could possibly happen next? But this time, there was one important difference – this time I was a little less drunk and a lot more determined not to submit to my animal instincts, whatever the provocation.

'So, English, going to join me for a nightcap?' Olivia purred, like a highly-sexed Siamese.

Instinctively, I found myself checking my watch. As if the time and my need to get home were the most important factors in making this decision. My conscience and good sense were being bombarded from every angle by the sound, sight and smell of her. If she'd reached out to touch me at that moment – if I'd felt the illicit sensation of her skin on mine – I might not have been able to resist. But she didn't and, thank God, I was. With a tremendous effort of will, I managed to find the strength to do the right thing this time.

'No, thank you very much,' I said. 'It's late. I have to get home.'

'"No, thank you very much!"' Olivia mimicked me in her excellent English accent. 'What do you mean, "No, thank you very much"? I'm not the Queen inviting you round for a cup of tea. I am Olivia Finch, inviting you up to my hotel room for a drink and then, if you're real nice to me, a repeat performance of our sensational New York opening.'

'No, Olivia,' I said, 'not tonight. I'm expected home – I've already stayed out longer than I should have. I'm sorry.'

I was starting to get used to Olivia's rapid change of moods, but was still surprised at how quickly she could switch from seductive charm to chilling anger. 'OK, English. Off you go,' she said, her voice rising along with the colour in her cheeks. 'You crawl off home to your wonderful family and tell them all about your lovely evening.' Suddenly she seemed like a small child, sulking because she couldn't have her own way.

Alerted by the raised voices, the doorman walked over to us, glowering at me from under his rather incongruous top hat. 'Is everything OK, Ms Finch? Would you like me to throw this gentleman out?'

'No, you idiot,' she replied, 'I want you to throw him in! Aw c'mon, English – what harm could one little drink do?'

She knew perfectly well, and so did I. I also knew that I had to keep her happy both for my own sake and in the interests of Askett Brown's relationship with Printing Press Productions – the calmer she stayed, the less likely it was that she would go blurting out the whole story to Buddy. 'I'm sorry, Olivia, I really can't stay tonight, but, I know, why don't we meet tomorrow? I could take you out for lunch or tea or we could go and see the Crown Jewels or take a cruise down the Thames or, well, whatever you want.' I was gabbling now, but it seemed to be having the desired effect.

'That would be lovely, English,' she said, a faint smile appearing behind the childish pout. 'I'd really like that.'

'Great. Can you give me a rough time?'

'Well, if you insist,' Olivia said, her smile broadening into a leer. 'I didn't think you were that kind of a guy, but sure, why not? What did you have in mind?'

'What?' I said, genuinely confused. 'Oh, I see! No, I meant, can you give me a rough time when you'd like me to get here. Shall we say one o'clock?'

'That would be spiffing, English!' she said, kissing me on the cheek. 'See you at one.' She took the arm of the bemused doorman and let him escort her through reception. I was off one hook but still caught on another. And, just as in all the best movies, with every twist and turn I impaled myself deeper.

# CITY OF LONDON

I didn't sleep much that night. The next morning I was in the office well before eight, bleary-eyed and too tired to think straight, the accumulated units of exhaustion stacking up like aircraft over Heathrow. Bill Davis had called me and Bennett in for an early meeting to find out how my presentation to Buddy had gone. With some of our other most important sectors in economic downturn, Bill knew we had to keep clients like PPP sweet. *Nothing Happened* was performing well in the States and was tipped to be one of the top three films internationally that year. There was already talk of a sequel.

Bill visibly relaxed as I explained that Buddy had been impressed by our figures and had sent them straight to LA so his team could start working on the possibility of a major refinancing package. He was looking to raise around $100 million to develop a slate of films and build his own distribution network in the US, rather than having to share profits with one of the studios. He was also considering buying a stake in a European distributor to boost their international revenues. Askett Brown stood to earn millions in fees from these transactions if they engaged us as their principal advisers this side of the Atlantic.

Bennett flashed me a look that could have stripped paint. Something didn't compute for him. How could I (of all people) have produced the goods when he (of all people) had failed so spectacularly to do so. But, before he could say anything, Bill was praising me as if I had just brought home peace in our time.

'Oh well done, West! Well done! That's an excellent result. I can see a decent bonus on its way to you – to both of you – if you pull this off. Was there anything else?'

I smiled and tried to look nonchalant about this praise. 'Not really,' I replied. 'Oh, except that last night, at the party, I managed to catch a few words with Olivia Finch. I offered to take her out today and show her a bit of London. You know, take her round a few sights. Would that be OK with the two of you?'

'That's a great idea, Joe!' Bill Davis beamed. 'If we can keep Ms Finch happy, it should help us keep Guttenberg on side too!' He turned to Bennett who was still gloweringly silent, like a gorilla brooding in the corner of his cage. 'What do you think, Joseph? I tell you what, it's a bloody shame that girl didn't take a shine to West instead of you, isn't it? Would have saved everyone a lot of bother.' Davis laughed heartily and even Bennett managed to rearrange his face into some sort of a smile. 'OK, Joe,' he said to me with a wink, 'you get off and plan your date. Joseph,' he said to Bennett, 'can you hang on a minute? There are a couple of things I need to go over with you.'

'Don't worry about all this,' I heard him say as I lingered for a few seconds before closing the door behind me. 'These film people aren't like the chaps you're used to dealing with in oil or gas. They have their own way of doing things – you'll pick it up soon enough.'

# WEST END OF LONDON

Olivia looked as immaculate as ever when I met her at the appointed hour. A brightly patterned, thin summer dress peeped out from under a Burberry raincoat. She was also wearing designer sunglasses and carrying a rolled umbrella, already aware that one had to be prepared for all weathers in London in early May. She showed no signs of fatigue after a tough morning of press and television interviews promoting the new film as she greeted me with exaggerated kisses to both cheeks, her expensive perfume, once again, evoking powerful memories of our earlier encounters. I found myself enjoying the sensation of being stared at by the other people in the foyer, who instantly recognised Olivia and wondered aloud who the hell was I.

'So, English, what treats do you have lined up for me today?' Olivia asked, using my nationality as a term of endearment now, rather than abuse. I was pretty sure she could remember my name by this stage – my first name anyway. 'I don't care what we do, as long as we get to spend some real good quality time together. We could always go back inside and have them deliver a bottle of something cold and wet to my room and, well, see what happens.'

It was an enticing thought, but not one that I, as a happily married family man could possibly entertain. I had considered all of the obvious places one might take a visitor to London: Buckingham Palace, the Tower of London, a spin on the London Eye, followed by lunch at Claridge's or an afternoon's shopping at Harrods – but all had the significant drawback that wherever we went, Olivia would be instantly recognised and mobbed. What I had in mind was something much more quintessentially English. Somewhere we could talk without being disturbed, and which, I was sure, would be a completely new experience for Olivia.

I took her to Lord's, where Middlesex were batting on the opening day of a four-day county championship match against Northamptonshire in front of a crowd of perhaps 200 bedraggled pensioners, students and truants. Here, in the hallowed grounds of the home of English cricket, there was no chance of anyone paying Olivia the slightest bit of attention, unless she suddenly developed a striking resemblance to Sir Ian Botham. She could have run naked across the outfield yelling 'I'm Olivia Finch' through a megaphone and the crowd would have cheered the stewards who sped on to apprehend her so that play could continue. It also helped that it was the least romantic place I could think of to bring her – I was determined to kill off any idea that our relationship had a future.

I didn't have to go through the usual complications of trying to explain cricket's idiosyncrasies to my American guest. Olivia displayed not one iota of interest in a single ball bowled. Apart from expressing, loudly enough for not only the sparse crowd around us but also the player himself to hear, her admiration for the taut, athletic buttocks of the thin-flannelled, jock-strapped fielder standing in front of us at deep square leg, she remained impervious to the action, content to be sipping a glass of wine, nibbling on crisps and chatting about life and other interesting subjects.

'Hey, don't get jealous, English,' she said, 'I bet you'd look great in a pair of white trousers and one of those funny little things for holding your nuts! Do you have any of that gear at home? Any chance you could bring it round to my hotel after the match?'

I didn't have the heart to tell her that the match still had another three days to run, by which time she would be safely back in Los Angeles. And I hardly had the will to resist her renewed advances as she snuggled closer to me. Without saying a word, she plucked my spectacles from my nose and started to wipe them on the hem of her dress, curling up the fabric to reveal six or seven inches of sleek, bronzed thigh. I found myself transfixed by the revelation and couldn't help but stare as she transformed the mundane act of cleaning a pair of glasses into a tantalisingly erotic experience. I had to work hard to resist placing my fingers on the exposed flesh as if I needed physical substantiation of how immaculate Olivia's skin could be, even without the benefit of airbrushing and CGI.

With great effort, I eased her away and sat up straighter in my seat. She looked at me, disappointment burning in those sugar almond eyes, but smiled to let me know that everything was still all right between us. Her attention scared and confused me.

'Olivia,' I asked, twisting my neck so I could look at her properly and putting on the earnest face that I used with the kids when they'd been naughty, 'what do you see in me? I mean, I'm oldish and fattish and baldish and Jewish. I have no money, by the standards of your usual circles. I'm not exactly Brad Pitt, am I?'

She fixed me with a sweet smile that went all the way up from the dimple on her chin to the tiny wrinkles in her forehead. 'I've got news for you, English. I'm not exactly Olivia Finch, either.'

'What do you mean you're not Olivia Finch?' I asked. Christ, it was confusing enough that I wasn't Joseph Bennett!

'Aw c'mon, English. You know the game. Olivia isn't really me. She isn't me at all. My real name is Cadillac McAllister. My sonofabitch dad always wanted a Cadillac, but every time he saved up anywhere near enough, Mum would tell him she was pregnant again and bang'd go the car. Fifth time it happened he'd had enough. He reckoned that if he couldn't buy himself a Caddy he'd grow himself one instead. So he saddled me with this stupid name and then skedaddled as soon as the shine had rubbed off the fender and the tyres had gone a bit flat. Can you imagine going through life named after a goddamn car? Putting up with all the jokes from guys wanting to take Cadillac McAllister for a spin around the block? I couldn't wait to get to LA to trade in that name and become someone different. Someone better.'

She sipped her wine and broke a slightly larger than average crisp in two and popped the smaller part into her mouth. 'Don't you see, Joe? It's precisely because you're not Brad Pitt – that you don't even *think* you're Brad Pitt – that

I'm crazy about you. Hollywood is full of phonies who'd like to be Brad, or Olivia. People like you – ordinary people who are completely honest about who and what they are – are a whole lot rarer. Buddy's not even really Buddy – did you know that? He's about as Jewish as I am! His family came over from Sweden. But how many Swedes make it in Hollywood? Even Bergman struggled in Lalaland and he was a fucking genius. I mean, I'm not having a go at Buddy – he's been like a father to me these last couple of years, helping me get established and looking after me and everything – but he's no more genuine than the rest of those guys.'

While we'd been talking, it had started to drizzle. Then it began to rain more heavily and the umpires led the players off to the safety of the pavilion. I envied them their sanctuary.

'Oh, great, it's finished,' said Olivia, snuggling up to me again until we were almost sharing a seat. Her breath warmed my neck as she spoke. A faint whiff of sea salt and white wine vinegar crisps rose up and tickled my nose. 'Hmm, London on a cold, wet afternoon – what could we possibly do now?'

'Well, we could take a look at the cricket museum,' I suggested. 'It's very interesting. They've got the original Ashes urn in there and one of W. G. Grace's caps and . . .'

'And I'm sure my hotel room could be a whole lot more interesting,' Olivia said. She opened her umbrella and gathered her things together, brooking no argument that we were leaving. 'And you can buy yourself one of those cute little ball-bag things on the way.'

We found a taxi on the St John's Wood Road. Olivia cuddled up to me as the cab meandered through the late afternoon traffic back down towards Park Lane. The driver looked into his rear-view mirror so often it made me feel very uncomfortable. This could have meant that he was taking care to watch the traffic behind him but, given that he was a London cabbie, it seemed more likely he was checking and re-checking that it really was Olivia Finch in the back of his cab getting all cosy with a baldy nobody. I could imagine him telling future fares, ''Ere, I 'ad that Olivia Finch in the back of me cab the other day and guess 'oo she was wiv? Fackin' nobody!' I prayed he wasn't connected through some bizarre twist of fate to anyone I knew. What if his very next fare was Bennett? Or Natasha? Or someone who knew either of them? London's a big place, but aren't we all supposed to be linked to everyone else through no more than six connections? What if his next passenger happened to be a lawyer doing some conveyancing work for a friend of Bennett's wife, who mentioned it to Sandra who asked Bennett if he'd been out with Olivia again? Bennett adds two and two together – even he can do that – and I'm busted. Or his next fare is the father of one of Helen's friends from school who tells his wife what the cabbie told him and she tells Natasha who then does 'the math' and 'Bingo!'– six degrees to separation; seven to divorce.

Then another thought struck me, right between the eyes. What if the bastard took a picture of us on his phone and sold it to the papers? I could imagine a charming picture of Olivia and her new man appearing as an exclusive in one of the tabloids under the headline: FINCH IN CAB CLINCH, followed by speculation about who the mystery man might be. The quality of pictures taken on those bloody phones was pretty good these days. My goose was, once again, being rapidly roasted in the hottest part of the oven.

I felt cornered. Like an antelope on the African plains at the moment it realises that the documentary crew isn't there to film him grazing but is actually focussed on the family of lions inching their way through the undergrowth towards him. Trapped by my own slow-witted ineptitude. I needed to drop Olivia back at the hotel and get away before I landed myself in any more trouble.

'You've gone very quiet, my fascinating English friend,' Olivia purred into my right ear, 'what are you thinking about right now?'

'Oh, nothing,' I lied.

'Aw, come on,' she said, turning up the Southern drawl a notch, making her voice even more huskily seductive than before. 'Y'all must be thinking about something with that huge, brilliant brain of yours.'

'No really, I'm not,' I lied again. I could sense the taxi driver straining to catch what we were saying.

'Well, you know what I'm thinking?' she asked, then told me without even giving me a chance to have a guess, 'I was thinking what a lovely day I've had.' She paused, ever the actress, waiting to deliver the pay-off line with expert timing, 'And wondering what I could do to say thank you for showing me such a good time.' This was followed by a couple of extraordinary suggestions breathed into my ear with such erotic fervour that I felt every hair on every inch of my body stand to attention. I doubt that anyone in the long and noble history of the beautiful game of cricket had ever received an offer quite like this one in return for a day out at Lord's.

'Are you all right, Joe?' Olivia asked, when I failed to respond. 'You look a little pale.'

'I'm fine,' I said. 'Well actually, you know, now you mention it, I could do with a little air. Listen, why don't I ask the driver to drop me a block or two from the hotel and I'll find my own way down in a few minutes? To be honest, I'm a bit nervous about being snapped coming out of the cab and going into the hotel with you. We've been out all day. People may start to talk. I'm sorry, Olivia, but I just can't risk being on the front pages of the world's press. I'm a married man, remember?'

These words hit her hard. The fire inside her stunning eyes burned even brighter – the first sign of an impending storm. 'How could I ever forget?' she said, turning away from me.

'I promise I'll come back. What room are you in?'

'Here, I'll write it down for you, English. Make sure you won't forget.' She reached inside her handbag and pulled out a small notebook and tiny pencil. She scribbled something down while I leaned forward to ask the driver to stop at the corner of Piccadilly and Park Lane. 'You will come back to me, won't you, English?' she said – Celia Johnson meets Scarlett O'Hara. 'Perhaps this will persuade you.' She popped the folded piece of paper into the breast pocket of my jacket, and planted a kiss on my cheek which somehow managed to be both chaste and teasingly erotic at the same time.

'Of course, I will,' I lied as I gave the driver twenty pounds to cover the fare and scuttled off towards the nearest Underground station, like the pathetic crustacean I now so closely resembled.

# MILL HILL, NORTH LONDON

I was home early. As soon as the children had been despatched to bed, I slipped out of my suit, threw on something more comfortable and got myself on the outside of a large glass of wine. I was already on my second when Natasha emerged from the kitchen with our dinner balanced on two trays and we settled down in front of the telly.

'You seem a bit tense tonight, darling,' she said as she swapped my food tray for her glass of wine and pressed the remote control to release *Coronation Street* from its frozen-framed paralysis. 'Tough day?'

I could hardly tell her that I had spent the afternoon watching cricket with a Hollywood A-lister and then resisting her amorous advances. 'Oh, you know,' I replied, 'the usual bollocks. Bennett's still on the warpath and giving me a hard time over that bloody presentation. Nothing I can't handle, love.'

'Well, you can understand him being a bit on edge, can't

you? He's probably terrified that Ms Finch is going to make another play for him. And he's in enough trouble at home already. Sandra's gone absolutely mental about it.'

I sipped my glass of wine and crammed some mashed potato and minted lamb into my mouth and contemplated my fate. In whichever direction I looked, the web of deceit and lies I had created was spinning out of control, strangling all those unlucky enough to be caught up within it. We finished our meal in silence as Natasha watched her favourite soap opera and I tried to think of a way to escape the one going on all around me. Then, emboldened by a third glass of wine, I attempted to cut my way out.

'Do you think you'd react like that?' I ventured, sticking a sacrificial toe in the piranha-infested waters. 'Like Sandra Bennett?'

'Pardon?' my wife replied.

'I mean, if I told you that I'd slept with Olivia Finch? Or you found out from someone. How do you think you'd react?'

'What, after I'd stopped laughing, you mean?'

'If the thought is that ridiculous, then yes.'

'You know exactly how I'd react,' Natasha said. 'I've always made it absolutely clear how I feel about adultery and it wouldn't matter if it was Olivia Finch or Polly or that barmaid at the King's Head with the large breasts and the lazy eye. The first thing I'd do is cut your balls off with the rustiest knife I could lay my hands on. Then I'd kick you out of the house and change all the locks and make bloody sure that the next – and final – time you laid eyes on the kids would be at the custody hearing. Which you'd lose. Why, dear? Was there something you wanted to tell me?'

'No, nothing,' I said as I started to clear away the dinner plates, 'just checking.'

Natasha settled herself back down in front of the telly and the waters closed over the conversation, consigning it – for now at least – to the depths. I settled down with my newspaper and made a half-hearted attempt at completing the cryptic crossword, but neither my heart nor my mind were really into the task. I was starting to contemplate giving up and heading for a hot bath and an early night when my mobile phone rang. I picked it up from the arm of the sofa and checked the display: 'Bastard' it read. 'It's Bennett,' I said, hoping Natasha would tell me not to ruin our wonderful evening by taking the call.

'Aren't you going to answer it then?' she asked, adding, 'In the other room.' I raised myself reluctantly from the sofa and pressed the appropriate button on the phone as I shambled through the door.

'You fucking useless twat!' Bennett roared as soon as the connection was made. 'You were supposed to be sorting this mess out and you've made it even worse, you moron. Listen to this text I've been sent now.' All was quiet for a few seconds, then the phone burst back into life. 'Right. I can't actually read the text while I'm talking to you so I'll forward it and you can ring me back when you've read it. I'm warning you, West, I'm taking this straight back to Bill Davis in the morning. I am fed up to the back teeth with this whole bloody business.' Then the phone went dead. Seconds later, I heard the polite ping of an incoming text and opened it to reveal:

> Thanx a bunch English. I waited 4 U all evening and
> U never showed up. So we've had some fun and now
> I'm dumped again?
> Well I'm not having it, U faggot. U'll pay 4 this.

The second I finished reading, the phone rang again.

'So what should I do now?' Bennett yelled. 'She's all over me. This is completely out of hand, West, and I blame you for the whole bloody thing.'

'I really don't understand this,' I stammered in reply. 'She was fine when I dropped her back at the hotel. Are you sure it's from her? On the other hand—' I started, but Bennett had already begun to talk over me.

'Your mate Guttenberg certainly seems to think she's behind it. Sounds like she's told him I diddled her. I tell you what, West – whoever is behind this, I'm going find them and have their bloody guts to restring my squash racquet.' Suddenly, and with an audible clunk, a penny dropped on the other end of the phone. 'What were you going to say then?' Bennett said.

'When?'

'Just then. You said, "On the other hand", but then you didn't say what was on the other hand.'

'What?'

'What is on the other hand, you cretin? You said "On the other hand" and then you stopped. What were you going to say? What is on your other fucking hand, West?'

'Oh, it's nothing really. It's just that as I dropped her back at her hotel, she said erm . . .'

'Said what?' Bennett insisted, the irritation rising in his voice again.

'Erm, well, she said that she would be in her hotel room that evening in case you wanted to drop by.'

'And what did you say? I take it you put her straight?'

'Not exactly,' I said after a lengthy pause, 'I told her I'd pass the message on to you.'

'You did what?' yelled Bennett. 'Why in God's name did you do that, you useless turd? You were supposed to be sorting this mess out not making it worse. Are you deliberately trying to stitch me up?'

'No, I'm not. I promise you I'm not, but, well . . .' I was skating bandy-legged on thin ice and it was starting to crack under the weight of my circumlocutions. 'I just said I'd ask you. I didn't promise her – I just said I'd try. I never had any intention of actually asking you. I was trying to get her off your back, Joseph. She's flying home tomorrow.' I could tell that Bennett had stopped listening to me. I could hear him cursing under his breath and occasionally more volubly.

'My wife is going completely crazy here, thinking I'm having an affair with this ruddy woman and it's all your fault, you imbecile,' Bennett raged. 'I'm going to call Bill Davis right now and suggest the three of us meet first thing tomorrow. I'll see you there at seven thirty.'

'What did he want?' Natasha asked when I returned to the living room.

'He wants me in early again tomorrow,' I said. 'There's more trouble in LA.'

# CITY OF LONDON

When I got into work the next morning, I made straight for Bennett's office. He was a few minutes late, which was unusual for a man who considered having to go home to his wife and children an inconvenient interruption to his working day. He looked like he hadn't slept for a week. I should have felt sorry for him, and guilty for what I'd done, but I couldn't. As well as being an arrogant bully, the man was a wanton and careless philanderer. He'd had affairs with at least five women in the office in the last few years (several of them simultaneously), not to mention his innumerable liaisons with clients, barmaids and pretty young students so eager to make a good impression at graduate recruitment fairs. Come to think of it, our trip to New York might have been the only time he *hadn't* slept with anyone while away on company business. If he was now being punished for a crime he hadn't committed, perhaps that was just God's way of evening things out.

He didn't even grunt a cursory 'Good morning' as he brushed past me to turn on his computer. His mood wasn't improved when he found another message from Olivia waiting for him. Taunting him.

From: CaddyMac@Wannabe.com
To: JosephABennett@Askettbrown.org.uk
Subject:

Evening, Mr Joseph A (as in Asshole) Bennett – or I guess it will be morning by the time you read this. Bet you're already all tucked up with the little woman at your cosy little English home. Well, I waited for you all night. I even got us a bottle of champagne which I had to drink all alone so that tomorrow when I leave this shithole country of yours I'll look like crap for the paps. But hey, that's OK isn't it? So long as we keep your picture out of the papers so the precious little woman doesn't find out what her precious husband's been up to.

Well, I'll tell you one thing for nothing, asshole – she will find out. If you keep treating me this way, she will find out, even if I have to go on Oprah and tell the whole fucking world.

Shit, English. I still don't know if I love you or hate you. Why are you doing this to me?

O

'I suppose you think I've asked for this, don't you?' Bennett said, turning away from his screen. He looked more unsettled – less Bennett-like than I had ever seen him, almost vulnerable. 'What with all the bits and bobs I've got up to in my time.' I shook my head vigorously as if this thought had never crossed my mind. 'Perhaps you're right. But I swear I never touched this woman. Never even spoke to her. So either she's a nutcase or there's something more sinister going on. I don't think anyone in the studio would take the joke this far.' His voice tailed off as he added, 'And it stopped being funny some time ago.'

Shortly before eight o'clock, we were ushered, like a pair of naughty schoolboys, into Bill Davis's office.

Bill was unusually brusque. 'Listen chaps,' he said without even going through the usual niceties of offering us a coffee, 'I've spoken to HR about this . . .'

'Oh, fuck!' said Bennett, then immediately corrected his mistake – just as in the military, swearing in front of a senior officer was frowned upon at Askett Brown. 'Sorry, Bill. But why did you have to get Human Bloody Remains involved?'

'Well,' said Davis, 'it is their job. You two are human resources, after all. This whole business is clearly affecting your work and that could impact on our results and I'm not having that. So, let's get it all sorted out and move on.'

'But if HR get involved, it will go on my file and I'll be marked for life,' Bennett whined.

'This isn't about punishing you, Joseph,' Bill replied. 'I'm trying to help you – both of you. HR will sort you out a bit of training or something and it will all be cleared up in no time.' He made it sound like a dose of the pox.

Bennett was not to be placated: 'With respect, Bill, the

only thing that needs sorting out round here is this fu— this flaming idiot. He told Madame Finch I'd go round and see her in her hotel room, for crying out loud!'

Davis turned to me. He looked exasperated and his normally T-square straight shoulders had sagged. 'Is this true?' he asked, his frustration pushing its way to the surface.

'Yes—' Bennett began, but Davis cut him off.

'Mr West?' he said in a tone that brooked no further argument from Bennett.

'I was only trying to help,' I said, after a long pause during which Bennett tried several times to fill the vacuum and was stopped by a glance or gesture from Bill. 'She wanted to see Joseph again,' I added, trying to piece together the same story I'd told Bennett. 'She was very insistent, so I said I'd speak to him and see if he would pop round to see her.' This was starting to make some sense to me but I wasn't getting any buyers in the room.

'And did you?' Davis asked.

'No, he didn't,' said Bennett.

'Mr West!' Davis demanded, turning his back on Bennett and fixing his gaze on me.

'No. No, I didn't,' I replied, much more quietly than the others. 'I knew that Joseph wouldn't want to see her and I didn't really want to tell him that I'd told her that I'd ask him if he would. I was just trying to buy us all some time. She's heading back to LA today – she's probably already up in the air. Perhaps the whole thing will blow over.'

'And perhaps,' Bennett cut in, 'you'll develop a brain sometime soon, you moron. She's not going to let this go, is she? You saw that e-mail. The silly cow's got it into her head that she's in love with me and you've done nothing but encourage her. You know what I think, Bill? I think we should ring Guttenberg and tell him that his Ms Finch is a lunatic and that if he doesn't get her to stop harassing me, we'll turn this over to the police. And at the same time, you can tell him that you've fired this useless little turd.'

Bill pulled a face that suggested he'd rather spread fish paste on his genitals and mud-wrestle a hippopotamus than have that conversation with Buddy. He thought for a moment, took a sip at an empty cup of coffee, then reached for the silver thermos jug in the middle of the table to pour himself another. His brow was furrowed like Solomon the Wise attempting the *Financial Times* crossword.

When he spoke it was with surprising certainty. 'This is what we'll do,' he said, his gaze steady and assured. 'I will ring Mr Guttenberg to apologise to him and Miss Finch on behalf of Askett Brown and the two of you specifically for yesterday's misunderstanding and any distress that might have been caused. I will also tell him that we have had one or two problems in the Entertainment and Media Division but that these are now being addressed. And I hope he'll be persuaded by the sincerity of my apology because, gentlemen, times are hard and I don't want to lose a good client because of some stupid cock-up like this. Is that clear?'

I nodded obediently. Bennett's intimation of agreement was more difficult to discern.

'So I will not be firing Joe here,' Davis continued looking pointedly at Bennett, 'or anybody else. Not for the time being at least. Now the pair of you get out of my ruddy sight and go and see HR. I'll tell Dai Wainwright you're on your way.'

*

135

Askett Brown's entire HR department consisted of a sinister little man named Dai Wainwright, who bore the title of Director of Human Resources with great pomp and importance, his secretary, Irene, and a single four-drawer cabinet into which were stuffed the thin histories of every person who had ever graced the company's payroll. From time to time, Wainwright would be wheeled out to fire someone – a task he performed with great relish – before being filed away back behind the door of his seventeenth-floor office. He was known throughout the company as 'Dai the Death'.

While the mere mention of the name 'Dai Wainwright' could reduce even the toughest of Askett Brown's alpha males to jelly, physically he was not a prepossessing man. Standing little more than five foot four in his stockinged feet, he only managed to break the socially acceptable five foot six threshold by wearing lifts in his shoes, which meant he had to walk carefully, like a trainee stilts-walker, especially when going downstairs. But within this small package beat the heart of an aggressive little bastard who had built up what little physique he had into something rather impressive and intimidating. As a teenager he'd had a trial for the Welsh schoolboy rugby team, punching above his weight as a pugnacious scrum-half, a snippet of his personal history he liked to remind people about as regularly as possible. Nowadays, he gave vent to his aggression by ending the careers of arrogant, high-flying City boys whenever the opportunity arose, which was all too rarely for his liking.

Bennett was already outside Wainwright's office when I arrived, pacing up and down like a disgruntled tiger, his face still contorted with rage. He wouldn't look at me, let alone talk to me, as we waited. Occasionally, he would sigh or 'tut' loudly, to let off a bit of steam, but apart from that we sat in silence.

After several minutes, Wainwright appeared at the door, apologised insincerely for keeping us waiting and invited us into his office. His voice had a characteristic sing-song lilt, but the song was a dirge – Uncle Fester performing karaoke at an Addams Family funeral. 'Coffee? Tea? Water?' he asked, making each sound as if it came laced with strychnine. We both declined. I looked across at Bennett as we sat down, but he didn't catch my eye. He was totally focused on Wainwright.

'All right, Wainwright,' said Bennett in a voice that to the Welshman must have shouted of centuries of English oppression, 'we all know why we're here, so let's get on with it. You've already kept me waiting fifteen fucking minutes and I don't intend to waste another second of my valuable time. So say your piece, write your report, and then let me and my fuckwitted friend get back to work. OK?'

Wainwright reworked his face into what might loosely be described as a smile, but one so lacking in warmth that you could have served sorbet out of it. His eyes were alive with the prospects of doing battle with a worthy adversary, not one of those lily-livered cowards who begged and cried and invoked their wives and children as he told them they had precisely one hour to clear their desks. Joseph Bennett was made of sterner stuff – and Wainwright was already enjoying this. He'd hardly even noticed I was in the room.

'This will take as long as it will take, Mr Bennett,' Wainwright said, glowering across the table.

Bennett stared back, refusing to blink or avert his gaze,

but choosing to say nothing. The Welshman stood up for maximum impact but, even with the two of us sitting down, he only towered over Bennett by a few inches.

'When Bill first asked me what we should do about this situation, do you know what I said? I said, "Bill, you should fire the pair of them. The reputation of this company is far too important to risk because of a couple of liabilities like Bennett and West."' He paused to check our reaction.

I tried to remain impassive, although I could feel my face reddening. Bennett shuffled uncomfortably in his chair and fought the urge to speak in his own defence or smash something heavy over the diminutive Welshman's head.

'Fortunately for the two of you,' Wainwright continued, 'Bill Davis is a far nicer person than yours truly.' He laughed an empty chuckle, like a repairman discovering your boiler needs an expensive new part. 'Not only does he want to give you another chance, but he's asked me to spend some of my precious training and development budget to send you on a course to improve your interpersonal skills. If you ask me, the only course we should be sending you on, Mr Bennett, is one on how to keep your pecker in your pants when confronted by a beautiful woman.' He allowed himself another smile.

Bennett looked fit to burst. I leaned forward and poured myself a glass of water.

'Still,' Wainwright went on, 'ours not to reason why, is it, lads? If Bill Davis says do it, then I like to think he can consider it done. I know a man who specialises in this kind of thing. Chap called Rodney James down in Balham. Wonderful man. Marvellous wing forward he was back in the day. I rang Rodney after Bill spoke to me and, bless him, he said he'd be happy to see you gentlemen first thing on Monday.'

Bennett could hold his tongue no longer. 'Now you listen here, Wainwright. I am a very busy man with a job of work to do, bringing money into this firm. I have a packed schedule on Monday and I have no intention of wasting any part of the day in fucking Balham. So you can tell your Mr James that he can do what he likes with this wanker,' he pointed exaggeratedly in my direction as if we'd otherwise be unable to work out who he was referring to, 'but I shall be at my desk as per normal. Do I make myself clear?'

'You make yourself crystal clear, Mr Bennett,' Wainwright replied. 'In fact, I thought you might say that. I said to Bill, I said, "If we offer Bennett some training, you know what he'll say, don't you?" and Bill said, "No," and I said, "He'll say words to the effect of 'Stuff that for a game of soldiers.'" I wish I'd had a little side bet with him now.' He chuckled again. Then, after a pause of several tantalising seconds, he added, 'And do you know what Bill said to me?'

Bennett shook his head, fists clenched, the impulse to reach over and strangle this annoying little man almost irresistible.

'Bill said, "Well, if he refuses to do what you ask, Dai, you have my authority to fire him!"' Wainwright sat down again, satisfaction tattooed all over his face.

Bennett looked dumbstruck. 'You can't do that,' he roared, rising from his seat, 'and you know it. You don't have the authority to fire me.'

'I can, I don't, I do and I will,' Wainwright sang back, relishing the moment.

Bennett stared at Wainwright, suddenly looking utterly

defeated. The thick veneer of undiluted success that he had worn like foundation all these years had been washed away, leaving a pale shadow of his former self. When he finally regained the power of speech, he said in little more than a whisper, 'Don't get me wrong, Dai. I didn't say I wouldn't go to Balham. I just said that I have a ton of work on right now, so if we could make it later in the week then that would be great. I'm very grateful for what you and Bill are doing to sort this mess out and I'd be a fool not to take every opportunity on offer. Perhaps we could check diaries and see when might be convenient for everyone?'

Wainwright scrunched up his face and nodded in admiration of Bennett's nimble footwork, like a hunter who had almost landed his prey, then seen it break free before he could deliver the *coup de grâce*. 'I'm so glad you see things our way, Mr Bennett. Unfortunately, Monday is the only day next week that Rodney is available, so may I humbly suggest that you try to free up your time? Let me know if this proves difficult and I'll have a word with Bill about the alternative options. Am I making *myself* clear now, Mr Bennett?'

Bennett nodded, defeated. Then, as an afterthought, as if he'd suddenly remembered I was in the room, Dai the Death turned to me and said, 'All clear, Mr West?'

'Yes,' I replied. It was the first word I'd uttered since I'd turned down the offer of a drink fifteen minutes earlier.

# BALHAM, SOUTH LONDON

Rodney James's residence was in a neat Georgian block in a quiet side street in that unfamiliar territory known as South of the River. Traditionally, it had been the East and West End of the city that had defined London, but more recently there had developed a north/south divide. People who spent their entire lives among the boulevards and terraces north of the River Thames could easily become lost if ever they ventured south. The city looked and sounded different down there.

I was the first to arrive and was greeted enthusiastically by Rodney, who showed me into his waiting area which doubled as a kitchenette.

'Would you like a coffee?' he asked.

'A straight black coffee would be lovely, thanks,' I replied.

'Fantastic,' said Rodney, as if making me a drink would somehow affirm the entire point of his existence. He seemed a pleasant man, which made me wonder how he could be so close to Dai Wainwright. He was tall, but walked hunched over as if he had spent too much time deferring to shorter people. His face was partially hidden behind large black-framed spectacles with lenses so thick and dirty that when you looked at him head-on his eyes all but disappeared. A conspiracy of opticians had obviously failed to tell him that he could have improved his vision appreciably just by cleaning his glasses every so often. I imagined him learning Braille for the day when the grime would block out the last vestiges of sunlight, rendering him completely blind.

He handed me the coffee and I thanked him and he thanked me for taking it from him and we sat quietly and waited for Bennett. As the minutes ticked by, I began to fantasise that Bennett wasn't going to turn up at all – that he'd found himself another job over the weekend and decided to stick two fingers up to Bill Davis and the loathsome Wainwright. But just as this marvellous scenario was taking hold in my consciousness, there was a loud chorus of 'Land of My Fathers' and Rodney leapt to his feet to open the door, thrilled by the chance to serve again.

Bennett walked into the room with all the enthusiasm of a cow being led to the abattoir. His face was set in a grizzly frown, eyes downcast so as not to have to acknowledge anyone. His shoulders were hunched – unusually for a man who normally stood so tall – and his hands balled into fists as if he was preparing to fight his way out. He grunted when our host offered him a cup of coffee, but Rodney poured him one anyway, determined not to let Bennett's indifference blunt his own enthusiasm for the day ahead.

'Welcome gentlemen and thank you so much for coming all the way down here to see me at such short notice. What

I thought we'd do today is that I'll have a quick chat with each of you individually to get a better picture of where we're at, kind of like a starting point if you like, and while I'm in there with one, the other – if you don't mind – will be out here completing a little questionnaire, what I call a "psychometric instrument". His high-pitched voice placed inverted commas around the words as if this was a concept he had invented specially for us that morning. 'It will help me learn more about each of you and, more importantly, help you learn more about yourselves. It's basically just a few questions I've developed which look at how you're motivated, how you relate to other people and so on. How does that sound? OK?'

Bennett's body language was screaming out 'No, it is not bloody OK!' while I sat forward trying to look interested but not too keen. Rodney ignored us both and ploughed on.

'Then, once I've had a chance to assess the results, we'll all get together for a debrief and see if we can identify which issues might be affecting your working relationship.' He spoke as if we were there voluntarily, but he knew as well as we did that we'd been press-ganged by Wainwright, with the threat of instant dismissal if we failed to comply. Bennett sat brooding like King Kong on Broadway, desperate to rip off his manacles and escape.

'I've known your pal Dai for donkey's years now, ever since we had our schoolboy trials together for the Welsh rugby. Cracking little scrum-half he was back then! Aggressive little sod, mind you! He'd often start fights, then expect me to sort them out for him. Still does in a way – sending me what he calls his "difficult buggers" to sort out.

But he hasn't beaten me yet! I've always managed to sort them out for him – or given him the bullets he needed to fire them.' He was still trilling away like a contented budgerigar but his words had taken on a more sinister edge. Perhaps he wasn't the pushover he appeared at first sight.

Rodney invited us to introduce ourselves and then looked at each of us several times in rapid succession as if repeating a rhyme in his head. Then, when he'd decided which little fishy to keep and which to let go, he turned to me. 'Joe W., why don't you come with me for a little chat? Joe B., would you mind filling in the questionnaire for me? It's quite straightforward. Just follow the instructions at the top of page two and answer all the questions as truthfully as you can. I'll pop out in a second to make sure you're OK.'

He showed me into his office and asked me to wait while he ran through the questionnaire with Bennett, who was still rumbling like a dark cloud carrying too much rain. I sensed there would be a storm before the day was out. I settled into a low-slung leatherette armchair and scanned the impressive array of framed certificates displayed in neat rows along two walls of Rodney's office. Rodney entered the room and closed the door behind him, then sat down and moved his chair closer to mine.

'So what I want to find out first, Joe,' he began, 'is what you would like to get out of today, hmm? What would a successful day look like for Joe West? I still get paid whether I help you sort yourselves out or go back to Dai and recommend he fires the pair of you, but I get so much more out of it personally if I feel I've actually made a difference. I hate to see fine young men like you and Joe B. slung out

144

in your prime because of some silly misunderstanding. So, what would be a good outcome for you, Joe, hmm?'

'Well, erm, er, I'm not sure really,' I said eventually. 'A good outcome for me would be, er, erm . . . I suppose a good outcome for me would be that Joseph and I manage to develop some kind of proper working relationship. You see, we've never got on, not since we both joined Askett Brown fifteen years ago. And now he blames me for this whole thing with Olivia Finch, as if I've been deliberately trying to set him up, which I haven't of course, but he doesn't have anyone else to blame. And, as he already thinks I'm completely useless, it's not too much of a stretch for him to pin this on me too.'

I was aware that I was saying far too much, but seemed powerless to stop myself. Without saying a word, Rodney was managing to carry out a meticulous interrogation. When I hadn't spoken for a while, he looked at me, trying to work out whether I was pausing for breath or had run out of things to say. He let the uncomfortable silence extend for almost a minute.

'So how would you describe your current relationship with Joe B.?' he asked when he was sure I wasn't going to say anything else.

'You know how it is, don't you?' I replied. 'Isn't that why we're here? We're not exactly best buddies. He's everything I'm not and I'm everything he can't stand. We took an instant dislike to each other the day we joined the firm and, now I have to work for him, everything is ten times worse. He's a terrible manager and bosses me about even though he hasn't a clue what he's talking about and expects me to do all the work while he takes all the credit.'

'And have you said any of this to him?' asked Rodney, sitting forward in his chair.

'Are you kidding?' I laughed, but it was clear he had no intention of answering my questions. He was the quizmaster on today's show. 'I'm sorry but that's just not a conversation I – or anyone – could have with Bennett. He'd throw me out of the building – probably from an upper-storey window.'

'You're making it sound like an unhappy marriage,' said Rodney, sitting back again.

'Oh God, no!' I said, laughing again, 'Not unless it was some kind of forced arrangement.'

'Let's imagine this is a marriage,' Rodney shot back. 'What options would you have now?'

'Well, I could leave him, I suppose. Or we could go to a counsellor for guidance. I suppose that's what we're doing today, isn't it?'

Rodney peered at me through his self-imposed gloom, waiting for me to say more, daring me to say more.

'What are you driving at?' I said. 'Are you telling me I should jack in my job because I can't stand my boss?'

'I'm not suggesting anything,' Rodney replied. 'I'm just trying to find out what's going on. So tell me, how long have you had this chip on your shoulder?'

'Pardon?'

'How long have you nursed this inferiority complex, Joe? Were you inferior at school? At university? With the ladies? Or is this a religious thing? Is it because you is Jewish? Hmm?'

'No,' I said, irritated both by Rodney's line of questioning and the stupid, childish intonation he had suddenly adopted, as if this was all a game to him. 'This has nothing to do with my religion – I'm not even really that Jewish – or with my upbringing. We just don't get on. Is that so unusual?'

'But Mr Bennett certainly went to a better school than you, didn't he? And a better university. And, I'll wager, he's had better luck with the women than you. Is that why you're trying to destroy him?'

He stared at me, trying to assess my reaction to his accusations, more like a detective playing both good cop and bad cop now than an over-qualified trainer. I wanted to shout back that it wasn't Joseph bloody Bennett who had bedded the beautiful Olivia Finch and driven her so wild that now she couldn't leave me alone, but me – little Joey West. I took a few deep, calming breaths, trying to gather my thoughts.

I hoped Rodney hadn't been able to read anything into my troubled expression, but feared that, as an expert in such things, he probably had. When I spoke, it was with an entirely artificial approximation of poise. 'I have no idea what you're talking about, Mr James. I have always worked hard to support Joseph Bennett and help him settle into his new role. I have never acted with anything other than total professionalism where he is concerned and I expect the same from him. There may be a few strange things going on in Joseph's life at the moment but they are nothing to do with me. Now, is that all?

Rodney stared hard at me for a few moments, then looked at his watch, smiled and said, 'OK. That will do for now, Joe. All most interesting! Now I'd like you to fill in my questionnaire while I have a chat with Joe B. Is that OK?'

I nodded, relieved. I'd survived the interrogation with my secrets safe, my honour intact. He explained to me how the questionnaire worked, then showed me out into the waiting area, inviting Bennett into his room at the same time. The door closed and I settled down to answer the thirty questions that would reveal the innermost secrets of my personality.

As I finished answering the questions, I became aware of raised voices coming from inside Rodney's office. The walls and door were thick enough to stop intimate conversations leaking out into the waiting area, but it was clear that Bennett was upset about something. After a brief pause, I heard loud grunts of exertion and what sounded like the smack of leather on leather, like boxing gloves hitting a heavy bag. Had Rodney annoyed Bennett so much that he was systematically beating him to death in there? No – not unless Rodney had changed into a pair of leather dungarees and gimp mask. I tried the door but it was locked from the inside. The sound of the handle being agitated must have disturbed them, though, because a few seconds later, before I had even regained my seat, the door opened and Rodney, looking hotter and redder than when I'd left him, appeared to assure me that everything was all right.

Breathlessly, he ushered me back into his office. Bennett was standing in the middle of the room, also looking a bit flushed. He was wearing an outsized pair of boxing gloves. On the floor in front of him were two of those large red leather pads that boxing trainers use for sparring with their charges.

'Sorry, Joe,' said Rodney between pants, 'that must have sounded rather odd from outside. I'm a great believer in the holistic approach to training, you know, bringing the mind and body together? I have various alternative techniques I use if someone seems a bit blocked and finds it difficult to tell me about their feelings, and that. So I thought I'd give Joseph here a chance to express himself in a different way – with his fists. Feel better for that, Joseph?'

'Actually, I do,' said Bennett, the first coherent comment I'd heard from him all day. 'You should try it, West. You look a bit uptight yourself.'

'That's not such a bad idea,' said Rodney, replacing his glasses, an action which probably diminished rather than improved his eyesight. 'I might come back to that later. But first I want to have a look at the results of your questionnaires. Give me a few minutes to go through them and do the scoring bit, would you, gentlemen? Why don't you go and refill your coffee cups and I'll call you back in, say, ten minutes? Lovely.'

'So what do you reckon so far?' Bennett asked while the coffee machine sputtered boiling coffee and a strange white, milk-like substance into his cup. He had clearly enjoyed the punching exercise and was finding it more difficult to maintain his earlier sourness. 'Complete bloody waste of time, if you ask me, but that last bit was fun. I could have got a damn sight more out of a session on the heavy bag down at the gym, mind you. Have you ever boxed, West? We must have a go later on – I only hope my hands can withstand the pummelling you'll give them.'

He laughed at his joke and I smiled back, glad to draw some of the chill out of the room. 'It will be interesting to see if this questionnaire throws up anything, won't it?' I said, trying to keep the mood pleasant.

'D'you think?' Bennett replied. 'I hate those bloody things. I must have done dozens in my time and they've never found anything of any interest.'

Our conversation exhausted, we sat in silence drinking our coffees until the door opened and Rodney emerged from his room, beaming from ear to ear. 'Come in, lads, come in!' he said with the fervour of a novice Boy Scouts patrol leader. 'This is all most interesting. Most interesting!'

We trooped back into his room and took our seats. He looked genuinely pleased to see us as if he had expected us to run away the moment his back was turned. Perhaps that's what most of his clients did. 'Right,' he announced, clapping his hands together, 'I have the results from your questionnaires. Are you happy for me to divulge them in front of one another?'

We nodded obediently. 'Yup, bring it on,' said Bennett.

'Splendid! First, let me explain again what this instrument is about. It is not a test of intelligence and there are no right or wrong answers. It is simply a set of questions designed to find out more about what makes you tick. The test has been validated and proven to provide reliable and relevant information. I am a fully qualified Stage 1 and 2 practitioner in the instrument—'

'Yeah, yeah, whatever,' Bennett said. 'Now, could you please tell us the results? Am I going to live, doctor?' Invigorated by the boxing, Bennett was starting to sound more like his old, insufferable self.

'No, no, Mr Bennett, it's nothing like that,' Rodney laughed. 'This just helps me – and hopefully you as well – see what kind of people you are and what might cause any difficulties in your relationship. And then, of course, gives us some ideas about what we can do about them. I must say, it's very clear from your reports why you might rub each other up the wrong way from time to time. You are very different.'

'With all due respect, Taff, I could have told you that an hour ago,' said Bennett.

'Yes, I appreciate that,' Rodney replied, 'but now we have some objective data to work with. This report considers your answers to the questions and then defines your character along two different axes: what motivates you and how you like to relate to other people. And then, to make it easier to remember, it translates this into a colour and an animal. For example, Joseph B., your results indicate that you are a Purple Stallion.'

Despite our general frostiness and recently glacial relationship, Bennett and I couldn't resist exchanging smiles at that. It didn't matter what kind of school you went to, having the teacher refer to someone as a purple stallion would always get a laugh. Rodney could see us smirking, but continued undaunted.

'Now, you see, this tells us that you are motivated by getting things done and are driven by a desire to win at all costs – that's the purple bit – but you are also something of a loner, happiest leading from the front and charging on, even when there's no one following behind you. That's the stallion. Does that sound about right?'

It sounded spot on to me and Bennett also concurred, no doubt enjoying the image of himself as a kind of modern Bucephalus, tougher and even more driven than the great Alexander on his back.

'Yup, that sounds like me, wouldn't you say, West?'

151

I nodded. I could already imagine his new business cards: 'Joseph Bennett, Head of Entertainment and Media Division. Purple Stallion', alongside an image of something suitably large, muscular and purple rising up to pursue a mighty quest.

'What about West then?' Bennett grinned, 'what's he?'

I ran through the possibilities in my mind: a Green Tiger, perhaps – sleek and powerful, yet environmentally friendly? Or a Scarlet Elephant – fiery and strong, but silent as the night? Or—

'Ah, now that's the interesting bit,' said Rodney. 'You see, Joe here comes out as a Yellow Meerkat . . .'

Bennett exploded into laughter. 'A yellow meerkat! Isn't that some kind of giant rat? That just about sums you up, West! A skinny yellow rat! That's priceless!' All of a sudden his day had become very worthwhile.

Rodney ignored Bennett's outburst and carried on. 'Yes, a Yellow Meerkat. Remember, Mr Bennett, there are no right or wrong answers or better or less good animals to be under this test. It simply provides a way of looking at the differences between people. Your Yellow Meerkat is motivated by helping people, is generally optimistic and enjoys working closely with others, but probably as part of the team rather than as the leader. All organisations need a few Yellow Meerkats scurrying around behind the scenes if they're to be successful. Does that sound like you, Mr West?'

'Absolutely spot on!' roared Bennett.

'But, remember, Joseph,' said Rodney, irritated by Bennett's triumphalism, 'a single meerkat can kill a deadly cobra if it is motivated to do so.'

'Yes,' said Bennett, 'and so can a stallion if it stamps on the fucker!'

Rodney made some notes on his pad, then handed us a copy of our individual reports. 'You can read through these at your leisure, folks,' he said, still retaining his enthusiasm.

In his world there really were no good or bad results, just more or less interesting subjects. Bennett flicked through his report, smiling occasionally. I placed mine on the floor and made a mental note never to look at it again.

'OK,' said Rodney, clapping his hands again to regain our attention and rubbing them together briskly like a vagrant searching for kinetic warmth, 'what do we learn from all this?' The question was meant rhetorically, allowing him the platform from which to announce his pre-prepared conclusions, but Bennett was too quick for him, striking like the cobra I would now dearly love to kill – metaphorically, of course.

'This completely explains why I find West here such a terrible drag. While I'm trying to get things done, he just wants to fanny about making sure everyone's happy. I mean, isn't that why we're here? He couldn't tell that American girl the truth, so he let her think I'd go and see her. For God's sake, even if I had diddled her in New York – which I absolutely did not – I still wouldn't have strung her along like this. It would have been wham bam, thank you ma'am – now fuck off! That's the Purple Stallion way.'

The most appalling thing about this analysis was that it was almost 100 per cent true. If I'd been more decisive, I could have stopped the whole thing weeks ago. Instead, I'd let it run out of control. Trying to please everyone and

153

ultimately pleasing no one. That, I'm afraid, is the Yellow Meerkat way. And that's why Purple Stallions rule the world.'

'That isn't exactly how I'd have put it,' Rodney replied slowly, 'but you are correct, Joseph, that your two types are so different that you may find it difficult to gel. The friendly, sociable meerkat will often find the stallion a little too, er, robust, whereas, as you've said, the meerkat can be a touch too reflective for your rampant, thrusting stallion.' Bennett sniggered and snorted but Rodney carried on. 'But that doesn't mean the stallion and the meerkat can't work together – you'll just have to put more effort into it. You may never be great mates, but you should be able to get along perfectly well. Do you follow me?'

'Absolutely,' said Bennett. 'West and I can work together fine as long as I lead and he follows and I try not to crap on him too often. And the slower he is running after me, the more crap he'll have to dodge.'

'Again, not quite as I'd have put it,' Rodney said, his enthusiasm finally beginning to wilt. 'What I mean is that you'll have to draw on the best aspects of both of your profiles to create a winning combination. It's like your forwards and backs at rugby. Different shapes and sizes and different roles and skills but all needed to get that ball over the try line. Do you see?'

'Got it! So it's for me to do all the hard grafting at the front, then get the ball out back to Westy to do the Fancy Dan girly stuff,' said Bennett. 'Is that it? Can I go back to work now?'

'Good gracious no,' said Rodney, smiling again. 'That instrument is only one part of the process I want to go through today – we've barely scratched the surface. There are a couple more exercises I want to do with you this afternoon but, right now, I think we could all do with an energiser. Why don't we go with Joseph's idea and get the old boxing gloves back on? Is that OK with you?'

'Actually, no, it isn't . . .' I started to reply but was quickly bulldozed into agreement by the others' enthusiasm.

'Oh, come on,' said Bennett as if he was talking to one of his mates, 'it'll be fun.' Without waiting for further instructions, he pulled on the sparring mitts and started slapping them together like dustbin lids.

'Here you go, Joe,' Rodney said, presenting me with the two enormous leather gloves. 'As Joseph says, this will be a bit of fun, but I also want you to get some learning out of it. What I'd like you to do is think of a succinct sentence that expresses something you would like the other one to do differently in order to improve your relationship. Then, as you punch the mitts, you announce that sentence one syllable at a time in time with your punches. Do you see what I mean? For example, let's say that I would like my wife to give the bath a wipe-down after she's used it, to get rid of all the hair and stuff she leaves behind. What I'd do is tell her what I wanted her to do differently and hit her to emphasise each syllable.' I was unsure now whether he was still explaining the exercise or confessing to being a wife-beater. 'So it would go: "Dar (he feinted a punching motion towards one of Bennett's padded hands and made the sound of a punch)-ling (whack), would (pow) you (smack) clean (bam) the (whop) bath (doov) prop-er-ly (a rapid left-right-left combination: bish-bash-bosh)?" Do you see?'

'Yes, we see,' said Bennett, stallionly. 'Come on! Let's get on with it.'

Still feeling some trepidation, as well as enormous sympathy for Mrs James, who I imagined was even now on her hands and knees polishing her bath to a state of show-room brightness in readiness for her husband's return, I sidled up to within two feet of Bennett, my fists so weighed down that I could hardly lift them. I wasn't sure what I feared most: the humiliation of not being able to land a meaningful blow on Bennett, or the pain of his reply. I conjured up the shortest sentence I could think of, hoping that when it was my turn to be his punchbag, Bennett would also go for something neat and pithy rather than delivering my full annual appraisal punctuated by bone-splintering punches.

I began my routine, spelling out the sentence one syllable at a time, landing an ineffectual blow to one of Bennett's hands with each utterance: 'Why (splat) can't (plop) you (nudge) be (thwat) nice-r (tap-tap) some (pat) times (pfff)?'

By the time I'd finished, Bennett was bent double with laughter. If it had been a boxing match, the referee would have had to stop it because he was incapable of defending himself. Rodney was trying hard not to join him, years of training and experience being stretched to the limit. Clearly, he had never before seen such a pathetic attempt at hitting anything.

'Are you ready to continue, Joseph,' he said, when he was certain he would not start laughing, 'or do you need a little longer to recover?' That set Bennett off again and, this time, Rodney joined him, convincing himself he was laughing at his own witticism rather than at the feeble joke standing in front of them.

When they had recovered some semblance of decorum, I swapped the gloves for Bennett's sparring pads and he took up his stance in front of me – six feet plus of well-honed muscle and properly drilled technique. My first instinct was to throw the pads down and run for my life, but I was comforted by the thought that his mood had improved a great deal during the course of the day. The Bennett who had arrived that morning would have been a murderous prospect indeed.

I held my hands up in front of me and prepared for the assault. What follows – like my teeth – has been pieced together from contemporary records. Bennett threw a flurry of punches with the rhythm and power of a professional cruiser-weight. He opened with a left cross into my left glove as he shouted 'West'. This was followed by a hard right to my right to illustrate the accusative 'Why', then a straight right to my left – 'don't' – followed by another left to my left – 'you'. The force of the successive blows was driving my hands back towards my body. A right to my right – 'stop', a straight left to my right – 'be-', another left, this time across my body to my left hand – '-ing', a powerful straight right that knocked me off balance – 'such'; then he took half a step forward to deliver another left, this time, I think, to my left but, by then, I'd lost all feeling in my hands – 'a'. Another straight right was followed by a flurry of punches – right, left, right, right – which backed me up against a wall – 'mis-er-a-ble', before another left/right combination stamped out the word 'lit-tle' on my battered palms.

'*SHIT*!'

*What the fuck was that? I didn't see no train coming. Did you see a train coming? Pardon me boy, was that the Chattanooga Choo Choo? Track sixty-nine, was that it? No,*

*that's not right. Thirty-nine? Twelve? Twelve Days of Christmas?*
Twelve Angry Men? *Henry Fonda. He was in* Twelve Angry
Men. *Daughter's called Jane, Saigon Jane.* Miss Saigon. *'On
the other side of the earth, there's a place for us'. No, wait.
That's* West Side Story. *Natalie Wood and what's his name?
What's my name? Where was I? Where am I? Who am I?'*

The room had turned horizontal: the walls were where
the floor and ceiling should have been and vice versa. My
head was scrambled and my face felt cold and wet. I ran
my tongue around the inside of my mouth and found a
gap where my front teeth had been when I'd brushed them
that morning. This knocked the crust off some semi-dried
blood and it started to run freely again out of my mouth
and down my chin where, because my face was lying at
90 degrees to its usual elevation, it took a right turn down
my cheek and dripped into my ear.

My vision was badly blurred, although I realised later that
was because the blow had knocked my glasses halfway across
the room. I could just about make out Bennett and Rodney
standing over me. They eased me up to a sitting position
with my back against the wall and Rodney pressed a pad of
toilet tissue to my mouth and offered me some water. I
sipped on it and let it dribble back into the glass, turning
the contents a washed-out pink. Rodney put my glasses back
on my nose, where they rested at a jaunty angle.

'Sorry old boy,' I heard Bennett saying through the fog.
'That last one got away from me. Softened you up with a
nice left-right combo and then sneaked one through your
guard. Went down like a sack of spuds, didn't he, Rodney?'

'Listen,' said Rodney, 'we're going to call you a cab and get
you home. I think we've done enough for one day. But Joseph

and I agreed that, given how things turned out, we should get together again some time to carry on. And this time, you can have one free hit at *his* face. How does that sound?'

I was incapable of speaking or of moving my face to show any reaction. It all hurt too much. Eventually, I flicked my watery eyes up and down in a gesture that could have meant anything from 'That would be lovely, thank you' to 'Call the police' and settled down to wait for the taxi.

When the mini-cab arrived, Rodney helped me down the stairs and into the back seat, explaining to the driver the reasons behind my dazed expression and blood-soaked clothes. As we were pulling away, Bennett came running out of the door shouting for me to open the window.

'Don't forget these, old boy,' he said, handing me a piece of blood-stained tissue paper. I opened the package as the taxi pulled away – and saw my two front teeth smiling up at me.

# MILL HILL, NORTH LONDON

The journey home seemed to take forever. The traffic, even in the early afternoon, was horrible, forcing the driver to weave through narrow side streets in desperate pursuit of a few feet of unoccupied road. As we drew nearer to my home, he had to ask me for directions, in response to which I could only mumble and splutter like the Elephant Man chewing a toffee. Every time I tried to speak, a crimson stream dribbled from my mouth into the sodden red paper napkin I was holding to my battered face. The cabbie checked occasionally that I wasn't bleeding on his upholstery, but otherwise seemed unperturbed by my plight.

When we got to within a few minutes' walk of my house, and tired of trying to make myself understood through swollen lips, I asked him to pull over. I handed over the contents of my wallet in settlement of the fare and shuffled home, engendering fear or laughter in the people who saw me, depending on their predisposition towards bleeding men in suits.

I eventually made it to my front door and fumbled for my keys with my left hand, while my right stayed pressed to my face, holding the napkin in place. I managed to hook them out of my pocket, but then dropped them behind one of the pot plants that adorned our front step. Even the thought of going down on my hands and knees to grope for them gave me a headache, so I rang the bell. There was no answer. Looking at my watch, I realised that Natasha must be collecting Helen from school. I was close to tears, not of pain – although my whole face felt as if I'd been used for batting practice by a Major League baseball team – but from the accumulated anguish of a day that had started brightly but had descended to my being labelled a cowardly weasel, punched in the face and made to struggle home only to find myself locked out.

I sat down on the step and rested my throbbing head in my hands. After what seemed like a lifetime, I heard the patter of excited feet and felt eager hands grabbing at me as Helen and Matthew, surprised to see me waiting for them, raced ahead of their mother to greet me. As I looked up, I heard the sharp scream, followed by the gut-wrenching sobs of my daughter and the maniacal giggling of my son who, while not used to seeing his father toothless and bleeding, was easily excited by blood and trouble.

Natasha heard the commotion and sprinted up the path, umbrella raised above her head, her face etched with the terror that only a mother can know: that the man on her front step whom she had assumed to be her husband was, in fact, a murderous, paedophiliac, Jehovah's Witness off his face on Special Brew or crystal meth. She was relieved to see that the cause of her daughter's alarm was only her husband sporting a face like a dentist's dream.

'What in God's name happened to you?' she asked, opening the door and pushing the kids into the house, then half-dragging me in after them. I mumbled something that was supposed to be 'Bennett hit me' but came out as 'Mwwaahh mwah mwa', which Natasha understood because she is my wife and not a taxi driver.

'Bennett hit you?' she reflected back with significantly better diction. I nodded. 'But why? No – let me guess. Could it be because you took his new girlfriend out last week?'

'Mwahh?' I asked. (I'll provide subtitles for those who find this hard to follow: 'What?') 'Mwahh mwah mwa mwa?' ('What do you mean?')

'Well,' said Natasha, stroking Helen's hair to calm her, while holding Matthew back with one knee to stop him dabbling his fingers in my wound like a pre-school Doubting Thomas, 'I'm no expert but I'd have thought that someone like Bennett might get upset if someone else took his newly acquired superstar girlfriend out for the day.'

'Mwwahh?' ('What?') I asked again. I wanted to ask, 'How the hell did you know I took Olivia Finch out last week,' but feared spraying my family like the audience at a Jackson Pollock sitting if I did.

Natasha ignored my question and carried on with her own line of enquiry. 'Just as the wife of that someone might get a tad annoyed if their husband came home one night complaining about what a crappy day he'd had at the office when in fact he'd spent the afternoon at Lord's with a piece of A-list Hollywood crumpet. Mightn't she?'

I lowered my head in shame, allowing Matthew to jab an inquisitive finger into my mouth.

'Look, Mummy, blood!' he announced, holding up a damp red fingertip for Natasha's inspection.

'Go and wash it off, dear,' Natasha said. She was still holding the sobbing Helen closely to her. 'Mightn't she?' she repeated.

'Mwah,' ('Yes') I replied quietly into my napkin, head bowed like a guilty schoolboy.

'I don't know what the hell is going on, Joe, but if Bennett hadn't hit you, I probably would have. How do you think I feel when I have to hear all this stuff from Sandra bloody Bennett because you haven't had the nerve to tell me yourself? She came round for a coffee this morning. She is so hacked off with you, it's untrue. She said you took Olivia Finch to watch cricket – cricket of all bloody things – and then set her Joseph up on a date with her. And all I can think while she's telling me this is, "Why didn't the lying swine tell me he'd been with Madame Finch all day?" Why don't you tell me what's going on, Joe?'

'Mwa mwa mwwahh,' ('I can explain') I started to reply before realising that that might not only be conceptually difficult but physically impossible.

'Not now,' she replied. 'Wait until the kids are in bed. You can write it down if it's easier. Here, let me take a look at that mouth. You may have to go to A and E and have that checked out. Make sure that bastard hasn't done any real damage.'

'Mummy, what's a "bastard"?' asked Helen, looking up from Natasha's lap.

'It's another word for a man,' said Natasha. 'But don't use it at school.'

Thankfully, Natasha decided, after much rootling around inside my mouth, that a trip to Casualty wouldn't be necessary, although she did book me an emergency appointment with the dentist for the following day. It was a relief to be spared the four-hour wait in some hideous wind tunnel, surrounded by fighting drunks and retching drug addicts, only to be told that I had indeed lost two teeth and should try to avoid being smacked in the mouth again until the bleeding had stopped.

By the end of the evening, the visit to the hospital seemed the better option.

'So,' Natasha began as she reappeared downstairs after putting the children to bed, 'let's begin at the beginning, shall we?' She had made no mention of dinner. I was going to have to sing for my supper. I had several ice cubes pressed to my swollen mouth, which had eased the pain a little but made talking even more difficult. My upper lip was so cold that it could play little part in the enunciation of most vowel sounds and many consonants. I had to let Natasha develop her argument while I tried to thaw myself out with a glass of red wine.

'Last Thursday,' she said, 'you went to work as usual but then, instead of spending your afternoon at the office, you took the most beautiful woman on the planet to a game of cricket – poor cow. Then you came home in a foul mood and told me you'd had a rotten day at work. Do stop me if I get any of this wrong.'

'I will,' I forced out from beneath my frozen lip, sounding like a mobster taking his wedding vows.

'Good. So I take it I've got it right so far?' I nodded. 'And, according to Sandra Bennett, you also told Ms Finch that you would ask Bennett to go and see her that evening. Which raises two questions: why didn't you tell me you'd spent the afternoon with Bennett's new lady friend? And then, why did you try to set him up again when you'd been explicitly told to get her to lay off him? What are you getting yourself mixed up in here, Joe? And why did you lie to me about it? What is it you're trying to hide?'

I wanted to point out that that was, in fact, many more than two questions, but thought better of it. Natasha held my gaze, waiting for my reply. I rubbed my injured face and winced to indicate that I would answer as soon as I could formulate an answer that wouldn't put too much pressure on my damaged mouth.

'I'm sorry, love,' I began, speaking slowly and mumbling even more than usual. 'I didn't tell you because I knew you'd get upset and . . .'

Natasha could see I was struggling to speak. She was also struggling not to interrupt. So she interrupted. 'Why should I get upset? If you'd explained the situation to me, why would I have had to ask any more questions? Let's face it Joe, you're not exactly a matinee idol, are you? And even if, in some parallel universe where overweight, bald Jewish accountants were considered a top catch for beautiful Hollywood actresses, Olivia Finch did decide to ditch Bennett for you, I very much doubt that a day at Lord's would be the quickest way to get inside her knickers. Or maybe that's what turns her on. Perhaps she lives such a glamorous life that she gets a perverse thrill from being bored senseless.'

'I'm sorry,' I said again. 'I should have told you.' I paused to wipe a trickle of drool from the corner of my mouth and prepare myself to attempt another complex sentence. 'I just thought it would be easier to blame my foul mood on a bad day at the office than on all this crap with Olivia Finch.'

'But now look where it's got you,' Natasha said, finally starting to sound a little more sympathetic. 'You've pissed me off because you lied to me and I had to hear the truth from Sandra Bennett, and you've made Bennett so angry that he's knocked out two of your teeth. I bet Bill Davis isn't best pleased either.'

'It was an accident,' I interrupted. 'Bennett hitting me, I mean. We were doing a stupid training exercise and he accidentally punched me in the face.'

'Well, however it happened, it's pretty obvious this isn't doing you any good at work, is it? So, sweetheart, if you'll take a bit of advice from me, cut out the lying. Stick to stuff you're good at like . . .' – she paused for effect, compounding my growing feeling of uselessness – 'like counting, or stalking celebrities. Now pour me a glass of that wine and let's consider the matter closed.' She was brooking no argument on this, and I was glad to let her draw a line under it. Another bullet dodged. 'I'd better go and sort that jacket out for you – it will have to go to the dry cleaners tomorrow to get the blood out. You'll be wanting to take it to Cannes, won't you? And you won't want to turn up looking like Bela Lugosi.'

I settled back in my chair, sipping the warm red wine and enjoying the thawing sensation it was having on my swollen and frozen face. I might have dodged this bullet, but I knew it wouldn't take long for Natasha to reload. When she came back downstairs, after she'd finished sorting out my jacket, I was sure to face further questioning. *The same jacket I'd worn to Lord's the previous week, with the pocket on the outside into which Olivia had stuffed her salacious invitation*; the jacket that Natasha was, at that very moment, emptying the pockets of in preparation for the cleaners. *Bollocks!*

I rushed out of the living room and up the stairs as fast as my swollen mouth would allow me. Every step jarred and I had to keep my hand pressed under my chin to reduce the vibration. I careered around the corner of the landing and into our bedroom. Natasha was holding the blood-stained jacket in one hand, methodically working her way through the pockets. The first had yielded a couple of taxi receipts, a crumpled chewing-gum wrapper and a folded flyer offering cheap off-peak phone calls to Nigeria, Botswana and Chad. The second offered up the rest of the packet of chewing gum and the stubs of two tickets for Lord's. Natasha seemed more relaxed since our chat and was humming contentedly to herself. She looked up in surprise when she heard me enter the room. I was panting heavily, making it even more difficult to speak.

'Stop!' I blurted out rather too insistently. Natasha was already ferreting through the inside pockets, from which she produced a pen and a few scraps of paper.

'What's the matter?' she asked. She looked concerned – like someone who is watching the man they love disintegrating before their eyes.

'Let me do that.' It was a demand rather than a request.

'No, I'm fine. I'm nearly done now.' She was equally adamant. She folded the jacket over one arm and went to put it in a carrier bag. I looked on the bed behind her for evidence of the contents of the outside breast pocket. As well as Olivia's note, I guessed there would also have been some business cards and, perhaps, a Tube ticket or two. There was no trace of any of these things in the little pyramid of detritus Natasha had carefully assembled in the middle of the duvet. I breathed a sigh of relief.

'Well, at least let me put it in the bag for you. Leave it on the bed and I'll sort it out.'

Natasha already had a perfectly serviceable jacket-sized plastic bag in her left hand, poised to take the garment as soon as her right hand let it go. Further delay seemed unnecessary. We stood looking at each other, me breathing loudly through my nose, her eyes wide in confused fascination. When it was clear she wasn't going to hand it over, I made a lunge for the jacket, but she ripped it from my grasp with a matador's flick.

'What is wrong with you?' she asked. 'Why are you acting so strangely? Perhaps we should go to the hospital and get you a brain scan.'

'I'm not acting strangely,' I insisted, fishing behind her back as she held the contested garment out of my reach.

'I'll be the judge of that,' Natasha replied. 'If you hadn't grabbed at me, I'd have stuffed the jacket in the bag five minutes ago and be back downstairs watching *Corrie* by now.'

'Just give me the jacket and go downstairs then. Please.' I had managed to get hold of an arm now and secured enough leverage to pull the jacket from Natasha's grasp. She gave a little huff of indignation as she let it go. 'Thank you,' I said, 'I'll pop it in the bag and join you in a minute. OK?'

Natasha walked out of the bedroom without another word. I listened for her footsteps descending the stairs.

When I was sure she was out of earshot, I unfolded the jacket and reached into the breast pocket with the thumb and forefinger of my right hand.

After a few seconds of fiddling about, I finally found what I was looking for. 'Got it!' I said out loud.

'Got what?' asked Natasha, who had sneaked back up the stairs and was now leaning against the door frame watching me.

I closed my eyes, hoping that might render the piece of paper I was holding invisible. If I couldn't see it, perhaps Natasha wouldn't be able to either. 'Nothing,' I lied. 'I was just checking you had the right jacket, that's all. So I unfolded it and had a look and, yep, it absolutely is the right jacket. Do you think the cleaners will be able to get these stains out? I hope so. This is one of my favourite jackets, you know. Didn't we get it from that outlet place off the M4? What's it called again?'

'Got what?' Natasha asked again.

'Hmm?' I held my mouth and winced to indicate that further talking might be uncomfortable. In fact, unless I could think of something plausible to say, any further talking might have been fatal.

'Joe, I can always tell when you're lying because you start to talk to me like a normal person – using proper sentences instead of grunting like a Neanderthal.' She spelled the next bit out slowly as if I was indeed something from an earlier evolutionary epoch. 'What is that piece of paper you're holding? Come on, show me!'

She was wearing her face that brooked no argument. The one she employed whenever the children needed scaring back into line. I handed over the piece of paper with all the desperate resignation of a recaptured prisoner of war presenting his badly forged passport to an SS Officer. Natasha opened it and read aloud:

Room 846 – can't wait to play ball with you again English!!! Love you, Ox

'Well?'

'Well, first, I think that's meant to be 'O' and then a kiss, not 'Ox'.

I didn't want my wife thinking I was carrying around a love note from some hairy-arsed biker who'd taken a shine to me.

'Oh, right,' Natasha said. 'So that would be "O" as in "Olivia", presumably?'

I nodded.

'And "English" would be . . . ?'

'Well, obviously,' "English" is Bennett, isn't it?' There were only two options and this was sure as hell the better of them. I was trying desperately not to portray every tic of the liar – the strange eye movements, sweating, too much hesitation, too little hesitation, nose growing longer with every word. 'That bloody madwoman gave me this note and asked me to pass it on to Bennett. But I didn't, which was when all the shit hit the fan at work. And by the way,' I mumbled on, 'Bennett still denies that he ever slept with her.'

'So if this note was meant for Bennett,' Natasha asked, eyeing me like a QC grilling a hostile witness, 'why were you so anxious for me not to see it?'

'What?' I asked, trying to look, as well as sound, incredulous. I even managed a short, derisory laugh to underscore the craziness of her suggestion. 'I wasn't trying to stop you seeing it, darling – I gave it to you, didn't I? Hey, why don't I run you a lovely hot bath? You look tired.'

Natasha looked me up and down again, far from convinced by this explanation, but unable to formulate a plausible alternative hypothesis. There was only one possible explanation as to why her husband would want to stop her reading a suggestive note from a beautiful woman – and that explanation just wasn't possible. I could sense the computer behind Natasha's cool blue eyes trying to work out other scenarios – but drawing blanks. There were still some fundamental truths in this crazy world: two and two must always equal four; water must always freeze at zero; no Hollywood superstar could ever want to sleep with her husband.

'And what does she say?' Natasha asked eventually when she had checked the situation out from every angle and assured herself that, despite everything, I might be telling the truth.

'What does who say?'

'Olivia, you idiot. You said that Bennett still denies he slept with Finch. What does she say about it? Don't tell me you spent the whole day with her and didn't ask her about what happened.'

'Erm,' I stalled (literally – my brain had slipped into neutral and the gears were spinning aimlessly, searching for yet another likely tale). 'Well, she might have mentioned one or two things, but, to be honest, I was mostly watching the cricket. You know what I'm like. Rubbish at remembering all the details.'

'So a guy in your office spends the night with the sexiest

woman on the planet – a woman you've admitted to me you fancy yourself – and you'd rather watch cricket than find out what went on? I don't believe you!' she said finally, taking herself out of the bedroom and off down the stairs.

I sat on the bed and slowly refolded the blood-spattered jacket and put it into the carrier bag. I was pretty sure Natasha meant 'I don't believe you' in the sense of 'I don't believe I married such a moron' rather than 'I think this moron I married is lying'. It was strangely comforting to think that my wife was convinced she had married an imbecile rather than an adulterous liar.

The painkillers were wearing off and my face was starting to ache again. Even the missing teeth hurt. I stumbled back down the stairs like a man descending blindfolded into the abyss, not sure anymore who I was or what the hell I was doing.

# CITY OF LONDON

irst thing that next morning, I found myself in a modern, well-appointed dentist's waiting room around the corner from my office, skimming through a well-thumbed magazine about high-performance cars, waiting for emergency treatment to sort out my missing teeth. Actually, I had the teeth with me, so technically they weren't missing they just weren't doing the job they were designed for any more. When I was called in to see the dentist, a brisk, efficient man named Hopper, I presented them to him like a cat offering its owner a dead bird. He looked at them, shook his head and announced, with all the mordant irony common to those who make a living from inflicting pain on others, that there was no more he could do for them. He invited me to sit down in his torture chair and open wide so he could examine what remained of my mouth. As I sat there with my jaw stretched to aching point, Hopper spoke swiftly in an indecipherable code to his baleful assistant, who looked as if she'd arrived at the surgery straight from a night on the town. Her stilettos click-clacked across the tile floor every time she delivered anything, an action executed with great reluctance, as if she hadn't become a dental assistant in order to assist dentists. There was a whiff of stale alcohol, cigarettes and garlic whenever she passed my chair.

Something about their demeanour suggested to me that they'd been out together the previous night and the evening had ended in a row. A week before, I wouldn't have cared less what they'd been up to – as long as it didn't impact on their ability to sort out my teeth as effectively and painlessly as possible – but now I felt some affinity with these casual fornicators. I was one of them. Perhaps there was a club I could join. With a crest and tie and monthly magazine – *Adulterer's Age*: this month – *Tackling Those Telltale Lipstick Stains* and *20 Great Lies to Tell the Kids*.

I was shaken from my reverie by Mr Hopper telling me, in the insistent way of one who has already given an instruction and had it ignored, that I could close my mouth. 'Well, Mr West,' he said, 'I'm afraid you've done quite a bit of damage to your upper gum. I can't do anything permanent for you in terms of replacing the missing teeth until the gum is strong enough to take a proper procedure, so I'll have to put in a temporary replacement to tide you over until I can do the full job. Is that all right?' He smelled of carbolic soap and mouth freshener and had the chairside manner of a man who was already counting off his patients until he could get back onto the golf course.

I nodded. Talking was still difficult and I tended to whistle every time I attempted a word with more than one syllable. I settled back in the chair, girding myself for the agony of my temporary 'procedure'.

'Great. If you could pop out to the front desk with Miss Stiletto,' (not her real name, but I can't be expected to remember every detail, can I?) 'she'll book you in for another appointment so we can get a temporary set fixed,' he said, snapping off his plastic gloves.

'I'm sorry?' I whistled. I was off to Cannes that Friday and could hardly travel to the greatest film festival of them all looking like a second-rate middle-weight. 'I need those teeth by Thursday.'

'This Thursday?' Hopper laughed as if this was the most bizarre suggestion he'd ever heard. 'I'm afraid that's totally impossible, Mr West. The very best I might be able to do would be next Monday – if I've any free appointments.'

'But it can't wait until then,' I whined. 'I'm going to France on Friday. Do you know anyone else who could do something this week?'

The smile drained from Hopper's face, strangled by the dreadful fear that he might be about to lose a lucrative piece of business. A temporary repair, followed by two new front teeth and all paid for by private medical insurance? There were some top-of-the-range titanium-shafted irons resting on this – perhaps a whole new set of clubs.

'I'll tell you what. Come back in last thing on Thursday and I'll see what I can do. It won't be perfect because I won't have time to order the new teeth. I'll just have to use what I've got in the surgery. But I like a challenge!' He turned to his assistant. 'Could you book Mr West in after my final appointment on Thursday afternoon and then come back and tidy up this mess?'

'Tidy it up yourself, wanker,' Miss Stiletto muttered under her breath as she led me back out to reception.

Rumours about my accident had reached Askett Brown before I did that morning. A wall of people greeted me as I emerged from the lift, as if they'd never seen an accountant with his two front teeth missing before. I had become a freak show. To the disappointment of the mob, I kept my mouth tightly shut as I made my way to my desk. The ever-faithful Polly was quickly at my side, clearing me a path through the throng like Moses traversing the Red Sea. 'I'll get us both a cup of coffee from the machine,' she said, helping me into my chair as if I'd had my kneecaps smashed as well. 'But first give us a flash of your teeth. I mean, the gap.'

When I was sure no one else was looking, I opened my mouth an inch or so and drew back my top lip. Polly gasped. 'Blimey,' she said, 'it's in a right state. He wasn't messing about, was he? Did you land one on him, too? No, wait. I'll get the coffees and you can tell me all about it.'

I turned on my computer while I waited for Polly to return. I knew she would be a while as she had a whole floor of people to update on the state of my mushed-up mouth on her way to the coffee machine and back. I opened my e-mail account to find the usual stack of miscellaneous rubbish, together with a couple of interesting messages about Cannes. Then I noticed one from Bennett, sent that morning. The subject line read: 'Fw: Sorry'. For one glorious moment I thought he might actually be apologising. In fact, he was simply forwarding someone else's apology:

From: Joseph Bennett
To: Joe West
Subject: Fw: Sorry

Hey, Joe. Hope the mouth isn't too bruised after yesterday. Good fun wasn't it? What do you make of this? My pal's back again but not quite as wacko as before!!!

Joseph A Bennett
Head of Entertainment and Media Division

From: CaddyMac@wannabe.com
To: JosephABennett@Askettbrown.org.uk
Subject: Sorry

Hey, English. I'm really really sorry about that horrible message I sent you the other day. I know it's not easy for you with the wife and kids and everything and I guess I'm just acting like a spoilt brat. I spoke to my analyst yesterday and he reckons that with what I've been through with my dad and all that shit I should respect you for the choices you've made and I know he's right but it's just too hard to let you go so easy. I'm just the poor girl who never got anything she wanted as a kid, and now I'm a rich girl who's used to getting whatever she wants.

And what I want right now is you, baby!

I'm flying into Cannes on Saturday – so exciting! I've only been once before and that was for like not even a whole day. Bet you've been loads of times –

want to show me around?!! I can give Buddy and the PR guys the slip and we can take ourselves off somewhere quiet. It sure would be good to have the chance to talk properly. I'm not trying to wreck your life, English, but I cant bear the thought of not seeing you. So what do you say? Friends again?

Olly xx

The first thing that struck me was that that overgrown school bully thought that knocking out someone's teeth was a bit of fun. Then I spotted a king-sized elephant trap: Olivia clearly wasn't so mad with me that she was going to do the decent thing and ignore me for the rest of her life – buoyed up by the advice of some quack therapist, she was going to make this work for her if it was the last thing she did. And, if Bennett replied to this e-mail, he would almost certainly tell her that he'd never been to Cannes before, whereas Olivia knew that I was a veteran of several campaigns.

I drafted a reply to Bennett explaining that my face was still aching like a bastard and that I was facing a series of long and painful dental procedures to sort the damage out, but I knew that would just add to his fun so deleted it again. Instead, I sent him a short note suggesting we talk about this at his earliest convenience, in the context of our overall strategy for the Cannes trip. Seconds later, my computer pinged to announce Bennett's reply:

From: Joseph Bennett
To: Joe West
Subject: Re: Re: Fw: Sorry

You must be a mind reader, mate! Bill wants to talk to us about that very thing this very afternoon. Head Honcho's office: 2 o'clock. See you there!

Joseph A Bennett
Head of Entertainment and Media Division

Polly had arrived back with my coffee and was reading over my shoulder – there could be few secrets between an accountant and his PA.

'He's very pally all of a sudden, isn't he?' Polly said. I explained that in Bennett's strange worldview, forged on the rugby pitches of Old England, the quickest way to a man's heart was to fight him, lose and take defeat like a man. I'm not sure that lying in a pool of my own blood, curled up like an agoraphobic foetus and moaning like a clubbed seal, met all his criteria for worthiness as an opponent, but he certainly seemed to have warmed towards me. To be fair, I hadn't actually cried when he hit me. Not in front of him anyway.

'Nah. I reckon he's shit-scared that you're going to press charges or insist Davis fires him. You've got him on the run now, Joe,' Polly said, easing herself off the edge of my desk. A group of sightseers had gathered around us, gawping at me as if I was the bearded lady. 'Jesus,' she called over her shoulder as she sauntered back to her desk, 'we should be charging 'em for a butcher's!'

I ate my lunch – two bananas mashed with a spoon and an orange and strawberry smoothie sucked through a straw – at my desk, then made my way up to Bill Davis's office. Ordinarily, months would go by without me seeing the inside of his executive suite and here I was making my third visit in the space of a week. I met Bennett in the outer office and we waited to be called in. He was happier than I'd seen him since before we sat down to watch the film in New York, proudly showing off his handiwork to Bill's secretary and the work experience lad who came in to deliver the afternoon mail. When we were invited into Bill's office, we discovered that Dai Wainwright was already there.

'Hi, guys,' Bill said cheerily. Bennett offered an effusive greeting of his own in reply, while I just grunted, trying to keep my mouth closed for as long as possible. 'Ah, Mr West,' Davis continued as we took our usual seats, 'I hear you've been in the wars!'

'Yeah, sorry about that, Bill,' said Bennett, before I could offer my explanation of this unfortunate chain of events. 'We were letting off a bit of steam with this boxing exercise and poor old West ducked into one of my better shots. I'd knocked him off-balance with a nifty little combo and then – bam! – he swayed straight into a right cross. Caught you flush in the old gob, didn't it, mate?'

I nodded, my remaining teeth clamped together behind tightly shut lips.

'I had a word with Roddy earlier about what happened, actually,' Wainwright chipped in. 'He said you caught him a real cracker, Joseph. Said poor old West's head snapped back like it was on a piece of elastic. He was a bit worried at first, what with the way he went down and all that blood, so he was relieved to hear it was all OK. It's a good exercise, that one, isn't it? Old Roddy does love that holistic stuff. *Mens sana in corpore sano* and all that.'

'*All OK*'? I'd lost two teeth because of that stupid bloody exercise and my daughter still couldn't look at me without crying. I felt as if I'd slipped into a parallel universe where punishment beatings were seen as a routine part of the working day. Where poor performers weren't fired – they were taken out and shot.

'Yah,' said Bennett. 'The problem was that West didn't make any allowance for the punch, didn't, you know, ride up with it from the floor.' He stood up to demonstrate what he meant, bending his knees and arching his shoulders and head back to reduce the impact as the imaginary blow landed. 'I don't suppose they teach boxing in the state sector these days, do they? People like West leave school with no idea what to do when someone thumps them.'

'That's true enough,' agreed Wainwright with a rueful smile. 'That's why the kids all carry knives these days. Mind you, I went to a secondary modern and I like to think I can handle myself. But then, you see, I had my rugby. If you couldn't look after yourself on the pitch you were in real trouble – especially as I wasn't the biggest. Had to get my retaliation in first, if you know what I mean. And if you belted one of those big buggers up-front, you wanted to make damn sure they didn't get back up again!' Wainwright laughed at the memory of unprovoked assaults on the rugby field and the other two joined him, recalling fond martial memories of their own.

I sat there aghast. Where I came from, having your teeth knocked out wasn't an anecdote – it was a police matter.

'I'm sorry, West,' Davis said once the nostalgia attack had subsided. 'With all this talk about what happened, I haven't asked how you are.' For a moment, a rare, fleeting moment, I felt cared for; that someone was actually interested in my welfare. Then he added: 'Go on – open up! Let's have a look at the damage.'

I opened my mouth and the three of them peered into it like Inuit around a fishing hole. Bennett gave them a guided tour, explaining with some pride how the force of the blow had probably reduced the collateral damage to the gums because the teeth were removed so cleanly. The others were equally impressed, 'oohing' and 'aahing' in all the right places. When I finally got the command to close my mouth again, I hoped that my humiliation was complete. It hadn't even begun.

'So,' said Davis when they had retaken their seats and helped themselves to fresh coffee, 'how was the rest of the day with, er, what's his name, Dai?'

'Rodney. Rodney James.'

'Ah yes. He's the fellow I did the session with last year, isn't he?'

'That's right,' smiled Wainwright, basking in reflected glory.

'Yes. Nice chap. One of your lot, isn't he, Dai?'

'What? Do you mean a sheep-shagger, Bill?' said Bennett.

Wainwright looked put out, but Davis laughed heartily at Bennett's witticism. A moment later Wainwright laughed too.

'As I was saying before I was so rudely interrupted,' Davis resumed with a smile and a knowing wink in Bennett's direction, 'how did the rest of the day go? Did you sort yourselves out? Listen, guys, you know you're both important members of the AB team. We really don't want to lose either of you.'

'Thanks, Bill,' said Bennett. 'Yah, the rest of the day went well. Didn't it, West? Well, just the morning actually. We had to stop after West's little accident.'

'Hear that, Dai,' Davis interrupted, 'make sure we only pay the bugger half his money!' Wainwright nodded, not sure whether Davis was joking.

Bennett continued with the zeal of the recent convert to the joys of management training. 'He did that thing where we answered a few questions and he told us what colour we were and what animal. It was pretty interesting, actually.'

'I bet you came out as something purple, didn't you, Joseph? A purple stallion? Am I right?' Wainwright asked.

'Spot on, Taff!' said Bennett, impressed. 'A mighty purple stallion, leading his people into battle!' Bill Davis also looked at his head of HR with paternal pride. As we had already established that Wainwright had spoken to Rodney James earlier that morning, it was clear, to me at least, that this was not some great feat of impromptu psychological profiling, but the less impressive achievement of remembering something he'd been told an hour before.

'I'm trying to remember what I was,' said Davis, smiling in the manner of someone who knew really but was too modest to say.

'You were a White Bear, Bill,' Wainwright cooed. 'White signifying wisdom, while the bear shows that although you are a warm and giving person, you're not to be messed around with.' I wondered whether the seal populations of the Arctic Circle would agree with this somewhat idealised view of the wise and cuddly polar bear.

'I,' Wainwright continued without waiting to be asked, 'I am a Red Kite. Rodney actually changed the name of that one just for me. Initially I was a Red Fox, signifying passion and cunning, but I've always loved the red kites, you know, those huge majestic birds of prey. I used to watch them circling over the hills and valleys back home like great eagles. Marvellous they were. So Rodney said, "You know what Dai, I'll recalibrate my instrument and you can be a red kite if that's what you want to be." Lovely like that, he is.'

I sat, silently hoping that if I didn't say anything they might forget I was there and move on to the next item on the agenda. They didn't.

'What was that other one?' Davis asked, 'That weird creepy one? Some kind of weasel, wasn't it?'

'You mean the meerkat, Bill!' Wainwright shrieked.

'That's the feller!' said Davis. 'Aren't they the ones that scurry around trying to avoid treading in everyone else's you-know-what?'

'That's it!' jumped in Bennett, 'Dreadful little creatures, aren't they, West, those little yellow meerkats?' He and Wainwright were laughing heartily now. Clearly you didn't need feelings to be a stallion or a kite.

'Oh no!' said Davis, joining in the fun, 'That wasn't you, was it, West? Oh dear, how funny!'

Or a sodding polar bear.

When the three of them had stopped chuckling and regained some semblance of professional composure, Wainwright brought the conversation back to the subject at hand. 'All joking aside,' he said, dabbing at his eyes with a monogrammed hanky, 'this does help us see where the problems lie with these guys. It's no surprise that a Purple Stallion and a Yellow Meerkat find it difficult to get along. Completely different mindsets, you see, your stallion and your meerkat.'

Davis nodded. 'Makes you appreciate why that bloody actress latched onto Joseph though, doesn't it? You can't see a foxy little number like her falling for a bloody gerbil or whatever the hell it was, can you?'

This set Bennett off again and soon his hideous cackle had been caught by the other two like some anti-socially transmitted disease.

Not for the first time since I'd returned from New York, I wanted to shout out to the disbelieving world that it was I who had slept with Olivia Finch. She was my celebrity conquest, not Bennett's. But discretion, once again, proved the better part of candour and I kept quiet. When the trio of oversized schoolboys had calmed down again, Davis moved the meeting forward.

'OK, chaps, now we've got you two sorted – for which, by the way, many thanks, Dai – we need to think about our strategy for Cannes. Joseph and I are flying in on Saturday afternoon for a couple of days. What are your plans, Joe?'

'Actually, Bill, I was thinking about giving it a miss this year,' I replied. 'You and Joseph seem to have it pretty well covered and, what with getting my teeth sorted out and everything, I thought that—'

'Nonsense,' said Bill, slamming the door shut on my hastily conceived escape plan. 'You're still our main man with these guys, for the time being at least, until Joseph can really get to grips with how it all works. You know how to talk to these people. So when are you flying out?'

'Friday, Bill,' I mumbled, defeated and deflated. 'I've got a couple of meetings and a lunch over the weekend and invites to see a few films. Then there's the out-of-competition screening of *Nothing Happened* on the Saturday night, followed by the PPP party.'

'The p-p-p p-p-p party?' asked Dai, generating another round of raucous laughter from the other two.

'The Printing Press Productions party. Buddy Guttenberg's company,' I explained as if I was trying to tell Matthew why it wasn't a good idea to stick his sucked thumb in the electric socket. 'And then I'm flying home on Tuesday.'

'Excellent,' said Bill. 'It's still really important that we keep Guttenberg sweet and you're definitely the man for the job. And Joseph,' he said to Bennett, 'I want you to build some bridges with Guttenberg as well – use some of your legendary charm on him. He's an important client for us and, as Head of Division, the lead on the relationship should rest with you. But do me a favour – stay well out of that ruddy Finch girl's way! You don't need the aggravation and I certainly don't need the hassle. There'll be plenty of other totty there for you if you must have a go.' He gave a short laugh – at once both supercilious and degenerate. Bennett smiled and pretended to be coy. He reached inside his jacket pocket and produced a folded piece of paper which he placed on the table in front of him, smoothing out the creases with a slow roll of his hand.

'I don't think that will be a problem now, Bill,' he said, pushing the paper across the table. Wainwright adjusted his seat so that he could read the mysterious message. I could see enough of it to identify it as a print-out of his latest e-mail exchange with Olivia. 'It looks like she knows she's overstepped the line and is trying to back down now. I wouldn't mind talking to her to find out why she started harassing me in the first place and make damn sure it really is all over. I mean, look, she even talks about Sandra and the kids – she's obviously been stalking me for some time.'

'Well, this is certainly more measured than most of her stuff,' Davis agreed. 'What do you think, Dai?'

'I don't know, Bill,' Wainwright said, stroking his chin to demonstrate how deeply he was thinking about this complex state of affairs. 'If I were Joseph, I'd still steer well clear of the woman. She could be crazy – psychotic even. Let West handle her and you two keep out of her way, would be my advice.'

'Yah, you're probably right, Dai,' said Bill. 'Joseph, you stay away from Ms Finch. West, could you get us tickets for the screening and the party so we can have a decent chat with Guttenberg? But keep that mad woman as far away from us as possible. OK?'

I nodded, although I wasn't confident I could deliver. Keeping Olivia away from Bennett wasn't going to be difficult, seeing as she didn't know he existed other than as a misattributed name on a business card. Getting a pair of tickets for one of the hottest parties of the fortnight, on the other hand, could be tricky.

The last couple of days before Cannes passed peacefully. I was still something of a tourist attraction, with members of staff I'd never met before bringing friends and relatives in to look at me. At last, that Thursday evening, I was able to return to Mr Hopper for the temporary solution to my dental impediment.

'Mr West,' he said, ushering me into his chamber of horrors, 'please sit down.' There was no sign of Ms Stiletto.

Their differences had obviously proved to be irreconcilable. She had been replaced by a slightly dumpier and more sensibly shod assistant. While Hopper fiddled around with all kinds of painful-looking equipment, she busied herself covering every surface within six feet of me with plastic sheeting. It looked like they were expecting a lot of blood. I wasn't sure I had much left to give them.

'Right, let's see what we can do with that gap. Miss Smith could you prepare the clamps for me? No, that's the hacksaw. The clamps are over there next to the scrapers.'

When Hopper loomed over me, I tried to tell him that I'd changed my mind – what's wrong with a little gap between the teeth, after all? – and would come back after Cannes, but as I opened my mouth to speak, he shoved in two clamps and a vacuum pump and I was rendered, literally, speechless. I felt the short sharp shock of a needle, followed by the longer ache of the anaesthetic entering my gum. The rest was drooling.

Once the anaesthetic had taken hold, Hopper worked like a master potter at his wheel, his fingers a blur as he cut and drilled and screwed and prodded and fiddled about for well over an hour. I sat in the chair with my head back, insensitive to what was going on in my upper gum, but still rendered nauseous by the mixed aromas of this oral charnel house: the antiseptic, the smell of seared flesh, the hint of last night's curry on Hopper's breath as he leaned over me – the new assistant's cheap perfume.

The complexity of the procedure meant I couldn't change my position, swallow or rinse. I gagged frequently, and was on the point of insisting I needed a drink before I threw up when Hopper stepped back, gazed lovingly into my mouth to admire his craftsmanship and, finally, invited me to rinse, gargle and expectorate to my heart's content. As soon as I'd recovered some semblance of poise, he handed me a small mirror and invited me to inspect the results.

After a pause to absorb the shock, the first words that came to mind were: 'They're a bit big, aren't they?' This was an understatement. I looked like I was about to gnaw down some trees to build a lodge.

Hopper was confused by my lukewarm reaction. 'Actually,' he said, 'they are exactly the same size as the two you lost. With the temporary structure they're sitting in, they do drop down a little further than before, I'll give you that. I've built a platform out of a light steel and tin compound, glued that onto your gum and then screwed the teeth into that. I say "teeth" but in fact they're made from the same compound and coated in enamel. Pretty ingenious really – I was up half last night working on them. But it does mean that, temporarily, your teeth will appear to protrude a little more than before. And they might clang a bit if you bite down on a fork or when you're drinking from a can. I meant to check whether they were magnetic but I ran out of time. So be careful if you go near any magnetic objects. Do you mind if I take a quick photo? It really is a brilliant piece of work, even if I say so myself! What do you think, Miss Smith?'

The assistant looked into my mouth and, although her facial expression suggested mild horror and major amusement, she held herself together long enough to congratulate her employer on his heroic orthodontic achievement. 'Very nice, Mr Hopper,' she said as he handed her the camera so that he could appear in the shot beside his masterpiece, like an angler with his catch of the day.

'Oh, there's one more thing,' Hopper added as I was about to leave. 'The fixing is quite fragile, so I've knocked this up to hold everything in place. Can I check whether it fits?' He pushed me back into the seat and asked me to open my mouth again. I felt something cold and hard being pressed against my teeth. 'There. That will do nicely. It might be a bit uncomfortable, but do keep this brace on whenever possible to make sure the bridge doesn't move. And always put it on when you are going to sleep so nothing shifts during the night.'

A few minutes later, I walked out into the cold evening air with teeth like Bugs Bunny and a bill to suit Daffy Duck. With the braces in place, I couldn't close my mouth completely, so I proceeded down the street and into the Underground like a whale eating krill. Cannes, I reflected, would be a nightmare with these teeth and Bill and Bennett for company. But first I had to survive the reactions of my family.

# MILL HILL, NORTH LONDON

Natasha laughed, Helen cried and Matthew tried to prise them out with a plastic fork.

'I'll get your dinner, darling,' said Natasha after the kids were safely filed away in bed. 'I've got us a lovely piece of liver. I thought we could have it with a few fava beans and a nice Chianti.'

# HEATHROW AIRPORT, LONDON

And so to Cannes. With a mouth full of temporary teeth and the worries of the world upon my sagging shoulders, I set off for five days of film, food and fun on the French Riviera. The Film Festival actually runs for a fortnight but only the hardiest of souls last the entire course – the hardy and the desperate, for in truth the whole world of cinema descends on Cannes for the middle two weeks of May: the superstars, the once-weres, the wannabes and the never-will-bes.

I arrived at Heathrow in plenty of time and mooched around the shops, wondering, as I always did, why anyone would want to buy new luggage at an airport. Hadn't they packed before they left home? I had managed to find a way to close my mouth over the braces which meant I no longer looked like Hannibal Lecter on remand, but now had a stiff protruding upper lip that was so stretched over the metal brace that I resembled a Bee Gee stifling a burp.

I still received funny looks from passers-by, but at least I didn't scare any children.

I walked down to the security gate, showed my boarding pass and joined the queue for the X-ray machines. Except there wasn't a queue – there was mayhem. Hundreds of people were trying to squeeze their way through the two available channels. A helpful sign told me that due to the heightened state of alert, fewer channels were available so that more officers could attend each one. This was little comfort for the people who were running late for their flights and were now trying to negotiate or simply push their way further up the queue. I wasn't due to board my flight for more than ninety minutes, so I watched amused as tempers frayed while no one appeared to gain any ground. Paschendale with carry-on luggage.

Forty-five minutes later, and still some distance from my appointment with the heavily manned X-ray equipment, I was starting to get worried. Soon it would be my turn to beg to be let through or to start manoeuvring the less physically robust out of my way. Arguments were starting to break out and one or two shoving matches had begun as people started to get desperate about making it to their departure gates. Realising that the situation was threatening to blow out of control, the officials opened a third checkpoint – and 300 people from behind me in the melee rushed forward to jump the queue. Somewhere deep within the belly of the Yellow Meerkat, a Purple Monster was aching to break free and smash the place down.

I finally made it to the security gate half an hour before

my plane was scheduled to take-off. I had already emptied my trouser pockets, removed my belt and shoes and made sure I wasn't carrying any liquids. I took off my (beautifully dry-cleaned) jacket and folded it into a grey plastic basket, then placed my briefcase in a second basket, having first removed my laptop, taken it out of its cover and placed that in a third tray.

'Beep!' The red light flashed and a piercing alarm announced I had failed the simple challenge of walking through the X-ray machine. Several guards turned to look at me. One rather portly officer, wearing a pale blue shirt stained with egg yolk and tomato ketchup from his breakfast sandwich asked me to step back through the gate and remove my shoes. I did as I was told, placing them in a fourth grey plastic tray, and walked confidently back through the gate.

'Beep!' The alarm seemed even louder this time. People in the queue behind me tut-tutted. They had waited more than an hour to reach this point and were now being held up at the moment of their liberation.

'Do you have you any other metal objects on you, sir?' the attendant asked. 'A watch? Jewellery?'

With an apologetic smile, I took off my watch and wedding ring and placed them in a fifth tray, a smaller one this time. Then I checked my pockets for any recalcitrant coins hiding deep within and passed through the gate once more.

'Beep!'

'Oh, for God's sake!' someone said. I looked at my wrist, worried I would be late for my flight, but saw only white flesh and a patch of damp hair pressed down by the weight of what had been there until a few moments before. The clock on the wall shouted that my flight was leaving in twenty-five minutes.

'Could anything else be causing the machine to beep, sir?' asked the guard, struggling to hide his irritation.

'My flies?' I offered, unable to think of anything else I was wearing that could be guilty – hell, I hardly was wearing anything else. Most of my clothes were already in grey plastic trays accumulating at the other end of the conveyor belt.

'Very funny, sir,' said the guard with no trace of amusement. 'You'd better come with me.'

There was a cheer from the gallery as I was led away to a small room to the side of the main security area. As we entered, my companion, who had now added sweat stains to the artist's impression of his breakfast on his shirt, reached into a drawer and pulled out a pair of clear plastic gloves.

'Would you mind stripping off, sir?' he asked as he pulled on the first glove with a resounding snap.

A wave of panic rushed through me. I could feel my brain function closing down. I was rooted to the spot, paralysed. I couldn't even move my arms to undo the buttons on my shirt. The sweaty one was staring straight at me, snapping the second glove into place. 'Well?'

'I . . . I,' I stammered, 'listen, I'm going to miss my plane if I don't hurry. Do I have to do this?'

Sweaty cocked his head and stared even harder. 'Say that again.'

'Do I have to take my clothes off, sir?' I stammered like a boy on his first day at boarding school.

'You stupid idiot!' he said, more in exasperation than anger. Then, remembering his customer service training: 'What I mean is, sir, I think I can see the answer to our

195

problem. You might have mentioned you were wearing braces. The way those machines are set up today that contraption in your mouth would light them up like a couple of pounds of Semtex.'

He removed his gloves and led me back to the gate. I took the braces off my temporary front teeth and walked through. The light shone silent green. I collected my possessions from the pile of grey trays that were causing a log-jam at the end of the conveyor belt, put on my shoes and raced to my departure gate. I heard my name being called over the Tannoy, asking where the hell I was, and, a moment before I arrived at the gate, threatening to remove my luggage from the hold. I presented my boarding pass and passport to the attendant and ran down the walkway onto the plane, avoiding the serried ranks of impatient faces looking up at me from their free newspapers and in-flight magazines. I buckled up my seatbelt as the stewardesses began their safety routine and, once I'd got my breath back, smiled at the close call I'd had. This would be a funny story to tell Natasha and the kids when I got home, I thought, as the engines roared and we pushed back from our stand.

I looked at my wrist to see exactly how close I'd come to missing the flight. And that was when I realised I was no longer wearing my watch – or my wedding ring.

# CANNES, SOUTH OF FRANCE

And so, eventually, to Cannes. The plane landed in Nice Airport on time, but after taking into account the one-hour time difference, the interminable wait for my luggage and the slow taxi journey into town, it was early evening by the time I arrived in my room. As I unpacked, I searched obsessively for my missing watch and ring, even though I knew they were, at best, in a grey plastic tray several hundred miles away and, at worst, already on eBay. For the past eleven years, I had worn it every day. I'd even kept it on during my one bout of adultery – there hadn't been time to take it off, and it hadn't got in the way. I already felt its absence and dreaded having to tell Natasha about its loss.

I was staying in an aparthotel a few hundred yards behind La Croisette, the legendary main street of Cannes along which, for the two weeks of the Film Festival, all manner of human and vehicular traffic would pass in noisy anonymity, while the huge crowds hunted their real prey

– the superstars of the film world. Despite the proud traditions of the Festival – and much to the chagrin of the French cinema elite – the real stars of the show would be flying in from Los Angeles and New York.

I didn't have anything to do that evening – no films to watch or parties to attend – so I went for a walk down past the Palais du Cinema to the Old Harbour, enjoying the spectacle of the people clamouring for attention – the hangers-on watching the desperate antics of other hangers-on. I was hardly an A-lister myself, but at least I had a reason to be there. I had meetings to go to, events to attend that I'd been invited to, films to see because I was on a studio's guest list, not because I'd queued to buy a ticket. I wasn't there simply to observe a moving Madame Tussaud's exhibit, waiting hours in the burning sun or pouring rain for a glimpse of Nicole Kidman's Manolo Blahnik-clad right foot. I had a purpose.

I also had a thirst. I found a small bar nestled just behind the main drag, a popular hang-out for the less glamorous members of the British contingent. Tired-of-life film critics huddled with independent cinema programmers in the narrow street behind the bar enjoying a relatively inexpensive beer and arguing about the best James Bond or the worst screen Jesus or discussing the amazing low-budget Albanian film they'd watched that afternoon. And I sat and sipped my beer and eavesdropped on their conversations and wondered what they would think if they knew they were sitting in the presence of a man who had once spent the night with the delectable Olivia Finch, had achieved something that most of them could only ever dream about – and turned his life into a nightmare as a result.

The next morning I woke up early and headed back down to the sea front. I had several meetings set up with British producers looking to Askett Brown for finance – meetings which could just as easily have taken place in London but which were so much more pleasant here on the Riviera. Most of the business during the Festival took place in the various hotels on a short stretch of one side of La Croisette or at the hotels' extensions onto the beaches on the other side. Cannes is, in effect, just an enormous office block turned on its side and opened up to the elements. Coffee and croissants were standard fare at every meeting, so I'd already eaten my way through three breakfasts by the time I headed down to the Carlton Hotel to meet Buddy for lunch.

I was first to arrive and was shown to a table out on the vast terrace by the outdoor swimming pool. I settled down with an orange juice, which I sipped through a straw while I flicked through the complimentary trade papers that lay around in huge piles at all the top hotels. The main titles all published daily updates on the major deals and rumours of deals at the Festival and reviews of all the films screened the previous day. All of them were reporting that Olivia Finch would be arriving in town that afternoon for the screening of *Nothing Happened*.

They were all pretty general, until I turned to one article clearly written by a columnist who fancied herself as a modern-day Louella Parsons. Under the headline 'Finch Set to announce Long-Term Transatlantic Commitment', the journalist reported that sources close to Olivia Finch had told her that she was madly in love with a mystery Englishman and might be about to announce her engagement. I felt cold beads of sweat prick my forehead, even though, with the sun almost directly overhead, the temperature must have been pushing thirty degrees. I read on, desperately hoping that the mystery Englishman would remain mysterious, and was so absorbed in this unfolding tale as it snaked its way through the paper's narrow columns that I didn't notice Buddy arrive.

'Hey Joey West!' he boomed from ten tables away. 'How the devil are you? As he reached me, he stretched out an enormous hand and almost tore my arm off with his enthusiastic greeting. Len and Diana were with him and I greeted them as they took their seats, trying to keep my upper lip stretched over my teeth when I said 'Hi!' – the shortest sentence I could get away with. I had left the unsightly braces in my room but still preferred to keep my dental upgrade hidden.

Buddy ordered an expensive bottle of Chablis and asked to see the food menu. Then he turned to me, asking 'So, how the devil are you, Joey? I haven't seen you for days. You don't write, you don't call . . .'

'Sorry Mom,' I replied and made the mistake of smiling.

Buddy exploded again: 'Oh my God! You've had your teeth fixed! Hey, look at this, guys – Joey's gone for the full Tom Cruise! They look great, Joey, but what did you do? Buy your teeth by the yard?'

I told them the story, stressing that it had been an accidental collision with Bennett's fist that had done the damage rather than retribution after the incident in the boardroom. Len and Di were sympathetic, but Buddy laughed loudly throughout my tale. Perhaps he and Bennett weren't so different. There were definitely traces of the Purple Stallion in Buddy.

Buddy ordered our lunch, then looked at me with a more serious intent. 'Hey, listen,' he said, 'speaking of your pal Bennett, we've got to do something about him and Olivia. The poor kid's really screwed up by the whole thing and I need her on top form for the next couple of days. We're already in talks with her agent about a sequel to *Nothing*, so she's got to be out there pushing the franchise, not moping around over some chinless English cocksucker, if you'll pardon the expression. Is he here?'

'Not yet,' I replied. 'He's flying in with Bill Davis later today.'

'Oh great! So we get Laurel *and* fucking Hardy. The point is, Joe, that although I can't stand the guy, I need him to play nice with Olivia while he's here. Whatever the hell he really thinks about her, I want him to make her feel special, OK? I don't care if he keeps his fingers crossed behind his back while he's humping her, I just don't want her upset again. You got it?'

I'd got it. But would Olivia get it?

Buddy hadn't finished. 'Have you got your ticket for the screening tonight? And the party?'

'I have,' I said, still mumbling in my attempt to keep my new teeth away from public view, 'but I need a couple for the other two. Is that possible?'

'Are you kidding me?' Buddy said. 'These tickets are like angels' farts. We must have got rid of the last of them weeks ago.' He paused, waiting for my reaction. A big part of me was relieved – it meant one less chance for Bennett to meet Olivia and for my whole paper-thin story to unravel. And one less chance for him to hurt her again. But I was also worried – how would I tell Bill and Bennett that they wouldn't be able to come to the event they were flying in specifically to attend.

Buddy let the uncomfortable silence drag on for another few seconds, then reached into his inside pocket, drew out an envelope and continued. 'Only messing with you, Joey. Here, I swear these must be the last tickets anywhere in fucking France. And the doormen have been told that nobody gets in without a ticket. Absolutely no one. The Queen of England could turn up arm in arm with the fucking Pope, they're not getting in, you know what I'm saying? So give these to Stan and Ollie and make sure your pal Bennett knows he'd better look after my girl, tonight, OK? Or he'll have me to answer to.' I nodded. 'Great,' Buddy said as a waiter arrived with a huge platter of fresh sea food, swimming in a lake of crushed ice, 'let's eat!'

Buddy was a generous host and I left the hotel a couple of hours later with the unruly gait of someone who had enjoyed a glass and a half too much hospitality. I hadn't taken any notes and wouldn't be able to remember a single word of what had been discussed when I got back to London. But that wasn't the point. I'd been building my relationship with a key client. Les and Di had drunk less and noted more and would be able to tell us everything we needed to know. The one thing I could remember was Buddy reminding me again to tell Bennett to be nice to Olivia.

I popped into a souvenir shop to buy some gifts for Natasha, the kids and Polly and bought myself a cheap watch with the Palme d'Or logo on its face to replace the one I'd lost, then I meandered back to my room to shower and rest in preparation for the big night. I could see disaster galloping up over the horizon, led by a rampant purple stallion, and it would be my job to protect the damsel he was almost certain to distress. It was a shame, I reflected, that they didn't sell pairs of balls in that souvenir shop, with or without the ubiquitous golden laurel wreath design. I was going to need to find a pair from somewhere.

As *Nothing Happened* was not entered into any of the official Festival competitions, the protocol for the screening was informal – lounge suits rather than black tie. I put on my favourite pastel green shirt and the trousers of my recently bloodied suit, slung the jacket casually over my shoulder and headed back down the hill.

Bill Davies and Bennett were staying at one of the better hotels on La Croisette. I reached the foyer a few minutes after eight and was relieved to see that they hadn't yet arrived. I ordered myself a beer and waited patiently, flicking through another of the daily trade magazines. My colleagues sauntered into the hotel lobby at quarter to nine, pulling their cases behind them and not looking too concerned about keeping me waiting.

'Sorry, Joe,' Bill said while Bennett diverted to the reception desk to ask after their rooms, 'flight was delayed. Spot of fog at Heathrow. What time does the film start?'

'No problem, Bill,' I replied. 'It doesn't start until ten.'

'Great. We'll dump our bags, get changed and meet you back here in fifteen minutes.' He walked over to Bennett, then turned back to me, 'Joseph's in room 485 – charge any drinks to that. Why don't you get a bottle of fizz ready for when we come down?'

I went back to my paper and then, when I anticipated their reappearance must be imminent, I ordered a bottle of champagne and three glasses. I was already enjoying my second glass, reading an enthusiastic review of a Lapp film shot entirely from beneath an ice floe, when they eventually appeared. As far as I could see, neither of them had changed. Bennett's breath suggested he had already introduced himself to the mini-bar, a fragrant combination of Scotch and peanuts.

'You all right, Joe?' he asked as he sat down. 'Love the new teeth! I've been telling everyone that story, haven't I, Bill? Always gets a good laugh! I thought that trolley dolly was going to wet herself. Pour us a glass of fizz then, there's a good chap.'

Looking back at all that's happened since, it's like watching the highlights of a sports match when you know what's coming next but the players don't – when a batsman looks in sparkling form but you know he's scored his last run. Or Kennedy smiling and waving as his Lincoln turns into Dealey Plaza. Bennett was at the height of his powers, guzzling champagne and regaling everyone in earshot with his stories, but the end of his innings was fast approaching. The lone gunman already had him in his sights. We finished one bottle of champagne and Bennett asked whether we'd like another.

I looked at my new watch. Quarter to ten. 'Er . . . actually, I don't think we have time for another drink,' I said. 'We really should be making our way to the Palais.'

'Nonsense!' said Bennett, clicking his fingers to get a waiter's attention. 'We've got plenty of time. Un autre bottle de fizzy plonk, see voo play,' he demanded in an accent of broken glass. When the bottle arrived, he poured three large glasses, each of which overflowed, but he carried on, ignoring the lesson like a backward child. When the bubbles had settled and we each had our half a glass, he raised his in a toast: 'To the AB team – here's to a blinding Festival!'

He topped up our glasses. 'You know what, Bill, I'm not sure I fancy seeing the film tonight. I saw it in New York and, to be honest, I slept through most of it. Not really my cup of tea. And it seems a waste of good drinking time, don't you think?'

'Well,' Bill replied, feigning annoyance, 'I wish you'd told me you didn't like watching films before I made you Head of Entertainment!' He paused, then added, 'But actually, I'm with you on this one, Joseph. Let's have a couple of drinks, recover from our flight and chat about our tactics for the Festival. Then we can pop down to the party nice and early. Would that be all right, West? We can tell Guttenberg our flight was delayed, which is kind of true. What do you think?'

What I thought was that, no, it would not be all right. It would be bloody rude. Buddy had gone out of his way to secure the last available pair of tickets for them and would expect to see us there. What I reckoned was that they were a pair of stuck-up, ignorant, inconsiderate bastards. But of course I didn't say that. I just mumbled that I was sure that would be fine and colluded in their egregious contempt.

'Don't get me wrong,' Bennett was continuing, still at full volume, 'I do like some films – but I prefer to watch them on TV so I can get a drink when I want one or take a leak without missing anything. You know what my favourite film is?'

My mind raced through all the possibilities – from the sublime to the more probable: *Les Enfants du Paradis*?

*Battleship Potemkin? Debbie Does Dallas – the Director's Cut?*
– while Bill consulted his memory bank and weighed up
the competing claims of the two films he could remember
the names of.

After neither of us offered a guess, Bennett roared on.
'Give up? It's that one with the old boy and his sons where
they've got a family business – selling fruit, I think, or
flowers – and they keep getting into scraps with all the
other businessmen. Oh, damn, what's it called? It's got that
guy in it who couldn't talk properly and the other one, the
little short-arse bloke. His name's Don – the dad in the
film I mean, not the actor. Don Fonzarelli, was it? They're
Italian but the whole thing's set in America – I suppose
that's where the money was. Sort of thing you'd know
about, West. What was it called? They made a few of them.
Come on, West, you must know.'

'*The Godfather*?' I suggested.

That's it!' yelled Bennett.

'Gosh! You really do know your stuff, West' said Bill.
'Well done!'

'Bloody good film,' Bennett continued, 'but I'd still prefer
to watch it at home rather than surrounded by a load of
other people blubbing into their popcorn every time
someone gets shot. Wouldn't you?'

Davis nodded in enthusiastic agreement while I shook my
head sadly. For me, few experiences could beat sitting silently
in a chamber of shared emotions, laughing, crying or gasping
in the company of strangers, linked only by our primal
responses to the action on the screen. Not for the first time,
I found myself asking what I was doing working for these
morons. Perhaps I could start again – at the bottom. Become

a runner on a movie and work my way up to being a producer. Or get a job as a production accountant, spending the money rather than counting it. I could have a word with Buddy – I'm sure he could get me a place somewhere, working on one of his movies. He'd be happy to look after me. Until he found out the truth about what had happened with Olivia. Once again, I felt the noose tightening around my neck, my room for manoeuvre evaporating.

'When you think about it, we're a bit like that family, aren't we?' Bennett was still going on when I tuned back into their conversation. 'Bill, you're like Don Fonza-wotsit . . .'

'Corleone,' I said, unable to bear it any longer. 'And his name wasn't Don. It was Vito. Don was his title – like Mr or Sir. And the family didn't sell fruit, they were—' but Bennett had had enough of this film buffery.

'Whatever,' he said, anxious to expand his metaphor. 'As I was saying, Bill's like Don Wotsit and I'm like his son – except I'm not a short-arse. What was his name, West?'

'Don Corleone had three sons. Which one do you mean?' I asked as if I didn't know. 'There was Michael, the youngest, played by Al Pacino, who comes back from the war and takes over the family business which, incidentally, was—'

'That's the one!' said Bennett. 'Michael. Mikey. That would be me. The real operator who makes sure everything runs smoothly, who takes care of business with just a hint of a ruthless streak.'

'And who would West be?' asked Davis, encouraging Bennett, even though he gave every indication that he didn't have the faintest idea what his protégé was talking about.

'Ah, West would have to be the other brother. What was his name?'

For a moment, I allowed myself to think that Bennett might be referring to Sonny, the big mean motherfucker with the vicious temper, who beat to a pulp anyone who got in his way. Sonny Corleone would know what to do right now, faced with these two annoying idiots. He'd pick up that champagne bottle and smack them with it before producing a handgun from under his chair and blowing them away, starting with that irritating jerk who knocked out two of his teeth. That's what Sonny would do.

But, of course, that wasn't the brother Bennett had in mind. He was thinking of poor doomed Fredo, played by poor doomed John Cazale. The brother few could remember, played by the actor few could remember.

'Not the big bruiser,' Bennett continued, as if reading my mind, 'the other one. The little snivelling one. What was his name?'

'Fredo?' I offered half-heartedly, but was drowned out by their simultaneous, glee-filled cries of 'the Yellow Meerkat!'

*'The champagne bottle!' a demonic voice inside my head implored me. 'Use the fucking champagne bottle!' As if on automatic pilot, I grabbed the bottle around its thin neck and lifted it from the table. It felt perfectly weighted. The remaining liquid fizzing away in the bottom half provided a natural amplitude and it gathered momentum effortlessly as it swung in my hand like a glass baseball bat. They were still chuckling away, delighting in their condescending wit. Preening themselves – masters of the universe. Catching them unawares, I brought the bottle down behind Bennett's head, just out of Davis's line of sight. It was now or never.*

'More champagne, Joseph? Bill?' I asked, filling their glasses without waiting for a reply.

No, it was wrong to compare me to Fredo Corleone, quite wrong. At least he had the guts to betray his persecutors.

I took myself off to the gents to regain my composure. When I returned, Bennett was staring intently at his mobile phone like an Egyptologist examining a set of hieroglyphics. He read out the cryptic message:

Didnt see u come in, asshole. I should be used to u letting me down by now but it still really hurts. You'd better be at the party later, English. Where the fuck are you? O

'She certainly has a lovely turn of phrase, doesn't she?' Bill said, trying to cut the developing tension. 'Where do you think she went to school? Roedean? Cheltenham Ladies College?'

Bennett smiled, but without amusement. 'Any idea what this is all about, West?'

'Ah,' I began. Always a good opening gambit. Buys a little time and gives the impression you're thinking about the issue at hand. 'Yes. I meant to tell you about that, sorry. When I saw Buddy this afternoon, he did mention he wanted you to be nice to Olivia this evening. He said she's very down at the moment and he wants her on top form while she's here, you know, to promote the film and everything. Did you know, they're considering a sequel?. So, as she seems to like you so much, he asked me to ask you to take care of her. I should have said something when you came in, but with all the great banter we were having, I didn't get the chance. Sorry.'

'I don't believe this,' said Bennett. 'Why didn't you tell him I want nothing to do with her? Why didn't you tell him that I've never had anything to do with her and that, in fact, I think she's insane? Are you completely useless, West, or is there still room for further development? Every time I think you've plumbed the depths of stupidity, you manage to outdo yourself with another bloody stunt. Are you deliberately trying to stitch me up – or are you just a fucking cretin?'

'OK, steady on, Joseph,' said Bill, saving me from having to answer his tricky question. 'I'm sure there must be some method in West's madness – although it's hard to fathom what it is from where I'm sitting. I still think that the best strategy is for you to stay as far away from Ms Finch as possible, but West may have been acting in the best interests of the company, trying to keep Guttenberg sweet. Is that right, West?'

'That's it, Bill! That's exactly what I was trying to do,' I said. 'I really don't think it would be a good idea for you to miss the party. Buddy went to a lot of trouble to get the tickets and he'd be very upset if you weren't there. We can get away with missing the film, but not the party.'

'You're right,' Bill said, 'but we'll need a strategy to keep Madame Finch away from Joseph.'

'I've got a strategy,' said Bennett. 'I'll grab the first piece of crumpet that comes within arm's length of me and use her as a human shield to keep that mad woman at bay. And you, West, can explain that to Goldberg, Finch and whoever else is interested. Shall we go?'

The party was on a private beach belonging to one of the hotels which, by day, served as an expensive and exclusive restaurant and, by night, provided a perfect backdrop for an event fit for the kings and queens of Hollywood. Half the floor space had been laid with boards to create a dancing and bar area, and beyond that the sand rolled away to the relentless sea. Somewhere in a distant corner, almost drowned out by the waves, a live band played soft rock. Two enormous heavies guarded the entrance to the covered walkway that led down to the beach. They eyed us suspiciously as they checked our tickets, presumably wondering what we were doing there so long before the film was due to finish. Another pair of bouncers waited at the other end. No one would be getting in without a ticket this evening.

The bar was virtually empty when we arrived. Pretty waitresses milled around with heavily laden trays of exotic treats and Bennett wasted no time getting stuck into the lavish offerings.

'Take it steady,' Bill said as Bennett took a third cocktail from a tray, 'you've already had a few glasses of fizz and we really do not want any more unsavoury incidents tonight. Bit of FHB, please, Joseph – Family Hold Back!'

'I'll be fine,' Bennett insisted although he was already starting to slur his words in a way that was vaguely reminiscent of me after he'd knocked out my teeth. 'You know me, Bill. I get even more charming when I've had a couple of snifters!'

We had been there almost an hour, and had long since run out of things to say to each other, when a sudden rush of new arrivals signalled that the film was over. Buddy was one of the first to arrive, making his way slowly across the beach, stopping every few paces to speak to a well-wisher or grab something to eat. When he reached us, he greeted me with a huge bear hug, shook Bill's outstretched hand and nodded peremptorily in Bennett's direction. He exchanged a few pleasantries with Bill and then, grabbing an elbow, steered me to one side.

'Joe, I need your help,' he said when we were alone. 'Olivia's in the car but she's refusing to come down. She's really pissed that your pal Bennett didn't turn up to see the film. Where the hell were you guys? Do me a favour. Go up there and persuade her to come down. This party's costing me a fucking fortune and I need her here playing the room, looking like she's enjoying herself. You've got to get her down here, then get that asshole to speak to her – put a smile back on her face. She likes you – you can persuade her.'

Getting out of the party proved even more difficult than getting in. A tide of glamour was sweeping down the walkway while I tried to rush up in the other direction like a spawning salmon. I emerged after several minutes with the painful legacy of a stiletto that had crushed two of my toes, and hobbled over to the huge limousine that had carried Buddy and Olivia the short distance from the Palais du Cinema.

'Ms Finch?' I asked the driver.

'No, she's in the back,' he replied. I explained to the wise-arse that Buddy had sent me to collect his passenger. He put down his newspaper, unfolded himself from his seat and led me round to the other side of the car. A thousand camera lenses peered over my shoulder as I leaned in. Olivia was curled up on the back seat, the life force that usually fizzed and crackled out of her apparently switched off.

'Hey, English! Thank you so much for ruining my big

night,' she said as I slipped into the car and closed the door behind me. We were enveloped by darkness, broken only by the flashes from the cameras, clicking away at the tinted windows in the hope of scoring a money-spinning shot. 'Buddy promised me you'd be there tonight. Where the hell do you get off treating me like this, asshole? Do you enjoy it? It's like you're two different people. One minute you're incredibly kind and lovely and the next you treat me like a piece of shit. I just don't get you, Joe.' She turned away from me, her eyes full of tears.

'I'm sorry, Olivia, truly I am,' I said. 'I had to wait for the other guys to get in from London and their plane was delayed so they were late getting to the hotel and, before we knew it, we'd missed the start of the film and we didn't want to come in halfway through and cause a fuss.'

'Nothing worse than causing a fuss is there, English?' Olivia said, carefully dabbing a paper tissue to her eyes. 'Well, it's lucky the theatre was so dark. I cried my eyes out all through the movie. The people sitting around me must have thought I was a complete wacko. I've been so looking forward to this trip and I so wanted it to be a special night and now look at the state of me. Half the world's press are lined up out there and I'm supposed to go into my own party looking like fucking Cruella de Vil.'

'Don't worry,' I said, 'you look fantastic and it can still be a great night. It's pretty dark out there and I can shield you from the cameras – I've done it before, remember? Come on, let's go and enjoy the party.'

After applying some make up to her tear-creased features, Olivia followed me out of the car, hunched over as if trying to avoid a series of low beams. Cameras flashed around us like mortar fire as she took my hand and we negotiated our way back to the top of the walkway. One of the heavies blocked our path, demanding to see our tickets as we advanced, pursued by the paparazzi. I flashed him a look at Olivia and he let us pass, taking immense delight in blocking the human tide behind us, turning them around and pushing them back in a manner that would have made King Canute sea-green with envy.

I led Olivia across the dance floor and through the soft sand to the edge of the beach where the tide lapped across the shore. I found a waitress and relieved her of two glasses of champagne. 'Cheers!' I said, 'and welcome to Cannes. What do you think of it so far?'

'Oh,' Olivia purred in reply, 'I think it's getting better all the time.' She chinked her glass against mine and gave me a dazzling white-toothed smile, which I returned, with a flash of my own remodelled grin. 'Oh my God,' she said, looking at me closely under the glare of the halogen flood-lights, 'what have you done to your mouth?'

'I had a bit of a training accident. My colleague Benn—' I stopped myself just in time. 'My colleague Ben-knee, Benny, er, Anderjets, I mean Anderson. Benny Anderson. My colleague Benny Anderson punched me, but, you know, it will be fine. This is just a temporary fix and . . .'

Olivia took hold of my left hand and held it up in front of my face. 'And does that also explain why you're not wearing your wedding ring any more, hmm? This Benny Anderson didn't chuck you out of the house as well, did she?' She sipped on her champagne and smiled, content in the warmth of her own misguided supposition.

My attempt to explain what had really happened was

cut short by the unmistakable sound of Buddy puffing and panting his way towards us. His heavy frame wasn't designed for walking across dry sand.

'Hi Joe. Olly,' he said when he'd got his breath back. 'How're you doing?'

'Hey Buddy,' said Olivia, 'Joe was telling me about his teeth. Isn't he brave? I didn't even know he boxed, did you?'

Buddy looked confused but carried on with his mission. 'Hey, Joey, don't you know someone who is simply dying to talk to Olivia? Why don't you fetch him over here?' He winked as subtly as an Italian footballer in search of a penalty and sent me off on my quest. By the time I found Bennett at the bar he was exceedingly well-oiled. One of the bouncers was watching him from a few metres away, itching to throw him out if he stepped out of line.

'Hey, Westy,' he said, 'you're just in time. It's your turn to get the drinks in. But don't worry – it's all free. You won't have to hand over any of your own precious shekels.'

'Buddy wants you to come and have a word with Olivia,' I said, meerkatly passing on the message, even though I could see disaster looming if Bennett acceded to this request.

'Oh, does he now? Is that what your pal Buddy wants, is it? Well, that's great. There's a few things I'd like to say to him and Ms Finch.' He knocked back the rest of his drink in one swig and attempted to place it on a waitress's tray, but missed and it shattered on the temporary wooden flooring. 'Let's go.'

Bill put a hand up to Bennett's chest, stopping him in his tracks. 'Come on now, Joseph, be sensible. You've had quite a bit to drink and this might not be the best time to make Ms Finch's acquaintance. Let's go back to the hotel, there's a good fellow.'

But Bennett was having none of it. He eased himself past Bill's hand and closely followed by myself, Bill and the bouncer, he strode out across the beach. When he arrived at the edge of the sea, he swept past Buddy and straight up to a shocked Olivia, grabbing her by one arm and pulling her away from the rest of us, towards the sea. Buddy, fancying himself in the role of Nurse to their Romeo and Juliet, wore the self-satisfied look of a man whose plans were finally coming together. He stepped in front of us and marched us back up the beach away from the action.

'Come on, fellers. Let's leave the two love birds in peace. I tink they vant to be alone.'

I stepped back, being careful not to tread on the bouncer's feet. Over Buddy's shoulder, I could see Bennett talking to Olivia, animatedly, taking charge. Too arrogant to be star-struck, he saw Olivia as just another pretty face – and he knew how to handle pretty faces. She looked back towards me – small, confused and alone. A few words were exchanged and she turned to walk away. I saw him reach out and grab her by both arms. She struggled out of his grasp and tried to run back up the beach towards us, but the sand was heavy and her heels high and Bennett had no trouble catching hold of her again. Instinctively, I went to intervene, pushing past Buddy to get to them, but I was too late. When I was still some yards away, I saw her draw back her right arm and smack Bennett around the face with all the force she could muster. He stumbled drunkenly on the uneven ground, then fell backwards into the soft sand just as a small wave broke at the edge of the sea and swept up over his prostrate form, drenching him from head to toe. A fusillade of flashes lit up the night sky as the photographers stationed back up on La Croisette captured the unfolding drama in the sights of their long lenses and shot away like a snipers' convention.

Before anyone else could react, the well-trained bouncer leapt into action. He grabbed Bennett under the armpits and yanked him to his feet, before pulling his arm behind his back in a half-nelson, and frog-marching his dripping form up the beach and out of the party. Bill hurried after them, threatening to involve the British Embassy if anything happened to his colleague. Olivia stormed over to us, shaking with fury. I was the first to reach her, putting an arm around her shoulders as she pressed her face into my chest and started to sob uncontrollably.

When Buddy reached us, he brushed me to one side, clasping Olivia to his far more substantial chest and using his bulk to shield her from the photographers. 'Hey baby,' he said, 'I'm sorry. It's all my fault. I thought you'd want to see him. I'm sorry – I got it wrong. Here, take a sip of this.' He handed her a glass of champagne and she took a drink. Then she took several deep breaths, trying to get her emotions back under control, but still her frame was wracked by sobs, the aftershocks of the eruption.

'What? Why in God's name did you think I'd want to see that arrogant prick? Who the hell does he think he is? Guys like him make me puke. Expect you to fall into their arms when they flash you a smile? I'm telling you Buddy, I have completely had it with assholes like that. This is the kind of guy I want to be with from now on. Ordinary guys like Joe here.' She threw her arms around my neck and hugged me tightly. I could feel the wetness of fresh tears on my face. Buddy smiled at us paternalistically in a 'yeah-but-girls-like-you-don't-really-go-for-guys-like-him-un-less-they've-got-money-like-me' sort of way. People were milling around us, looking belatedly for the action as if the whole thing would now be repeated in slow motion.

'Let's get you back to the hotel, Angel,' Buddy said to his star attraction with genuine affection, prising her out of her one-sided embrace. 'The press are going to be all over this now – the sooner we get you out of here and back to the States the better. Come on, let's go find our car.'

He wrapped an enormous arm around Olivia and guided her towards the exit. I could hear her faint protests as she asked to take me with her, but Buddy was too busy comforting her to listen to a word she said, repeatedly muttering 'there, there' as if he was dealing with a fright-ened child. I suppose, in many ways, he was. He guided her up the gangway, flanked by the bouncers' guard of honour, towards the safety of their car and away from the limelight that was her lifeblood but also her Kryptonite.

She had been at her own party for less than fifteen minutes.

The next morning dawned bright and sunny. A typical Cannes morning, just as the mornings when one woke to dark, rain-filled clouds were also somehow typical of the French Riviera in May. I lay in bed, hoping that the ice caps would melt a few years ahead of schedule and carry me off to a watery grave. I sensed the walls closing in around me. At that precise moment, or one just like it, Olivia would be telling Buddy that the nutter who accosted her at the party had claimed to be Joseph Bennett, which he couldn't possibly be because I was Joseph Bennett. In another hotel, Bennett would be telling Bill what had happened and more pennies would be dropping. My goose was cooked and all that remained was for someone to lay their hands on some apple sauce.

As I lay there with my head under the grey, tobacco-smelling pillow, trying to find the guts to suffocate myself, I heard my mobile phone ringing from inside my jacket. I let it ring itself out so I could check who was calling, then put on my glasses and read the display: 'You have one missed call from Bastard'. Reluctantly I pressed redial and waited for the verbal barrage. What I got was a very flustered Bill Davis.

'West? Glad you're there. It's Bill, Bill Davis. Listen, the smelly stuff has really hit the fan here. The place has gone crazy. Have you seen the papers? They're all running Joseph's contretemps with that madwoman as their lead story, pictures and everything. He doesn't know what to do with himself, poor soul. He hasn't a clue what's going on – one minute she's sending him erotic texts, the next she's sending him to the canvas. The woman is clearly crackers.'

I took comfort from the fact that he wasn't, as yet, pointing the finger at me. 'Where's Joseph now?' I asked, surprised to find that I was genuinely concerned for Bennett's welfare as well as my own.

'He's here with me. We're getting out of this madhouse, first plane we can get on. What a bloody shambles! I want you to stay here and sort things out with Guttenberg. But not a word to the press, d'you hear? Strictly no comment. If they ask you about anything, just tell them to mind their own bloody business, right? When are you flying home?'

'I've got a ticket for Tuesday evening.'

'I want you in my office first thing tomorrow. Got that? We have to sort this mess out once and for all.'

I nodded in that inane way we do sometimes when we are on one end of a phone line, invisible to our interlocutor. I ran through the engagements I would have to cancel to comply with this demand. On balance, it was better for me to be in London than in Cannes right now. I had to be at home with Natasha when the story broke. To be there to comfort her and explain myself and apologise for my stupid, destructive actions as best I could. To do whatever I could to save my marriage. Either that or go and hide deep in the Amazonian rain forest.

I took a quick shower, threw on some clothes and headed down to La Croisette. I stopped in the lobby of one of the big hotels to pick up copies of the trade papers. All of them were running the events of the previous night as their front-page headline, illustrated with full-colour photographs of Olivia landing the blow or Bennett hitting the deck. I tucked the papers under my arm and took myself off to a small café where I bought a coffee and a croissant and sat down in a dark corner.

I folded out each of the papers in turn. Above a picture of Olivia's right hand connecting with Bennett's shocked face, *Variety* ran the headline: FINCH BEAU KO OK FOR BO? I had to read four paragraphs before I worked out that, in *Variety* speak, they were wondering whether Olivia knocking out her unnamed suitor would boost the film's box-office prospects. Beneath this headline, Buddy was quoted as saying that Olivia was very upset about what happened and would be cutting short her visit to Cannes.

*The Hollywood Reporter* carried a picture of Bennett lying at Olivia's feet as the sea lapped over him under the headline: SOMETHING HAPPENED! FINCH MAKES WAVES AT 'NOTHING' PARTY. They had found out who Bennett was and were speculating whether this would mean the end of Printing Press Productions' relationship with Askett Brown. Buddy had told them that it was far too early for any decisions about future working relationships at this stage and that Ms Finch would like to be left alone at this difficult time.

Finally I turned to *Screen International*, a paper with a more European focus. Their lead photograph was of a clearly distressed Olivia being led away from the fracas by Buddy. The headline was: THE SLAP HEARD AROUND THE WORLD, under which they ran the teaser: WILL FINCH FALL-OUT MEAN STUDIOS RECONSIDER USE OF EUROPEAN PROFESSIONAL SERVICES FIRMS? SPECIAL REPORT: PAGES 7–11. Their report noted that the Askett Brown accountant at the centre of the storm, Joseph Bennett, had gone to ground. His colleague Bill Davis had offered only a terse 'mind your own bloody business' when asked about what had happened and whether it would have any impact on his company's plans for expanding their business in the film and media sector.

I chewed disconsolately on my croissant and sipped my bitter coffee. My phone rang again. It was Buddy. My end was nigh.

'Hey, Joey. How're you doing?' He seemed surprisingly upbeat, his tone carrying no suggestion that he'd spent a long night with Olivia trying to convince her that my name was West not Bennett. 'Have you seen the papers this morning? We're all over them!' He made this sound like a good thing. 'That Clint Eastwood picture was supposed to be the big event yesterday, tipped for the Palme d'Or and all that shit, and we knocked it out the park. That doesn't make that jerk pal of yours any less of a jerk – and I'll still beat the crap out of him next time I see him – but, I'm telling you Joey, you cannot buy publicity like this. We're going to clean up over here now.'

I managed to stop him long enough to ask how Olivia was. 'Has she said anything more about what happened last night?'

'I tell you, Joey, that girl is so fucked off it's unbelievable. I've seen some women pissed in my time, but never like this. She absolutely refuses to talk about what happened. She won't look at the papers, she just wants to get the hell out of here. It's like she's in complete shock. She just keeps mumbling to herself and bursts into tears every time I ask her about it. That's why I called. We're taking a Lear out of Nice in an hour, probably spend a couple of hours in Paris and then head straight back to LA. I'm gonna give that stuck-up schmuck Davis a call and tell him to keep that sonofabitch away from me, my people and my company from now on. I still want to keep our business with you, Joey, cos you're the tops, but the rest of that crowd, I wouldn't give you a nickel for the lot of them. First chance you get to ditch them, you let me know and I guarantee you'll be taking my business with you. Enjoy the rest of your stay and I'll see you Stateside some time soon. Take care now.'

I wished him a safe journey and pressed the red button

on the phone. A long exhalation of air signalled my relief. I was still riding the wave. If Olivia didn't see the papers and no one spoke to her about the events of the last twenty-four hours, then she might not discover that the man who accosted her on the beach was Joseph Bennett and I wasn't. I wasn't out of the woods yet but I'd avoided another elephant trap – for now.

I finished my coffee and gathered up my newspapers. Then, just as I was leaving the café, my phone rang again.

'I cannot believe I've had to read about all this in the *Sunday Times*,' my wife yelled across the time difference. 'Why the hell didn't you tell me?'

'It's in the *Sunday Times*?' I asked. Cocooned in the special atmosphere of Cannes, I hadn't thought about the more general newsworthiness of last night's events.

'And the *Sun*, the *Express*, the *Mirror*, the *Observer*, the *Independent*, the *Mail on Sunday* and the *Telegraph*. I've bought them all. It's only their later editions that got the story, but their websites are full of it. And the TV news this morning. Cameras outside Bennett's house and everything. They're all saying that he accosted Finch at the party and she decked him. Most of them say they'd been having an affair but now, by the look of it, it's over. So what really happened, Joe? Were you ringside? And why the hell didn't you tell me about it? What's the point of you being in the middle of all this stuff if you never tell me anything? You're the worst bloody gossip ever.'

'It all happened very late, Nat. I couldn't say anything, could I?' I replied when she paused for breath. 'I'm sure you'd have been delighted if I'd woken you up in the middle of the night to give you the latest on Bennett's love life.

And this morning's been totally crazy. My phone hasn't stopped ringing. I've been talking to Bill and dealing with Buddy and everything. It's mayhem over here. In fact, I'd better go now in case any of them are trying to get hold of me. Bill Davis and Bennett are heading back to London today and they want me back tomorrow. I'll have to go straight into the office, but at least it means I'll be home a little earlier than planned.'

'That's great. I can't wait to see you,' Natasha said, possibly sincerely but it was hard to tell. 'And if you do happen to witness any more major news events, please try to let me know before I read about them in the papers.'

It's amazing how quickly the glamour of La Croisette can be replaced by the everydayness of a small provincial French town lifted above the humdrum only by the smell of the sea and the screeching of the gulls circling overhead like vultures on vacation. Cannes *ordinaire*. While I'd been talking to Natasha, I'd wandered off the beaten track and now realised I was lost. I meandered through narrow, twisting streets in what I hoped was the direction of the sea, but all I found were more small streets and, sometimes, the same small streets encountered from different angles.

I ducked into another café, hoping to find someone who could direct me back to what passed for civilisation in Cannes in May. I sat brooding over a strong, black coffee for the best part of an hour, considering my future. As I weighed up the various scenarios now facing me, I was confronted by the growing realisation that I'd had it. I was fucked. All roads led inexorably to my exposure and ruination . . .

224

Buddy talks to Olivia on their flight home. She tells him that I'm Bennett and not West. Buddy laughs and explains her mistake. She convinces him that it was me she slept with. Buddy is appalled by my lack of integrity. He calls Bill Davis. Tells him everything. I'm fired. Natasha kicks me out. My life is over.

Or – Bennett swears to Davis that he has never touched Olivia Finch, has never even spoken to her before Buddy insisted on it last night. He has no idea why Finch should be texting him and telling people they're lovers. All he knows is that she and Joe West seem pretty close. Perhaps West set the whole thing up. Davis agrees. I'm fired, kicked out of my house when Natasha finds out, etc.

Or – Bennett is interviewed by a switched-on investigative reporter. He denies the whole thing. She looks more deeply into the story. Quick word with the doorman at the restaurant in New York where the party took place. Quick scan of some photographs. Quick conclusion – nah, that wasn't the guy Ms Finch left with. He was a short, fat, baldy guy. I remember cos we were all wondering how a woman like her could leave with a short, fat, baldy guy like him?' Reporter puts together two and two, makes four. I'm exposed. I'm fired and so on as per earlier scenarios.

By the time I left the café, still none the wiser about where I was or how to get where I wanted to be, I was convinced of one thing – I had to get back to London as soon as possible and confess everything. At least then I could control how Natasha heard the news and do my best to save my marriage. Maybe even keep my job, although I imagined that Bennett would claim the right to knock out the rest of my teeth as the minimum price for letting me stay on.

Once I'd made that decision, an incredible thing happened: all the tension that had been building up suddenly left me. I stopped panicking and became reconciled to my fate. The future might still look unimaginably bleak, my whole life still in ruins, but at least I was back in control – I could now walk with my head held high towards the gallows, not wait to be shot in the back, trying to escape. I'd pack my bags, take a taxi out to the airport and get myself on the first flight home. That's what I'd do. It was the right thing to do, the brave thing to do. The only sensible thing I could do.

I decided to spend the day watching a few movies, then sleep on it and make my mind up in the morning. That, of course, was the Yellow Meerkat thing to do.

# CITY OF LONDON

I arrived at Heathrow just after eight on the Monday and took a cab straight to the City. I dropped my bags at my desk and, ignoring Polly's pleas for more information, headed up to Bill Davis's office where an emergency meeting was already in session. Bennett sat hunched over a cup of black coffee, crumpled like a man who hadn't slept for thirty-six hours. Strewn across the table in front of him were the news sections of all the main Sunday papers and several from that Monday morning. All were leading on FINCH'S FRENCH FRACAS – war, pestilence, famine and other less important matters had all been relegated to the inside pages.

The front page of the *Daily Telegraph* in particular caught my eye. It showed two pictures of Olivia: one in her beautiful prime, dressed to the nines and dripping with jewels on the night of a premiere or awards ceremony; the other taken late on Saturday night, her face streaked with the mascara tracks of her tears. The fear I had been feeling all the way back to London, the nervousness of knowing that I was soon to be found out or forced to confess was suddenly replaced by an even more primal, painful emotion: guilt at what I had done to this totally blameless person. Even when I looked away and my eye caught the stricken figure of Bennett in the corner, I saw only the reflection of my culpability in his crumpled form.

I wasn't alone in feeling the tension of the occasion. Bill Davis was standing in one corner, too wound up to sit down, as if his body physically wouldn't be able to bend enough to let him take a chair. Only one man seemed impervious to the dread-filled, dreadful atmosphere. Lounging in the two-seater sofa under the picture window with its extensive views across the City of London sat Dai Wainwright, in his element at the centre of this storm of human suffering.

'Mr West,' said Wainwright as I was shown into the office, 'glad you could make it. Please grab a beverage and pull up a chair.' I sat down at the table and poured myself a coffee from a silver thermos jug, then offered it to the others. Bennett avoided making eye contact with me while Bill shook his head.

'Now then, Joe,' Wainwright said when I was settled, 'I'm sure you don't need me to tell you that we have a very awkward situation here. The good name of Askett Brown has been dragged through the media slime and it's my job to find out what's gone wrong and who is to blame. And then,' he paused like an executioner at the top of his upswing, 'what action should be taken against said person or persons.'

'This is bloody ridiculous,' Bennett mumbled. 'Can we

please get on with it so I can get back to work? I have to meet a client in half an hour.' The words still bristled with his need to be in control, but his defeated posture left them empty of impact.

Bill spoke for the first and last time. 'Yes, you're quite right, Joseph. Let's get on with it. Dai, over to you. I want you to get this sorted and report back to me when you're done. Take as long as you need. You can stay in here – I'll go for a bit of a wander. Make sure the troops are coping OK with all this publicity.' When he reached the door, he stopped and looked back over his shoulder. 'Goodbye chaps,' he said with such chilling finality that Bennett and I instinctively looked at each other for reassurance and support.

Wainwright was offering neither. He picked up two buff folders from the floor and walked slowly to the table, like a sadistic games teacher about to force the fat kids to run another mile. There was a hint of 'this is going to hurt me more than it's going to hurt you' false sympathy in his expression but he couldn't hide what he was truly feeling. He was a cat with two mice for playthings and his only dilemma was which one to disembowel first.

'More coffee, gentlemen? No? OK, then let's get down to business.' He reached for the fatter of the two folders and placed it on the table in front of him. 'Joseph Bennett,' he read from a label on the front cover. He opened the file and took out a pristine sheet of white paper, which he lifted to his chest like an old maid playing gin rummy, concealing his hand. Then he took a sip of his coffee, cleared his throat, and sat forward in his chair.

'Joseph Bennett,' he repeated, 'I have here a memorandum

listing several misdemeanours allegedly committed by you in the past few weeks. I intend to read you the complete list and then we can look at each incident in turn. OK?' Bennett blustered and tried to cut in, but Wainwright continued undeterred. 'Number one: that, whilst on company business in New York City, State of New York, United States of America—'

'Oh, get on with it!' snarled Bennett.

'. . . United States of America,' Wainwright continued unperturbed, 'on 23 April this year, you performed sexual intercourse with Ms Olivia Finch, a well-known actress and, for the duration of the making of the feature film *Nothing Happened*, a contracted employee of Printing Press Productions, an important Askett Brown client.'

'That's a load of cobblers,' said Bennett, 'and you know it. I had never even spoken to that bloody woman until Saturday night.'

'I had planned to read through all of the allegations against you first, Mr Bennett, so that we could consider them in the round, as it were,' said Wainwright, 'but if you'd like to discuss this one now I'm happy to do so. I take it that you are denying that you slept with Ms Finch?'

'Absolutely. She may be cute but she's also a fucking nutter. I wouldn't touch her with a ten-foot pole.'

'I would kindly ask you to refrain from using inappropriate language, Mr Bennett, or I may have to add that to my list,' Wainwright said, making a note on his piece of paper. 'In that case, can you please explain why you contacted Ms Finch confirming that you had slept with her and suggesting that you do it again some time? We have records of several texts and e-mails sent by you to

Ms Finch, all of which appear to confirm that you enjoyed carnal knowledge of her.'

'That was because I thought she was one of the studio guys,' Bennett replied.

'You thought you'd slept with one of the studio guys?' asked Wainwright, leaning forwards as his line of enquiry started to get more interesting.

'No, you bloody idiot! I thought the texts had been sent by one of the guys at the studio.'

Wainwright made another note, then said: 'You thought one of the studio guys was texting you so you replied by commenting on his sexual performance?'

'No!' The veins in Bennett's neck were standing out proudly as the blood pumped into his brain. 'I thought the studio guys were playing a trick on me, so I replied in kind.'

'And which studio guys would these be?' Wainwright asked.

'Oh, you know,' said Bennett. 'Just guys – from the studio. I thought they were having a bit of fun to welcome the new kid on the block – you know, yanking my chain. So I thought I'd give them a bit back. Show them I wasn't going to be dicked around with. That's right, isn't it West? You were there. Tell him.'

'Well, West?' Wainwright asked, looking at me as if at the key witness who could make or break his case.

'Well, I did think it was a bit odd,' I stuttered. 'I know most of the people at Printing Press pretty well and I didn't think this was the kind of thing any of them would do. But Joseph definitely did say at the time that he thought it was the studio guys who'd texted him.'

'Mr Bennett,' said Wainwright, disappointed that I hadn't supplied him with his smoking gun, 'can you please tell me the names of these "studio guys" with whom you were enjoying such a riotous time?'

'Not as such,' Bennett said, after a lengthy pause while his brain rifled through its filing system but produced only the sparsest pieces of information about the 'Chinesey Girl' and the 'Poofy bloke', 'but West knows them – don't you, West?'

'I hardly think that is relevant to the issue at hand, is it?' Wainwright insisted. 'You are claiming that when you texted Ms Finch, you believed you were in fact texting one of your pals from PPP, but you can't name a single person who works there. That's not a particularly compelling argument, is it?'

'Now look here,' Bennett roared back, rising from his chair and leaning forward to close down the space between himself and Wainwright, 'this is not a court of law and you are not a ruddy QC. I don't know what the hell you think you're playing at, Wainwright, but you're really starting to annoy me. So let's cut this crap and get to the point. Or I shall go straight out to Bill and tell him to call off this ridiculous charade. Is that clear?'

Wainwright had not budged an inch during this tirade. He stayed as close as possible to Bennett's advancing frame, almost goading the bigger man to punch him. My temporary teeth ached vicariously. 'Mr Bennett,' he replied, craning his neck to look up into Bennett's half-crazed eyes, 'let me explain something to you. Bill Davis has asked me to carry out this investigation and report back to him when I have decided what actions need to be taken. He is staying out of it because he may be called upon to hear an appeal against whatever remedies I deem it necessary to apply. Do I make myself clear?'

Bennett slumped back down in his chair and started to nibble on a nail.

'Right,' continued Wainwright, brandishing his Mont Blanc pen with a flourish and scribbling another note on his piece of paper. 'I will record here that you deny the first allegation. May I now read through the rest of my list?'

Bennett nodded, his resistance wilting in the face of Wainwright's fastidious prosecution.

'OK. Number two: that at a meeting with the client, Printing Press Productions, in London on Wednesday, 4 May this year, you did embarrass Askett Brown by delivering a presentation so banal and unintelligible that it damaged the reputation and credibility of this firm and left our client feeling angry and confused.'

'What?' Bennett exploded. 'That was West's fault. He gave me a load of rubbish data. It was a miracle I managed to make anything of that presentation at all.'

Wainwright ignored this outburst and continued in the same relentless, deathless prose. 'Number three: that at a training event in Balham, South London on Monday, 9 May this year, you did deliberately and wilfully strike one of your subordinates, Mr Joseph West, with such force that you knocked out two of his teeth and left Askett Brown's insurers with a sizeable sum to pay out to enable Mr West to rectify the damage caused.'

'This is preposterous,' gurgled Bennett. 'That was an accident and you know it. We all had a bloody good laugh about it at the time, didn't we? You and me and your pal – what's his name? And Bill. Even West saw the funny side of it eventually, didn't you, West?' I stared at the table trying to keep my head as still as possible. I wasn't going to be the one to hang Joseph Bennett, but nor would I lie to help him. That punch in the face had bloody hurt and been bloody humiliating. Even if it hadn't been entirely deliberate, it had been completely avoidable.

'I said we'll discuss all this when I've finished my list,' said Wainwright, his irritation showing for the first time, 'but, for the record, I do have a statement from the trainer, a Mr Rodney James, of Balham, South London. He says that in more than fifteen years of facilitating executive development training solutions of this kind, he has never before seen someone hit a fellow participant with such force and accuracy. While he could not say for certain that the blow was deliberate, he said he thought it unlikely that a man with your pugilistic skills could accidentally miss his target – i.e. Mr West's hands – by such a large margin.'

'He moved his bloody head!' Bennett shouted, more now from resignation than conviction.

'Number four: that on the evening of Saturday, 14 May this year, in Cannes, France, having consumed an inappropriate amount of alcohol while participating in an official business engagement, you did place your hands on the actress Olivia Finch in such a way that she feared for her safety and felt compelled to strike you to prevent you causing her any further distress.'

'Guttenberg told me to be nice to her,' Bennett muttered to himself.

'Number five: that upon being struck by Ms Finch, you

did fall to the ground as if felled by a second-row rugby forward, creating a spectacle that was captured by the world's media, bringing Askett Brown into further disrepute.'

'I slipped!' said Bennett disconsolately.

'And finally, number six: that on Monday, 16 May this year, in this very office, you did verbally abuse and attempt to physically intimidate the Director of Human Resources of Askett Brown with a view to perverting the course of his investigations into the above alleged misdemeanours.' I had to admire Wainwright's technique. That last one had been added off the top of his head but rivalled any of the others in its casual, pedantic vindictiveness.

'This is a bloody joke,' Bennett snarled. 'You can't make any of these accusations stand up and you know it. None of this is the way you've made it sound. I've been set up all along – I assumed just by West but perhaps you've been involved as well, Wainwright, you little piece of shit. You two have always been jealous of my success and now you're trying to stitch me up in front of Bill. Well, it won't work.' He stood up to leave. 'I'm Joseph Bennett, not some knob you can jerk around.'

'Sit down, Mr Bennett,' said Wainwright, adding, when Bennett ignored him, 'sit down and calm down right now or I will have to call security.'

Bennett, checked in full flight by Wainwright's refusal to be intimidated, sat down. I glanced momentarily into his eyes and saw, behind the anger, real fear.

'Thank you,' Wainwright said, looking directly at his prey. 'Now then, Mr Bennett, you have heard the list of allegations against you and you have been given the opportunity to speak in your defence. Is there anything else you would like to say?'

Bennett fiddled with a pencil and breathed deeply. 'Is there any point?' he asked. 'This whole thing is a bloody farce. I did not sleep with Olivia Finch. I've been set up by West and his Hollywood pals, and probably by you as well. I will not forget this and, believe you me, I will have my revenge. I will make you pay for this, Wainwright. And you, West. Now is that all?'

'Not quite, Mr Bennett. Wait here a second, would you?' Wainwright crossed to the door and popped his head out to whisper something to Bill's PA. I suddenly felt very exposed alone in this room with Bennett, more Raging Bull now than Purple Stallion. He stared at me with unconcealed loathing – jaw jutting, teeth grinding hatred.

'Sorry,' Wainwright said as he sat down again, smiling at both of us. 'Had a bit of admin to sort out. OK, here's the tough bit.' He paused again and shifted in his chair, drawing in two good lungs full of air. 'Joseph Bennett: you have heard the accusations of misconduct levelled against you and have been given the opportunity to explain your actions and contradict any of the charges that you consider to be unjust. You have failed to convince me of your innocence in respect of any of the matters raised with you by me this morning. It is, therefore, my duty as Director of Human Resources to inform you that you are hereby and with immediate effect dismissed from your position of full-time employment at Askett Brown.'

'You what?' spluttered Bennett.

'You're fired!' repeated Wainwright, never once taking his eyes off his victim.

I have never seen anyone spontaneously combust but it can't be very different to what I witnessed that day. As he heard his sentence passed, Bennett's face crumpled like a sandcastle under the onrushing waves. He produced a cry of inhuman volume, a dozen expletives all rolling into one single cloud of abuse as he lunged across the table at Wainwright, who, able to anticipate Bennett's reaction to the news, slipped backwards to evade his grasp.

Right on cue, two burly security guards stormed into the room, grabbed Bennett and, with some difficulty, dragged him away from the table and back towards the sofa. They pushed him down onto its black leather upholstery and stood guard in front of him.

Wainwright wasn't finished. 'I have set out fully and clearly the allegations against you and you have failed to provide a satisfactory explanation for your behaviour. Indeed, you have compounded the accusations by acting in an aggressive manner and threatening me physically and verbally. You now have precisely sixty minutes to clear your desk and leave the building. If you are not off the premises by . . .' – he looked at his watch with an exaggerated flourish – '11.28, Jim and Darren here will be happy to escort you.

'Mr West, Bill Davis and I have decided that, as an interim measure, you will take over Mr Bennett's duties as Head of the Entertainment and Media Division. I don't suppose he'll require any handover from you in the next, er, fifty-nine minutes, Mr Bennett, but I'm sure he'll be in touch once he has his feet under the table.'

'He can go to hell!' Bennett shouted, 'and take you with him.' Commanded by a subtle nod of Wainwright's head, Darren and Jim yanked Bennett up off the sofa and marched him out of Bill Davis's office. 'You haven't heard the last of this, Wainwright,' Bennett shouted back into the room. 'Half the bloody Board were at uni with my father. I'll be back and when I am, I'll have your scrawny arse kicked from here all the way back to the fucking valleys.'

Wainwright took a deep breath, cracked his knuckles and smiled at me, implicating me in his dreadful deed, co-opting my approval of his smooth handling of another man's destruction. I had just witnessed the dismantling of my bitterest rival, the only person on the planet I could claim genuinely to hate, but I felt no sense of triumph. Just insidious, gnawing guilt that I had brought this essentially innocent man to this undeserved fate. Dai looked at me, waiting for some kind of reaction. 'So, what do you think, Joe? Will you take the job? It'll mean quite a big step up in salary.'

'It's all very sudden,' I replied, like a girl receiving a marriage proposal on her first date, 'do you mind if I pop out for a bit of fresh air? Clear my head a little.'

'Of course not,' replied Wainwright, all smiles and unctuous buddiness. He curled an arm around my shoulder as I stood up and guided me to the door. Suddenly, I was one of Dai Wainwright's best mates. 'Bill will want to see you as soon as possible, but you pop out and come back when you're ready. And please don't talk to anyone about any of this for now. We have to make sure that all the correct procedures are observed.'

That ruled out going anywhere near my desk. Polly would want to know all the details and was sure to find a way to force them out of me. I scuttled out of the office and into the nearest toilet.

My head was spinning. I took refuge in one of the two

cubicles, locked the door and sat down on the wooden seat. I placed my elbows on my knees and my head in my hands. I'd been sitting like that for several minutes when I heard the door open and the footsteps of two men entering. I heard them walk over to the urinals, the gentle ripping sound of flies being undone, the shuffling of feet and then the faint percussion of pee on porcelain. Dai Wainwright was clearly one of those men who enjoyed a good communal slash and he held forth as he went about his business.

'Yes, it all went very smoothly, Bill. Bennett was upset, of course, but he must have seen it coming. He's no fool. He knows you can't go dragging the reputation of a company like this through the muck and expect to come up smelling of roses.'

'Well, thank you again for carrying out this horrible business with your usual professionalism, Dai,' Davis replied. 'It must have been ghastly for you. I hope you told poor old Joseph how deeply I regret what's happened and wished him well for the future from all of us on the Board. I don't want him leaving with any bitterness towards us. He is a good chap, you know. One of us. I always had really high hopes for him.'

I heard the zipping up of flies. Wainwright continued the conversation as they made their way to the wash basins. 'Don't worry, Bill, it was all done with the utmost dignity and respect.'

'I must say though, Dai, there are a couple of things about all this that still bother me,' Bill said as he washed his hands.

'Hmm?' hummed Dai.

'Yes. Well, first, it does seem odd that Bennett still categorically denies sleeping with that blasted woman. He's hardly the kind of chap to deny a conquest of any kind, let alone bonking a fabulous piece like her. But even when we've been on our own and totally on "tour rules", he's still been absolutely adamant that he never touched her.'

'That's because he knows that he's – if you'll pardon the expression, Bill – shat a bit too close to his own front step, don't you see?' Wainwright replied. 'Being new to the film business, he probably didn't appreciate how much fuss one little hump would cause – he might even have thought it was a way to prove himself to someone like Guttenberg.'

'You're probably right,' said Davis, 'but he should have known that it's one rule for "them" and another for the rest of us. He's absolutely convinced it's all down to the usual Jewish thing – you know, that they're all in it together, with our friend West right in the middle of things. Perhaps he's right. Which brings me to my other worry. Are you sure West's the right person to take over from Bennett? I know he's pretty good with individual clients, but can he really grow the business? My worry is that we're letting that loathsome Guttenberg fellow twist our arm over who we appoint to a very important job.'

'Listen, Bill,' Wainwright said, dropping his voice conspiratorially as one of them opened the door back out to the corridor, 'like we agreed, I've only offered it to West on a temporary basis. Let's see if he can paper over the cracks in the short term, land that next deal with Guttenberg and then we'll see how the land lies. And Bill,' Wainwright was saying as the door swung shut again, 'try to be a bit more positive when we meet with the annoying little twat.'

When I was confident they had gone, I flushed the toilet and emerged from the cubicle. I washed my hands and splashed some water on my face, trying to make sense of the past twenty-four hours. Things couldn't get much worse, I thought. Then I felt my mobile vibrating inside my jacket pocket.

'Hello, sweetheart,' Natasha said in unusually honeyed tones, 'how's your day going? Anything interesting happening?' Her voice became more strident as she ended the sentence and I sensed trouble. 'Anything to add to what Sandra Bennett's just told me?'

*Bugger!* Natasha had already heard the whole story from Bennett's wife. Now my life really wouldn't be worth living.

'She's just been on the phone,' Natasha went on. 'According to her, her Joseph's been fired and you've been given his job. Is that right? Were you planning to tell me this sometime? I mean, I know I'm far too busy cooking and shopping and cleaning up after your kids to be interested in all your complicated business stuff, but don't you think it would have been nice to let me know? Hmm? So I didn't have to hear the whole thing from Sandra bloody Bennett? She's in a terrible state. She said she's never heard her Joseph so distraught. She's scared he might do himself some damage. Still, it was nice of him to call her, wasn't it? You know, to let his wife know what was going on before he topped himself. I was so embarrassed – she was going on and on and I didn't have the slightest clue what she was talking about.'

'I'm really sorry, love,' I said, 'but I honestly haven't had a moment to call you. I had to stay in with Dai the Death after Bennett was taken away and since then I've been hiding in the toilet, listening to Bill and Dai slagging me off and blaming the whole Bennett situation on me and the International Jewish Conspiracy. I'm going to tell them to shove the job. I can't take it under these circumstances, can I?'

'Oh, I think you can, love – and you should. They should have given it to you in the first place. Now you can show all those anti-Semitic tossers exactly what you're capable of.'

'I'm really not sure, Nat. Bill clearly doesn't think I can do it and—'

'Just give it a go, love. I'll support you. And if you really don't like it after you've tried it for, say, fifteen years, you can leave and do something else. OK?'

'Yes, OK,' I agreed. 'I'm going in to see Bill now. I'll ring you later to tell you how I got on. Promise.'

'Thank you, darling,' Natasha replied. 'That would be lovely. Oh, and one more thing. Be careful on your way home tonight. Sandra thought her Joseph might come looking for you to finish reorganising your dental work. He still blames you for the whole thing, apparently. So typical of him not to take responsibility for his own mistakes, isn't it? Better take a cab straight home. We can afford it now, Mr Director.'

# MILL HILL, NORTH LONDON

When I got home that evening, Natasha greeted me with a kiss, and a glass of cold champagne. We sent out for a meal from our favourite Chinese restaurant and, over our meal washed down with a few more glasses of wine, I brought her up to date with everything that had happened in the past few days. Everything, that is, except the rather important details that Olivia Finch had flattened the wrong English arsehole, and Dai Wainwright had sacked the wrong man.

Natasha's good humour soured a little when she noticed that my left hand was one gold ring short of a marriage and I was quizzed at length about what had happened to my wedding band and why, once again, I had failed to mention this important fact to her. On any other day I'm sure I'd have been despatched straight back to Heathrow to find the missing symbol of our love. That evening, though, she was so delighted by my promotion that she was willing to overlook even this cataclysmic failure of attention. We even made love that night. Natasha said it was much better doing it with a Director. Perhaps, she said, that was why Olivia Finch found Bennett so irresistible.

# CITY OF LONDON

With the press all over the company looking for new angles on the Bennett Affair, I had to hit my stride quickly, reassuring clients that everything was fine in an endless series of breakfasts, lunches, dinners and even occasional meetings without any food attached. It was good to be following in the lumbering footsteps of a man who had been as disliked by our clients as by most of his colleagues. They welcomed me like a long-lost son and no accounts were lost.

The only news of Bennett over the next few weeks came from what Natasha picked up from Sandra, occasional gossip procured by Polly through the PA grapevine, and speculation in the tabloid press which ranged from suggestions that he had fled the country to an exclusive report that he had been booked to appear in the next series of *Celebrity Big Brother*. All we knew for sure was that Sandra had kicked her now infamous husband out of the house when he couldn't explain to her satisfaction why a top Hollywood actress had laid him out in front of the world's media. This wasn't the first of Bennett's affairs that Sandra had got wind of, but now she had decided that enough was enough. No sooner had he slammed the door on his home for the final time than she had instructed a top divorce lawyer to take him for every penny he had. Bennett was rumoured to be staying in a plush West End hotel, still in denial about the loss of his job, wife and family and motoring through his cash faster than a horny teenager in a lap-dancing bar.

With no one to replace me in my old job, I had to work every hour under the sun, plus a few that took place after dark. I didn't see much of Natasha and the kids, often leaving home before they were awake and returning long after they had gone to bed. Our weekends were punctuated by phone calls from all around the world and requests for urgent pieces of analysis. Natasha remained positive that this was the right thing to do – for me to put the hours in and make a good impression – but it was hard on her and the children and even harder on me. I soon realised that jobs like these were meant for people like Bennett – people who preferred working to living.

My main priority at work was putting together a new finance deal for PPP. Flushed with the success of *Nothing Happened*, Buddy was keen to move ahead with a slate of new films. I pulled in funds from all over Europe, exploiting government subsidies and intricate tax-offsetting schemes wherever possible to sweeten the deals for the investors. By the time I'd finished, Buddy had the capital he needed to give the green light to the impressive list of projects he'd been holding in development and Askett Brown had earned a healthy commission.

# LOS ANGELES, CALIFORNIA

And so, just a few weeks into my new role as Director of the Entertainment and Media Division (temporary) – and complete with a new set of properly fitting teeth (permanent) – I found myself boarding the red-eye to Los Angeles to seal the deal with Buddy. I would be away from home for a week but, I thought as I boarded the plane and turned left towards Business Class, I might as well not be seeing my family in America as not seeing them in London.

I spent my first full day in LA at my hotel acclimatising and relaxing by the swimming pool high up on the rooftop terrace. After a refreshing wake-me-up swim, I took breakfast by the pool, still wearing just my swimming shorts and a hotel robe: orange juice, coffee, French toast with maple syrup and bacon, all consumed whilst reading complimentary copies of *Variety* and *The Hollywood Reporter*, sitting in the shade of a palm tree, warming in the Californian sun. All I needed was the big cigar and I was Sam Goldwyn.

Over the next few days I had several meetings with Buddy's people at PPP to iron out the final details of the financing package and made a trip to Rodeo Drive to buy some decent presents for Natasha and the children. When everything was sewn up, I went for lunch with the big man himself. Buddy drove me out to the coast at Santa Monica where we ate at a fabulously extravagant seafood restaurant right on the pier. He ordered a bottle of the best Californian wine on the menu and we drank a series of toasts to our friendship, to the greatest deal in the history of the movie business and to the conjoined futures of Printing Press Productions and Askett Brown.

'So how's your dick-for-brains pal, Bennett?' Buddy asked me as he paid the bill and we rose from the table. 'You know, I still haven't got to the bottom of what really went on between him and Olivia. She absolutely refuses to talk about it, but the funny thing is that, whenever she has, she absolutely swears blind she'd never set eyes on the creep before that night on the beach. She must have been drunker than I thought that night. Or off her face on something stronger. It's such a shame. She's a beautiful and talented actress but it's difficult to work with someone when you don't know what they're sticking up their nose after the director's shouted "Cut!"'

I'd already ruined Bennett's career and now it looked like I was going to take Olivia down too. I knew I had to say something – to tell Buddy the truth and let him know that all this was my fault, not Bennett's. That Olivia was neither mad nor off her face on drugs. But, once again, my courage failed me. 'It was pretty dark on the beach,' I said, 'so she could have made a mistake. Or perhaps she's been so traumatised by the whole thing that she's trying to deny it ever happened at all. Isn't that what some of these therapies recommend you do?'

'I wouldn't know, Joey. You could be right,' said Buddy, wrapping an arm around my shoulders and steering me towards the exit. 'I don't go in for that head-shrinking stuff myself. If I get depressed I just eat cheeseburgers.' He patted his enormous stomach to underline his point. 'As you can see, I've been pretty down these past few years.'

On my final evening in LA, Buddy threw a party at his palatial home high up in the Hollywood Hills. The house boasted five large bedrooms on two levels, all of which offered incredible views across the valley. Extending out of the main entertaining room – neither 'lounge' nor 'sitting room' did this vast space justice, it was simply a room designed for throwing huge parties – was a decked terrace offering even more spectacular views, not least from the enormous hot tub, easily capable of swallowing ten people, built slightly off to one side to afford the occupants some privacy should they wish to do more than simply soak their cares away.

A gang of hired staff roamed around serving drinks and canapés and, in one case, performing close-up magic to the delighted guests. All of them – male and female – wore the same uniform of long white frockcoats over red striped trousers – which was supposed to suggest Uncle Sam but in fact made them look like they'd escaped from an ice-cream vendors' training school. All of them – male and female – were young, slim and strikingly attractive: foot-soldiers in the army of out-of-work actors, willing to do anything for a little money and the chance to meet a Hollywood power-broker. All of them, that is, except one. One guy looked much older than the others, with a shock of ginger hair smeared untidily across his head, and, while most of the staff seemed eager for any opportunity to serve – scrambling to deliver a cocktail or barbecued tiger prawn to their next big chance of breaking into the movies – he stood idly, watching proceedings, serving those who approached him with all the enthusiasm of a London coffee-shop barista.

When Buddy saw me, he called me over to join him and the small group he was standing with, introducing me with his usual hyperbole – I was the 'miracle man' who had saved his company and so on. The rest of the group seemed unimpressed. Miracle men are ten a penny in Hollywood.

'I was just telling the guys this great story I heard about one of the studio tours,' Buddy said after the introductions were complete, 'you know, the ones where they take a bunch of fat rednecks around the studio lot on a golf cart? Apparently, there were these guys going round the Warner Brothers' lot the other day, and they're sitting in the back of the cart while the driver's going through his spiel about what films were made on which sound stage and trying to keep his front wheels on the ground. Anyway, when they're about halfway round they get to Sound Stage, I dunno, let's say Ten and the driver, who's just a college kid, says: "This is the famous Sound Stage Ten where Oliver Stone shot *JFK*." And one of these fat pischers in the back shouts up: "I thought it was that commie guy who shot JFK. Whatsisname? Lee Haley Osment." And his mate leaps in and says: "Yeah, and it wasn't in LA, you dipshit, it was in Dallas, Texas. Don't you know your American history, boy?" So the poor kid's sitting there trying to remember the script and not knowing what the hell to say, when another guy chips in from the front, "Aw, lay off him, you guys. And anyways you're both wrong. It wasn't JFK who got shot in Dallas. It was J. R. Ewing. Now come on, already, let's get on with the tour!" Priceless, isn't it?' Buddy asked, flakes of pastry flecking his lips and chin. 'True story, I swear to God.'

I left Buddy to his entertaining and went for a wander around his sumptuous pad. Everywhere I looked, I saw legends of every kind: demi-Gods I'd grown up with through the magic of the movies and younger stars with whom I hoped to grow old. Then I saw the one person I would rather not have bumped into that evening, the person who possibly still harboured some bizarre hopes of growing old with me. Fortunately, I spotted Olivia before she saw me and was able to duck out of sight while she handed her jacket to one adoring flunkey and accepted an extravagant fruit cocktail from another. She looked stunning. Her blonde hair was cut shorter than before, while the simple diaphanous dress she wore fought a losing battle to look casual as it flickered gently above her smoothly naked knees. Every pair of eyes turned to greet her as she entered the room, a low murmur following her casually balletic move-ments. An awestruck bubble of admiration for perhaps the most beautiful person in this city of beautiful people. I hunkered down behind a group of slack-jawed, junior studio execs and hoped that she might walk on by.

She didn't. The guys in front of me could barely contain their excitement as she advanced towards them, nor hide their disappointment when she continued past. They turned around, probably expecting to see a star of similar luminescence to Olivia, but found themselves instead looking at an ordinary bloke like them. A bloke who, unlike them, was silently praying for the floor to open up so he could fall straight through it and keep going all the way down to Hell.

'Hi Joe,' she said, beguiling and threatening in equal measure. 'Buddy told me you wouldn't be here tonight. In fact, he promised me I'd never have to set eyes on you again as long as I lived.'

All other conversation around us stopped. The strange ginger waiter approached us and almost forced Olivia to give up her half-full glass for another that was barely fuller. He didn't offer me a drink but didn't move away either. His uniform didn't quite fit, as if it had been handed down to him by an older but smaller brother.

'Hi Olivia,' I said as calmly as I could, 'how are you?' I kissed her on both cheeks. 'Not here,' I whispered when my mouth was close to her ear, 'not with so many people around.'

She stepped back, ever the actress, in complete control of the scene. 'We must have a proper chat sometime soon, Joe. Real soon.' She leaned towards me and hissed in my ear: 'John 8:45'. Then she turned on her delicate heels and disappeared back into the party.

I had no idea what she was talking about. It sounded like another biblical reference, like the tattoo on her arm. Something from the New Testament – the Testament I hadn't had to study in my pre-bar mitzvah Hebrew classes and had paid scant attention to in my Religious Education lessons, which I'd mostly spent playing games of pencil cricket with Nick Spencer. I could remember Don Bradman's batting average from our all-time greatest Ashes Tests, but not a single word of the Gospels according to anyone.

I circulated around the room and chatted to a few people, but I couldn't stop thinking about what Olivia had said. Intrigued, I went in search of a bible.

Almost every wall in Buddy's house was fitted with built-in bookshelves, all of which were crammed to overflowing – with DVDs. As a voting member of both the US and British film academies, Buddy would have received hundreds of them every year, sent by the films' distributors to encourage him to vote for their movies. Technically, these screeners remained the property of the distributors who could ask for their return at any time, and they couldn't be loaned or given away to anyone else, but they were never recalled. So the collections of Academy members grew and grew until eventually they provided an extra layer of insulation for every wall in the successful movie executive's house. The only printed materials I saw anywhere were dog-eared scripts, evidence of Buddy's homework, casually littering almost every available horizontal surface.

My search for the good book eventually took me into Buddy's master bedroom. It looked like the kind of room you see in films about Las Vegas high-rollers. An enormous bed, draped in black satin sheets, dominated the room, which was also large enough to accommodate a three-piece red velour suite and a gigantic television, complete with cinema sound system. More DVDs and scattered scripts filled the shelves and tables. I searched for ages for any books and then found what I was looking for. Tucked in at the bottom of a small bookcase beside the bed, filed ironically between DVDs of *The Ten Commandments* and

*The Greatest Story Ever Told*, I discovered an elderly, leather-bound book adorned with gilt images of six-pointed stars and seven-branched candelabra that could only have been a bible. I opened it carefully, noting from an inscription on the inside cover that it had been a bar mitzvah gift (to someone named Sidney Schulman) in 1954, and flicked through the pages in search of the Gospel according to St John – forgetting, like a schmuck, that not only would this bible stop short of the chapter I needed, but also that the whole thing was written in Hebrew, a language I remembered only sketchily, and back to front.

I replaced the book where I'd found it and stepped back into the corridor. I'd been looking for Jesus for half an hour and it was now nine o'clock. Emerging into the bright lights of the party, I saw the funny ginger waiter holding an empty drinks tray and, beyond him, Olivia Finch being talked at by an eager young studio executive with a pony-tail. I smiled and mouthed a hello, then tried to sidle past her on the pretext of having someone else to talk to.

She grabbed my arm and dragged me towards her. 'Where the hell were you?' she breathed, 'I've been waiting in that goddamn bathroom for fifteen minutes.'

For once I didn't have to feign incomprehension – I genuinely hadn't a clue what she was talking about. She interpreted my open mouth, shrug-shouldered gesture perfectly and enlightened me. 'I told you to meet me in the john at quarter to nine, you dummy. Don't you understand the Queen's English? Meet me there now, OK? You go in first and I'll join you in two minutes.'

I wandered back down the corridor, found the 'john', went in and locked the door. Then I thought I should leave it open for Olivia, so unlocked it again, but then wondered what would happen if someone else, unconnected with our arrangement, needed the facilities, so I locked it again, but then couldn't see how she would announce herself, so I unlocked it and whistled the British national anthem loudly enough to be heard outside, so that if anyone disturbed me, I could pretend I hadn't noticed the lock.

Like every other room in the house, the bathroom was enormous, with a large white porcelain throne perched on top of a red velvet dais. There were twin his 'n' hers vanity units, linked by a black marble top and a marble shelf which supported a forty-inch plasma screen and DVD player. Across the room was a two-seater wicker sofa with plump red cushions that could have been used as a vantage point either to watch the TV or observe Buddy at his toilet. Perhaps he conducted meetings while he was taking a dump. I shuddered at that thought giving an interesting vibrato to the final bars of 'God Save the Queen'.

I heard a faint knock at the door and was relieved, when I opened it, to see Olivia standing there rather than members of a coprophiliacs' convention. She peered over both shoulders to check that no one had seen her joining me in the smallest (relatively speaking) room, then locked the door behind her, stepped towards me and slapped me hard across the face.

'Ow! What was that for?' I whined. In the movies I would have grabbed her arms and shaken her a bit until she melted sobbing into my embrace. But this wasn't the movies. The bathroom wasn't a film set and that slap hadn't been a carefully choreographed miss accompanied by a man clapping his hands off-camera. It had been real and it had really hurt.

'That was for all the horrible texts you've sent me since Cannes, you bastard. And for all the e-mails you didn't even bother replying to. Why didn't you look after me, Joe? After that awful man attacked me on the beach. I trusted you.' There was a pause, which could have been for her to catch her breath or gather her thoughts or simply for dramatic effect, before she added, with perfectly under-stated passion, 'I loved you.'

I had no idea what texts and emails she was talking about. They would have gone to Bennett who would have answered them in his own inimitable style, fuelled by the terrible anger of his abrupt fall from grace. Then, when the company took away his phone and cancelled his e-mail account, he would have stopped receiving her messages – and stopped replying at all. While I was contemplating this, Olivia landed another ferocious smack on my left cheek.

'Please stop hitting me,' I said like an abused child, raising my hands to protect myself. 'That's not going to do anyone any good, is it?'

She hit me again, this time around the back of the head, causing my glasses to fall forwards and my expensive new teeth to rattle in their moorings. 'You speak for yourself, asshole. I'm finding it surprisingly therapeutic.'

'Well, I'm not just going to stand here being slapped,' I said, backing away from her towards the door. 'I'm going back into the party. I'll be happy to talk to you, Olivia, happy to explain why things are the way they are, but only where there are witnesses so you can't hit me again. This isn't getting us anywhere.'

She lifted her hand again and I tensed myself for another

blow. This time, though, when she brought her fingers down to my face it was to stroke the backs of them across my reddening cheek. 'I'm sorry, Joe,' she said, 'but you make me so mad. Please don't leave.'

'Let's go out on the terrace and get a drink. It won't matter if there are people out there if all we're doing is talking, will it?' I said. She nodded. 'And keep your hands in your pockets.'

She slid her hands down the sides of her shimmering, skimpy dress and shrugged. 'Could be kinda difficult,' she said with a smile. She stepped past me and planted a delicate little peck on my livid cheek. I felt a delicious tingle spread from the top of my head down to my toes, taking in all stations in between. Once again, I found myself torn between the need to do the right thing and the equally strong impulse to rip off her dress and throw her to the floor. A battle royal was being fought for my body and soul, and this time I – the real me: the caring, loving, happily married, ordinary Joe West – had to win.

A small crowd had gathered outside the bathroom, some waiting to use the toilet, others investigating the rumours that a scuffle had been heard inside. I dare say it's not that unusual for two or more people to emerge from the same toilet at a Los Angeles party, but people were clearly confused to see Olivia Finch emerge with a flushed, red-cheeked nonentity.

Our friend the waiter was there, still holding an empty tray and coughing expansively into the sleeve of his jacket, like one of those royal protection officers talking into a hidden transmitter. I wouldn't have put it past Buddy to have allocated a personal attendant to Olivia – but surely not the most disorganised, useless member of staff. Then it dawned on me. He wasn't a waiter at all. The funny hair, the ill-fitting uniform, the implausibly poor service – Buddy must have hired a comedian to add a bit of spice to our evening. I leaned towards him and whispered discreetly in his ear. 'I'm onto you, pal! I know your game. But I won't say anything as long as you leave me and Ms Finch alone. So bring us a couple of drinks out onto the terrace and then bugger off. OK?'

His eyes swivelled nervously in his head. He nodded, then backed away from me defeated. It must have been important to him to remain incognito for as long as possible; an insult to his craft that I had picked him out as an imposter so easily.

I followed Olivia out onto the deck and we found a spot by the railings where the views down into the lush valley were at their most incredible. The cacophonic symphony of the gazillion insects living in the woods below filled the air, making it almost unbearably noisy, even when nobody was talking. Across to our left, some people had stripped down to their underwear and climbed into the hot tub. I took a deep breath of the warm air. Somewhere along the way – from being slapped to standing here – I had decided to tell Olivia the whole truth. To tell her that I was West not Bennett, and to apologise for the lying and all the hurt I'd caused her. That's what I planned to tell her, but I didn't get the chance.

'Look over there, Joe,' Olivia said, 'in the hot tub. You see those guys? You may recognise a couple of them. Good actors but never quite made it. Guys who'll do anything to land a part in a movie or TV show – even a commercial. You see them? I could walk over there now and take my pick of whichever one, two or three I fancied and steal them away from whoever they arrived with – just like that. And look in there.' My eyes followed hers into the house. 'You see all those people enjoying themselves? The studio chiefs? The players? The talent? I could have any of them too. All I'd have to do is click my fingers.'

I didn't like to spoil her speech by pointing out that pretty well anything in a skirt could have taken her pick of the drunks in the jacuzzi or most of the other guests. The comedy waiter returned with our drinks, which he managed to hand us without spilling, and then retreated again.

'Heck,' Olivia went on, 'I don't want to sound big-headed but I could walk into any home in the valley or over there in the city, or out to Santa Monica or across the whole of the USA from sea to fucking shining sea, and have more or less any man I choose. I could probably walk into the goddamn White House and pluck the President right out from under the First Lady's nose.' She paused and sipped her champagne. Then she looked me square in the eyes until I had to avert my gaze for fear of being caught forever. Turned into a pillock of salt. 'But I can't have you, Joe. I can't have the one man I really want. Why did I have to fall for the one guy in this whole stupid industry with any morals? The one guy who really understands me, who's interested in me for my brain and what I have to say as much as for my body and the way I look. I've spent most of my adult life being dicked around by guys who only wanted me as a trophy – something to stuff and mount and display on their Facebook wall. But you really seem to care for me, Joe – at least some of the time. When we're together you are always so gentle and lovely and then we go our separate ways and I try to tell you how I feel and you shut me down.'

I shuffled uneasily, afraid to look her in the eye. She seemed to read my thoughts.

'I know you're scared, Joe. I'm scared too. I swear I've never felt this way before. Right now I can't decide whether I love you or hate you. Maybe I don't even know what love is. I've known plenty of hate in my time, but not too much of the other side of the coin. You must love your wife and children very much, Mr Joseph "A is for Asshole" Bennett. They're lucky people.'

As she'd been talking, tears had pooled in her eyes and now they started to skitter down her cheeks. I wanted to put my arms around her, but was still scared my resolve would crumble if I laid as much as one finger on her exquisite form. I handed her a paper napkin and she used it to dab her eyes, which glittered like fresh frost behind the thin veneer of tears. 'Yes I do,' I said. 'But I'm the lucky one, not them.'

'Aw, don't go all modest on me now, Joe. I bet they really miss you when you're away.' From somewhere deep inside, Olivia had found a character called Dignity and now performed her role with consummate skill.

I looked out across the valley. 'Perhaps,' I said, 'but nowhere near as much as I miss them – especially the kids. I miss Natasha too, of course, but that's different. At least we can catch up on lost time when I get back. With the kids it's different. When I'm away I'll miss them doing something for the first time or saying something cute and I'll never get that chance again. They grow up so much in a day, let alone a week. Still, I'm heading home tomorrow and I'll see them the next day. And I'll probably be sick and tired of them by the weekend.'

Olivia looked at me, a faint glimmer of hope in her sparkling eyes. 'Really?'

'No, just joking. It's a shock when they come bouncing in on you at God knows what time in the morning but I wouldn't want it any other way.'

'I will never understand your English sense of humour, English,' Olivia said, sadly.

I looked back towards the room – anything to break eye contact with Olivia – and noticed the red-haired comedian hovering in the doorway, training his beady eyes on us and rudely brushing aside requests for drinks from thirsty guests. I pointed two fingers at my eyes and then jabbed them towards him, the internationally acknowledged signal for 'I've got my eye on you, buster'.

From behind him, Buddy came ambling towards us. 'Hey Olly, Joe! How's it going? Enjoying the view?'

'Hi, Buddy,' Olivia replied, through clenched teeth, 'you didn't tell me Joe was going to be here tonight.'

'Oh, didn't I? Well, I wasn't 100 per cent sure he'd make it. We didn't firm up the dates for our meeting until pretty late in the day. You know this man has come up with the goods for us again? You, young lady, are going to be a few million dollars richer thanks to this young man, so be nice. OK?'

'Aren't I always nice to our English friends, Buddy?' she said with a humourless smile.

'Just don't you go smacking Joey here, OK?' Buddy said. 'He can't afford another set of teeth, can you, pal? Is everything OK out here? Want me to knock the humidity down a couple of degrees for you? Tell the bugs to shut the fuck up?'

'Everything's fine, thanks, Buddy,' I said. 'Great party. When's the comedian coming on – or is this his whole act?'

Buddy looked back at me, puzzled.

'That guy over there in the badly fitting outfit. Is he going to do a bit of stand-up or is impersonating a dodgy waiter his whole act?'

'I swear I have no idea what you're talking about,' Buddy said. 'I'll find out who he is and what he's doing. If he's goofing off on my time, I'll have him chucked off the fucking terrace.'

Olivia smiled as Buddy disappeared back into the house and we were left alone again. Some of the hot-tubbers were climbing out, whooping and laughing as, still dripping wet, they got themselves dressed and headed back to the party.

'Where were we?' I asked.

'You were at home with your wife and family having a wonderful time,' she said. We stood in silence for a couple of seconds, then she carried on. 'It's just not fair, Joe! I really, really want you! I don't want to sound like a spoilt-brat bitch actress, but I am kinda used to getting what I want. You're the first man I've met that I've ever really liked, let alone loved. And that includes my two fiancés. Is what you've got back at home really better than this?' She struck a glamorous pose, one long, sleek leg pushed forward to expose a perfect thigh, but she was smiling rather than pouting, acknowledging the irony of attempting to use her beauty to entrap the man she wanted because he respected her for so much more than that. 'We could be Tracy and Hepburn, Bogart and Bacall. We could be anything we wanted to be, Joe. I could give up all this shit and we could go live on a farm out in the Midwest, and you could write your brilliant novels and I'd learn to paint and we'd have dozens of kids and we'd raise buffalo and make amazing pizzas using our own fresh mozzarella! Wouldn't that be wonderful?'

For a moment – one terrible, tantalising, tempting moment – that image filled my mind, pushing what I knew to be right into the wings. Domestic bliss and the freedom to do what I wanted to do, be who I wanted to be without the chains of a mortgage or the pressures of everybody else's lives to deal with. And all the fresh, delicious home-made pizza I could eat! The chance to write meaningful words instead of counting meaningless numbers, to fulfil my dreams, not work to help other's fulfil theirs. There was just one problem: beside me in that perfect idyll wasn't Olivia, sitting on a stool milking buffalo in her Versace gowns and Jimmy Choo stilettos, but Natasha, and the gentle murmur of animals in the pasture was punctuated by the cries and laughter of happy children – my children.

The story was a good one – it was just that the casting was all wrong.

'But you can't have me, Olivia,' I replied after a long pause, risking taking another look into those incomparable eyes. 'You can't have the me that you want because that me is the ordinary guy who does a dull job and lives a dull life with his ordinary, average family. Ordinary to everyone else, I mean, but not to me. To me they're everything and without them I'm nothing. Without them I couldn't be the person you want me to be. So even if you did have me, as soon as I left my family – the one thing that actually makes me me – to be with you, I'd stop being me. Do you follow me? I'd be despised by everyone and especially by Natasha and the children. And I'd hate myself for making haters out of the people I love the most. I'd lose any remaining trace of what it is that makes me who I am. I'd still be Joe West – I mean, Joseph Bennett – but I wouldn't be the man you thought I was. The man you think you want.'

I finished my champagne and placed the empty glass on the top of the railing separating the terrace from the precipitate drop into the valley below. 'So, if it's all the same to you, Olivia, I'll leave now. I'll go home to my family and every time I watch one of your movies, I'll have the wonderful private excitement that will be my special secret until the day I die. Or until I get so old that I can't remember whether that incredible night in New York really happened or I just imagined the whole thing.'

Olivia looked back at me, her eyes wet with new tears. 'Oh, go on then!' she said eventually. 'Go back to your precious family and I hope you all bore each other to death. No, I don't mean that, English. I'm sorry. But somehow I have to convince myself that I don't need you if you don't want me.' She paused and her hand sought out mine. Our fingertips touched and it felt electric – there even seemed to be a flash of light at the edge of my vision. For a moment it felt like I was falling in love. Then the mood was broken. 'Shit!' Olivia said, 'I think that guy's a pap!'

'Which one?' I asked, but I should have guessed.

'That funny-looking waiter over there. Either he's got a camera hidden under his tray or he's got a fluorescent tip on his winky, because something sure as hell keeps flashing.'

She smiled at her own joke. 'Still, we're only talking, aren't we, Joe? It's not as if we're doing anything wrong, is it? It's not like we're lovers or anything like that.' She put down her glass and straightened her back as if a golden thread was pulling her upright – as if she was suddenly transported to the centre of a stage, with bright lights shining on her and everybody hanging on her every word. Ready for her close-up. 'But it is a shame he is standing there, English, because, if he wasn't, I would love to give you a nice friendly hug, wish you well and send you on your way. Because I am Olivia Finch, a classy sophisticated lady and the greatest actress of her generation. And you should be fucking glad that it is Olivia whose heart you've broken, Joseph Bennett, because I know a girl called Cadillac McAllister who would have kicked your sorry Limey ass all the way back to England if you'd pulled this shit on her.'

Olivia forced another smile onto her lips but her eyes told a different story. I said goodbye and walked away from her (though not, as it would turn out, for the last time). I found Buddy at the door, where he was organising the eviction of the phoney waiter. He gave me a bear hug, thanked me again and wished me well. I walked out into the warm evening and straight into one of the elegant white limos that Buddy had laid on so that nobody would have to worry about being too drunk or stoned to find their way home. I could get used to this way of life, I thought, as the driver pulled away from the kerb, but right then what I wanted – what I really, really wanted – was to be back with my wife and children in the dull comfort of my ordinary home.

# MILL HILL, NORTH LONDON

Iflew out of LA the next afternoon, arriving back in London the morning after that. I slept most of the flight, feeling more relaxed than I had for months. Natasha and the kids were delighted to see me – especially when I handed them their expensive, well-thought-out gifts rather than the usual cheap last-minute tat – and Bill Davis was equally delighted with my report from my meetings with Buddy. He was already hinting that my promotion would be made permanent. I had managed to sort out the situation with Olivia – and Bennett, although harshly treated, was at least out of my life.

That Saturday we took Helen and Matthew into town for a spin on the London Eye and a movie at the BFI IMAX cinema. Then we went up to Hatton Garden and bought a new wedding ring for me – flasher than its predecessor, with three colours of intertwined gold – and a matching pair of diamond earrings for Natasha. For the first time since I'd slipped through the screen into my own private pornographic disaster movie, it was starting to look as though, somehow, things might work out all right.

But that would be a pretty boring end to the story, wouldn't it?

The next morning, I was sitting trying to concentrate on the *Sunday Times* while Matthew clambered all over me, flying model aeroplanes into my ears and landing them on the sleek runway of my head, when my mobile phone rang. The screen said 'Private number'. The voice I heard was horribly familiar.

'West, is that you? It's Joseph, Joseph Bennett. I need to talk to you.'

'*Shit!*' I thought. 'OK,' I replied, hesitantly, 'I've got a few minutes before we take the kids swimming. What can I do for you?'

'Not on the phone,' he hissed, 'I need to see you in person. When can we meet?'

I wasn't especially keen to see him *mano e mano*, given the reasonable probability that he would take the opportunity to rip my head from my scrawny shoulders. 'The thing is, Joseph, I'm just back from LA and things are completely mad at the office. After swimming, I was planning to pop in for a few hours to go through the backlog. Then next week it's meetings, meetings and more meetings. You know how it gets. How about next weekend?'

'Yes, I know exactly how it gets, thank you,' he replied. 'But I have to talk to you urgently – today.' He heard my silence and quickly identified my concern. 'I'm not going to hurt you, West, I promise. I'm in enough shit already. We can go somewhere where there are plenty of other people if it would make you happier.'

# NEAR HENDON, NORTH LONDON

I agreed to meet him at a public golf course a few miles from the house. I got there first and, about ten minutes later, Bennett arrived in his sporty little Audi, still clinging to some of the trappings of his former life. He was dressed immaculately in a navy blazer and dark slacks, but he looked a shadow of his former self. His normally grenadier-straight back was bent and his eyes were cast down as if he was looking for loose change on the pavement. The uncharacteristic stubble on his face suggested that his last shave had been several days ago. We grunted our 'hellos' and shook hands. We had never known what to say to each other at the best of times – and this, for him at least, was not the best of times. I went to the bar and ordered us both a cup of coffee and a bacon sandwich. Before I'd paid, Bennett appeared at my shoulder and asked for a double whisky as well. We found a table and sat down in silence. Bennett stared at me as if he was mulling over various opening lines in his head but, not knowing where to start, said nothing.

To break the permafrost, I began to tell Bennett about my visit to LA. I was careful not to mention Olivia, but the damage had already been done.

'Buddy Guttenberg! Don't talk to me about Buddy bloody Guttenberg! Loathsome fat bastard! Jesus Christ, West, I wish I'd never set eyes on him. Why did I ever leave oil? What was I thinking of?' He sounded like a modern-day Lear, railing against the inexplicable forces that had brought him down. He was speaking loudly, inviting everyone else to look round to see what was going on.

'I wouldn't mind, West, I really wouldn't mind any of this if I'd actually done something wrong. You know I haven't always been whiter than white. But I swear I never touched that ruddy woman. I'd never even spoken to her before that night on the beach and look where that got me. She's a bloody psycho – ought to be locked up. It's just not fair, is it, West?'

I held tightly onto my coffee cup, trying hard neither to nod nor shake my head. Bennett stood up abruptly and sauntered to the bar, returning a minute later with a tumbler half full of whisky and ice. Perhaps that should be half-empty.

'Well, is it, West?' he said, getting rid of most of his drink in one gulp. 'Is it fair? Come on, you should know. I reckon you know more about this than anyone, don't you?' His tone had changed. From being self-pitying and abject he had suddenly become aggressive and accusatory.

The barmaid arrived and placed our bacon sandwiches on the table in front of us.

'Bacon, West? Bennett sneered. 'You really are full of

surprises, aren't you? And I don't just mean your eating habits.'

'What do you mean?' I asked. All of a sudden, I wasn't feeling very hungry.

'I think you know exactly what I mean,' said Bennett, taking the upper slice of bread off his sandwich and slathering tomato ketchup all over the bacon. 'You know me, West. You must have known I wouldn't take a thing like this lying down. Have my whole career ruined by some miserable little slapper? So, you know what I did?' His eyes darted like mayflies over a pond as he recalled the details. 'I hired a private eye. I got this guy to go over to LA and follow Madame Finch around for a couple of weeks. Followed her all over the place, he did. Restaurants, bars, the lot. He even managed to get into that fat bastard Guttenberg's party disguised as a waiter. Bloody good tracker, I must say.'

I stared into the steamy black contents of my mug, wishing I could dive in. Weighed down by a plethora of heavy emotions, I'd have had no trouble sinking to the bottom.

'Unfortunately, he was a bloody lousy photographer,' Bennett continued through a mouthful of sandwich, 'but he got a few half-decent shots.' He reached inside his jacket and produced a manila envelope. He tore it open, slid about a dozen 6 x 4-inch photographs onto the table and pushed them towards me. 'I think you'll find these interesting.' Bennett was smiling now, watching me, monitoring my reaction. He finished his sandwich and took a long sip of his whisky.

I looked at the first print, then turned it over to check the other side. As far as I could make out it was completely blank. The next two were the same. Bennett grabbed them, and a couple more from the pile, ripped them in half and threw them to the floor. 'Not those! That was when the stupid sod kept snapping away with the camera under his apron. They get better.'

Gradually, the quality of the photographs, and the clarity of the tale they were telling, improved. First, there was a picture of my shoes talking to Olivia's shoes. Then our knees locked in earnest conversation – not that anyone could have recognised them as belonging to us. Then one of our thighs, followed by our groins, both of which would have been far more interesting had they been taken in New York rather than Los Angeles. The next picture was of two champagne glasses which might have been held by us – or someone else, or sitting on a table. The next one did make me start – if you knew what you were looking for, you might have recognised our hands: her long, elegant fingers outstretched to meet my short, stubby digits, and touching almost like lovers. Without that knowledge, though, the picture could have been of any two acquaintances about to shake hands. Then there was one of our chests, perfectly properly a few feet apart. Finally, I saw the dome of a balding head similar to mine, bending to put a glass down on a tray, while the more shadowy figure of a slim and elegant woman (who might possibly be identified as Olivia Finch with the application of advanced forensic techniques) looked on in the background.

When I looked up from the last of the pictures, Bennett was staring at me.

Well?' I asked, fighting to keep my voice steady.

'Well,' Bennett bellowed, 'that's you, isn't it? That's you and Finch at Fatty Gutbucket's party, chatting away like old friends, isn't it? Old friends who've just carried out the perfect crime: to stitch me up so you could take my job. That's right, isn't it? Somehow you managed to get her to make the whole thing up, hassle me, then smack me right under the nose of the world's press. And bingo! No more Joseph Bennett. I should commend you on your excellent plan, West. But I think I'd rather smash the rest of your teeth out.'

Bennett sounded controlled as he said this, but I could see he was getting more and more agitated. He emptied the contents of a hip flask into his whisky glass and sank the lot in one effortless swig. I feared he would hit me despite the number of witnesses in the bar.

'No, it wasn't like that Joseph, I swear,' I said, hoping I didn't look as hot as I felt. 'We were just talking. I was only at the party about an hour and I only spent a small part of that time chatting to Olivia Finch.'

'My man tells me you were hardly away from her from the moment she came in to the moment you left. He says you even went to the loo with her. I suppose you were paying her and didn't want anyone to see. So, how much did it cost to wreck my life, you stinking little worm?'

Backed into a corner, I had no option but to fight – the meerkat desperate to avoid being trampled under the stallion's hooves. 'Do you have any idea how much Olivia Finch earns in a year?' I asked. 'She makes $10 million a movie. Do you really think she'd get involved in some ridiculous plot for a few quid? This is crazy. I did not go into the toilet with her.' (Liberated by the private eye's incompetence, I risked an outright lie.) 'I bumped into her when she was coming out and we chatted about how the film was doing. I didn't cook up any plan with Olivia Finch. The whole idea's absurd.'

Bennett looked at me for a long, long time, *really* looked at me. Stared at me and forced me to hold his gaze as he tried to unpick the locked entrance into my innermost secrets. I gave him my version of the look that Matthew always did when he was swearing blind he hadn't drawn on the wall when he still had the smoking crayon in his hand. Then I raised my hands in something approaching a papal gesture and shook my head slowly from side to side. I chose my next words very carefully: 'I swear to you, Joseph. I never planned any of this with Olivia Finch – on my children's lives.'

I watched him closely as he assessed what I'd said. I was teetering on the edge of the abyss. If I failed, I would be lucky to get away with just a hell of a beating. At worst, I faced total ruination. Bennett looked at me as if he knew I was lying but couldn't quite put his finger on it. After what seemed like an eternity, he picked up his glass and turned it upside down to let the last few drops drain into his mouth. Then he leant forward, scooped the remaining photographs off the table and put them back in the envelope. He went to put it back inside his jacket, but then let out a strangled, involuntary cry and ripped the whole package into a hundred tiny pieces and threw them down, like confetti, onto the sticky, threadbare carpet. 'Oh fucking hell!' he yelled, causing everyone to look round again. His eyes were sprinkled with tears of despair as he stood up, sending his chair somersaulting across the room. Without another word, he turned and walked out of the door. I hadn't been acquitted, but at least the case had been adjourned due to insufficient evidence. For now.

Leaving my sandwich untouched, I followed him out

into the car park. It was starting to rain. 'I've lost every-thing, West,' he said as he folded himself into his car. 'My job. The house. My pension. The kids. Sandra. Everything. This car's got to go back tomorrow. And there's you, happy as Larry, doing my job, earning my money. I haven't even done anything wrong. You know that and I honestly think Bill Davis and that little Welsh cunt Dai Wainwright know it too. I never laid a hand on Olivia Finch. I just provided a face for her to hit. What was it? Prearranged publicity for the film? We certainly made all the front pages, didn't we?' He was ranting now, his words slurred by the combi-nation of anger and alcohol. 'If I had actually done some-thing wrong, I'd think "OK, fair cop" – but I haven't. I didn't even mean to hit you, you know. If I had, I promise you, you would never have got up again.'

'I'm sorry, Joseph, I really am,' I said, hoping Bennett would interpret this as a conversational platitude rather than an indication of guilt. 'If there's anything I can ever do for you, please call me. Here's my new card with all my contact details on.' He had one hand on the steering wheel, while the other held the key in the ignition as he prepared to leave, so I pushed the card into the breast pocket of his blazer.

Bennett looked down at the pocket, then back at me. His eyes were knotted in concentration and his mouth fixed, a thin line underscoring his patrician nose. It was as if the hourglass icon you see when a computer is processing something had been transposed onto his face, spinning slowly around, crossing and uncrossing his eyes. Three times he looked down at his pocket, then back up at me. The third time, his expression had changed – his eyes opened wide in realisation as he slowly raised his head. The hourglass had changed back to an arrow: the processing completed. The riddle solved.

'It *was* you, wasn't it? Oh my God! It really was you.'

I started to repeat my often rehearsed denial of any involvement in any kind of a plot, but he talked straight through me.

'I don't believe it! You screwed Olivia Finch, then pretended to be me and gave her *my* card so she'd pester me, not you. And while my whole life gets flushed down the toilet, you calmly take my job and carry on playing happy families. Un-fucking-believable. I have no home, West. Because of you, I have no home. My wife's kicked me out. My boys won't speak to me. The captain of my golf club – who happens to be my ex-father-in-law – is having me blackballed. Askett Brown have fired me and I'm a laughing stock throughout the City. Every useful contact I had came from Sandra's old man, so my chances of future employment are pretty well zero.

'My own family are no bloody help because none of them has spoken to me since my father died. OK, so I didn't go to his funeral. He was dead, for Christ's sake! He wasn't going to miss me, was he? It wasn't cheap sending that wreath from Klosters, I can tell you, but for all the thanks I got I might as well not have bothered.

'So I'm screwed and you're sitting pretty – your secret safe as long as I'm taking all the blame. Very neat, West. I never thought you had it in you.'

He stared at me as if he was waiting for me to say something – to deny it all, perhaps. When I remained silent, unable to think of anything to say, he rambled on with the eerie calm of a lunatic wandering the streets, telling total strangers about Jesus.

'Do you know what I'm going to do now, West?' he asked, but I understood this to be even more rhetorical than his usual questions and kept quiet. My stomach flipped and knotted and I was glad I hadn't eaten that greasy sandwich or I might well have thrown up. 'I'm going to drive round to your house and I'm going to tell your lovely wife – what's her name? – what you've done. Or should I let you tell her? What do you think? Would that be better, seeing as you know all the details? I'd love to know exactly what went on that night. How a little piece of shit like you got Olivia Finch into bed. Did you get her so drunk that she was powerless to resist your advances? Or drug her? Fair play, though, you must have given her a fair old seeing-to to make her react like she has.' He was warming to his theme now, genuine enjoyment infiltrating his voice, all his hideous self-confidence returning.

'Then, after she's kicked you out of the house and locked the kids safely indoors to stop them saying goodbye – don't worry, you'll see them again at the custody hearing – I'll call Bill Davis and tell him what you've done. I'll ask if I can watch him fire you before he begs me to take my old job back. He owes me that at least. And then do you know what I'll do?' Again, he expected no reply and I obliged. 'Then, when I've fucked up your marriage and lost you your job, I'm going to take you somewhere nice and quiet – just the two of us – and kick your fucking lying, conniving head in.'

Bennett smiled, like a catless Blofeld. 'You've gone very quiet, Mr West. All out of answers?'

I had no doubt he would carry out each element of his

plan. My life was over. Before I could even begin to beg for mercy, he turned the ignition key and the powerful engine roared into life. His right foot stamped on the accelerator and he screeched out of the car park, flinging loose stones into the air and forcing a couple of middle-aged ladies to take evasive action as they wheeled their trolleys towards the first tee.

The two ladies glowered as they walked past me, as if Bennett and his inconsiderate actions were my responsibility. Perhaps they had a point. I stood and watched the departing car, kicking up dust as it sped away, paralysed into inaction. There was a throbbing in my brain that felt like a whole battery farm of chickens coming home to roost. Directed by Alfred Hitchcock. For a fleeting moment, the comforting thought that Bennett didn't know where I lived lodged itself in my mind, but just as fleetingly it was gone: he had called round to pick Sandra up from Natasha's book group several times over the years, and men like Bennett never forgot an address or a set of directions.

# THE NORTH CIRCULAR ROAD, NORTH LONDON

I got into my car and sat for a while, contemplating my fate. I considered every possible angle before reaching the obvious conclusion: I was fucked. Bennett had a head-start on me and would be driving much quicker than I would ever dare around London's crowded roads. Then it struck me – my one chance. Bennett might know where I lived, but he might not know the quickest route to get him there. If I turned off the North Circular Road and cut down through the back streets, I might still be able to get home before him. What I would do when I got there was still not clear, but at least that gave me a chance. I fired up the ignition and roared out of the car park like a latter-day Starsky or Hutch.

As I drove, I began to formulate a plan. I would ring Natasha and tell her to get the kids ready so we could all go out to lunch – somewhere with decent food but plenty for the kids to do. Once we were safely away from the house,

I would tell her that Bennett had gone crazy and I feared for our safety. I'd persuade her to take Helen and Matthew to her mother's for a few days while I dealt with the situation. This was starting to sound almost heroic – 'a man's got to do what a man's got to do' kind of stuff. It was starting to feel like a movie. And it could still have a happy ending.

I had been making good progress for a couple of miles and wasn't far from the junction where I would turn off the main road to weave my way, London cabbie-like, through the intricate network of residential streets, when the traffic started to slow and then ground to a complete halt.

'Bollocks!' I yelled over the radio's attempts to calm my soul with gentle Sunday tunes. I looked behind me to see if there was any way I could turn around and find a different route, but I was already hemmed in on all sides. It was possible, of course, that if I was caught in this then so was Bennett, but people like him didn't get caught in traffic jams. His car probably turned into a helicopter to fly above the melee of ordinary folk. Or perhaps he had arranged to have the traffic stopped for him by one of his mates in the Masons to make sure he could get to my house as quickly as possible.

A traffic bulletin came on the radio and I turned up the volume to listen as it made its leisurely way down from the northernmost tip of Scotland to the part of the country where all the people actually lived. There was no mention of my hold-up – this was just normal London congestion, even on a Sunday. Not as newsworthy as a tractor driving slowly towards Pitlochry. I turned off the radio and tried to think.

Bennett had left a couple of minutes ahead of me and

would have been driving faster to this point. If he had got through here before the traffic became impassable, then he would be arriving at my house any time now and there wasn't a damn thing I could do about it. I rested my head on the steering wheel, inadvertently sounding my horn. The thickset, bald-headed man in the car in front of me made an obscene gesture into his rear-view mirror and for a moment I feared he might get out of his car and attempt to pull me out of mine. Actually, at that moment, being beaten to death by an irate motorist didn't seem such a bad way to end my day.

Still not sure what I would say, I picked up my mobile and speed-dialled home. Natasha answered after three rings. Except that it wasn't Natasha but a digitally remastered, electronic version of my wife's voice telling me she wasn't there. Of course she wasn't there. She'd already be on her way to her mother's, having paused only to slice up all my suits with her dressmaking scissors and flush my treasured stamp collection down the toilet. Or she was there but was still listening to Bennett ruining my life – her life. Or perhaps he'd started to tell her his story, she'd tried to throw him out and he'd beaten her and the kids to death with one of his top of the range golf clubs.

I was starting to hyperventilate. I wound down my window to let some fresh air into the car and into my lungs and was immediately deafened by the wail of a siren as a police car flew past, travelling the wrong way down the opposite carriageway. The noise receded and then stopped altogether, suggesting that the car itself had come to a halt not too far ahead. A few moments later, another, even louder siren signalled the arrival of an ambulance. The traffic was still at a complete standstill and people had started to get out of their cars to see what was going on. I stumbled out of my car and pulled my jacket around me against the insistent drizzle.

The flashing lights of the emergency vehicles were no more than two hundred yards ahead, competing for attention with the red, amber and green of the traffic lights that marked the junction. It looked like a macabre seventies disco. I overheard one van driver explaining to the man in the Range Rover in front of him that it looked as if 'some twat had gone straight through the lights into the path of a bus'. As I walked a few yards further forward, his account was corroborated by the sight of a red double-decker leaning drunkenly against some badly damaged parked cars. Most of the windows in the front half of the bus – on both the upper and lower decks – were smashed and glass was strewn all around. A huddle of smartly dressed ladies, perhaps on their way home from church, stood nearby, shaking their heads or gently weeping. This wasn't what they'd spent their morning praying for.

A few yards further on I saw the shattered remains of a midnight-blue sports car, littering the road like a child's toy on Boxing Day. Police officers and paramedics were huddled around the wreckage, shielding its contents from the growing crowd as they worked out what had to be done. As I moved closer, drawn inexorably to the scene, I felt a sickness start in the pit of my stomach and then work its way down my legs until I could hardly propel myself forward. Somehow I knew, even before I saw the four interlocked rings on the grille, that the car was an Audi. Bennett's Audi.

A young policewoman walked towards me, clearing

people out of the way so that more emergency vehicles could get through.

'Can you tell me what's happened, please, officer?' I asked, my voice emerging as a thin, reedy squeak.

'Yes, sir. There's been what we call in the policing business a car crash,' she replied. 'Idiot thought he could beat the red light. We've been bloody lucky, mind – a second or two later and he'd have cut that bus clean in half. God knows how many casualties we'd have been looking at then.'

'So is everyone all right?' I asked, although I already knew that couldn't possibly be true.

'Everyone on the bus is,' she replied. 'Thank God. Driver's got a few cuts and bruises, but nothing to worry about.'

'The car driver? So he's going to be OK?'

'The car driver? Are you kidding me? You try driving into one of these bastards at sixty, mate. He's jumped his last red light, that's for sure. No, I meant the bus driver. He's pretty shaken up, of course, but he'll be fine in a day or two. Are you in this queue, sir?' she added, keen to get back to the job in hand. 'We're going to have a job clearing this lot.'

I walked slowly back to my car, sat down and rested my head on the steering wheel, taking care not to depress the horn – and wept.

# NEAR BRAINTREE, ESSEX

It was raining at Bennett's funeral, as it always seems to be at funerals. Weddings, too, come to think of it. The service was at a small church in a village near Braintree where Bennett had been born and grown up until he was exiled to boarding school, aged seven. The congregation was small, too – just immediate family, a handful of friends and acquaintances and a few representatives from the firm, led by Bill Davis. Dai Wainwright was also enjoying a day out. Clearly he needed to verify Bennett's death personally before he could close his HR file with a big black 'DECEASED' stamp and make sure that any unpaid bonuses were cancelled. Bennett's mother was there, of course, looking confused and forlorn, standing with a man I assumed to be Bennett's brother, who held an umbrella solicitously over her bowed head and hunched shoulders. Sandra was with them, shepherding her three boys, all dressed in matching deep blue suits, which would serve equally well for her cousin's wedding the following weekend.

We joined the huddle of people filing into the church and found a couple of seats on the end of a row a few pews from the front. Bill and Dai sat down behind us and we exchanged stage-whispered greetings. Bill leaned forward across the back of the uncomfortable bench. 'West, really glad you're here. Listen, Bennett's brother's asked me if I'd say a few words on behalf of Askett Brown about, you know, what poor Joseph was like as a colleague, but it's a bit embarrassing given how we parted company and everything. So I've told him you'll do it. Hope that's OK? I mean, you've known Bennett longer than anyone, haven't you? Dai tells me the two of you joined AB on exactly the same day. I bet you've got a few stories of your time as trainees together, haven't you? Nothing too near the knuckle, though, OK? Time and a place and all that.'

Natasha placed her hand on my thigh and squeezed it sympathetically, but I could see the amusement building in her eyes. 'Go on, love,' she whispered, 'I bet you've got some great stories to tell about your old pal Joseph Bennett!' In truth, the only anecdote I had from our halcyon days as young bucks learning the ropes together was hardly very amusing, even though it did give an accurate impression of the man we had definitely come to bury, not to praise.

It was our first day at Askett Brown. I'd been so keen to make a good impression that I hadn't even sat down on the Tube to make sure I didn't crease my new work clothes. I was scared to death as I walked into the office in my trainee accountant's uniform of blue pinstripe suit, light grey tie and black brogues, proudly carrying the real leather briefcase my parents had bought me to celebrate my first day of work, complete with the solid brass, six-number combination lock and my initials – J. E. G. W – embossed in gold letters below the handle. It was almost entirely empty, of course, except for an over-ripe banana, a new Parker rollerball pen and an old scientific calculator I'd had since my schooldays. But no one else needed to know that.

Bennett was one of the first people I saw – all six foot plus of him, dominating the room as if to the manor born – completely at home even on his first day, dominating every conversation, oozing confidence from every Aramis-infused pore.

When I came back from lunch my briefcase, which I had left under my desk, was now lying on top and I could see as I got closer that the corners, which had been in mint condition when I left it, were now scuffed, as if it had been used as an impromptu cricket bat while I had been gone. Then I saw that something was wrong with the gold mono-gram. Someone had scratched out the 'G' – not just Tippexed it or covered it with a sticky label, but scratched it out, permanently and irreversibly defacing what had been my proudest possession for the five hours since my parents had given it to me that morning.

Of course, I couldn't prove it was Bennett. Couldn't prove that he'd been the one to turn Joseph Edward George West into just plain J.E.W. I didn't have to. When he came back from lunch an hour later and the worse for several pints, he called everyone around to admire his handiwork. Inviting them to decide whether to laugh along with their new, self-appointed leader or condemn him for his hate crime. So they laughed, of course. No point getting on the wrong side of the alpha male on day one, was there?

I'll never forget the look on my parents' faces when I

told them I'd left the briefcase on the Tube. Mum cried, while Dad just shook his head sadly as if this confirmed everything he'd ever thought about me. But it had still been better to tell a little white lie than to tell them the truth: that the gift they'd saved so hard to buy and had presented to me so proudly that morning was already swimming with the fishes down the Thames.

No, that probably wasn't the right story for this occasion.

The vicar asked us to stand and the coffin made its sad journey down the central aisle, followed by Bennett's mother leaning on his brother for support as if her own legs wouldn't carry her, and then Sandra and the boys, her head held high, their shoulders weighed down by the tragedy that had struck their young lives. I wonder whether there's a physical limit to the number of emotions one can feel at any one time. That day I felt guilty, anxious, tired, melancholy, frightened and a dozen more – each one burrowing into my consciousness.

Sandra and the boys sat down at the front next to Bennett's mother and, after a few uninspiring words from the vicar, Nigel Bennett stood to pay his respects to his dead brother. The poor man tried his best but even on this saddest of days, he struggled to evoke any sense of fraternal closeness. There were no intimate family details or special nicknames to suggest youthful fun and good times; no amusing tricks played on each other or their parents. Just one quite chilling story about how his older brother had failed to stand up for him when he'd been bullied at school, preferring instead to stay in with the very boys who were doing the bullying. He spoke like a disengaged television reporter about Bennett's accomplishments at every sport to which he had ever turned a hand, whilst also being a brilliant scholar and prize-winning church chorister.

He didn't speak for long. After a few minutes, I heard him say 'and now we'd like you to join us in singing Joseph's favourite hymn and, after that, we'll hear a few words from Joseph's colleague and close friend, Joe West'.

Natasha couldn't help snorting at this, but managed to cover it up as a manifestation of grief escaping through her nose. As the sparse congregation slipped self-consciously into 'Onward Christian Soldiers' – an attempt so lacklustre and Godforsaken that I realised for the first time why the phrase 'extraordinary rendition' is often associated with programmes of state-sponsored torture – I tried to focus on what I would say. I had to choose my words carefully. I couldn't bear to see a hypocrite staring back at me in the shaving mirror every morning – as well as an adulterer, coward and liar. Our bathroom wasn't big enough for a party.

As the congregation tried valiantly to bring their song to a heavenly climax, I became aware of a disturbance at the back of the church. The background noise gradually rose from a polite murmur to an intense chatter and then a full-scale hubbub. The hymn petered out singer by singer until just one woman remained, blissfully unaware that hers was the last steadfast voice praising the Lord. Perhaps, I thought, she was deaf. She certainly sang as if she was.

Looking around, I immediately saw the cause of the commotion. A woman was walking down the central aisle of the church as if she was on the catwalk in Milan, wearing the kind of exclusive designer mourning apparel rarely seen outside of a Royal funeral or Goth wedding. Her simple black dress was short and cut tight around her thighs. Sleek black stockings drew the eye down to shiny black patent-leather shoes with three-inch heels. Removing my eyes, with some difficulty, from those legs, I looked up to where the apparition's face had been obscured by a heavy black veil protruding out of a black pill-box hat. Encased in black from head to toe, she looked like Darth Vader after an expensive makeover. The phrase '*Luke – I am your mother!*' arrived uninvited inside my head. The vision stopped a few rows behind me and took a seat at the end of the bench. The guy next to her, who I recognised from our Oil and Minerals Division, shuffled along to get even closer, grinning despite himself as if he'd won the Lottery. Two words could be heard now above the clamour, passing around the church like a rumour of war: 'Olivia Finch!'

I could see Sandra talking animatedly with her erstwhile mother-in-law, presumably explaining to her who this woman was, why she was there and why the hell she shouldn't be there. Nigel looked shell-shocked. The vicar talked excitedly with the organist, who may have been the only person in the room who didn't recognise the Hollywood superstar. I suddenly felt a desperate need to go to the toilet, preferably on Alpha Centauri. The only person who retained any semblance of composure was Natasha, who prodded me in the side and whispered, 'Oh my God! She's here! Go on, Joe, you'd better say something. And no jokes – OK?'

Panic, trapped, terrified, abject, with an uncomfortably full bladder – I was feeling many things but an urgent need to make jokes wasn't among them. I stumbled to the front of the church and stood beside Bennett's coffin, fervently wishing to be somewhere else – anywhere else but here. I felt like Bugs Bunny staring down both barrels of Elmer Fudd's shotgun. No, not Bugs Bunny – Bugs always got away. I was like that hapless halfwit Daffy Duck, and any second now Elmer was gonna blast every last feather from my scrawny body. Halfway back, the exquisitely dressed lady peered intently at me through the tight gauze of her veil. She cocked her head slightly to one side like an inquisitive spaniel, then lifted the dark mesh to get a better view.

Her first scream filled the church like thunder trapped in a barn. Each of the next three was louder and shriller than the last. After the second, the vicar, demonstrating the reactions of an octogenarian sloth, threw himself to the floor, as if convinced that the wrath of God had finally caught up with him. By the fourth, I imagine, he'd vowed never again to help himself to even a small percentage of the collection plate.

All eyes were now on Olivia, while I stood pinned to the spot like a frog in a science lab, scarcely able to breathe as I was dissected by her screams. Slowly she stood and stepped into the aisle. She advanced towards me, her veil still raised, her face a mask of confusion. Then she stopped and stood rooted to the floor in the middle of the church like a misplaced statue. Starting in a whisper that quickly rose to a statement, she looked straight at me, slowly raising a finger in accusation: 'Oh my God, it's him. It's you, isn't it? It is you.'

Only her eyes moved, swivelling in her head like Ophelia's in a drugs project production of *Hamlet*. I felt the ancient stone walls closing in around me as she inched her way forwards, closing the gap between the two of us with each tiny step. 'Oh English,' she said, 'oh my darling, lovely Englishman, what's it like? What's it like on the other side?'

Suddenly remembering how to move my legs, I shimmied behind the coffin, hoping to confuse people about whether Olivia was talking to me or my namesake in the wooden box. She was still moaning to herself as she tottered forward, asking over and over again what was happening on the other side, like someone who had mislaid their TV remote control.

Just when I thought the game was up – just when Olivia was almost close enough to reach out and touch me to test whether I was real or a ghostly apparition – I saw the expression in those mesmerising eyes go blank and every drop of colour drain from her face. And then, confronted by the spirit of her dead lover right there on the stage beside the coffin he was supposed to be occupying, Olivia's composure, decorum, and finally her legs, gave way and she tumbled in a dead faint to the floor.

Her head made a disconcerting clang as she hit the ground. She lay there for a moment not moving, her eyes open but expressionless. For one brief, horrible moment I thought that she, too, might be dead. That my selfish, vile, casual, unthinking act of adultery was turning into a massacre of the innocents.

A small crowd gathered around Olivia, and a man I didn't know, claiming some knowledge of first aid, felt the prostrate actress's wrist for a pulse and, having found one and established that she was still alive, started to loosen her clothing. An old lady stopped him when she felt that Olivia's clothes were quite loose enough and a posse of sturdy mourners was enlisted to carry her out of the church to the sanctuary of fresh air. The vicar announced in a shaky voice that everyone should proceed immediately to the cemetery for the committal. In the midst of the chaos, Natasha appeared at my side, grabbed my arm and led me out of the church.

'What was all that about?' she said as we walked towards the cemetery. 'What a nutcase! It was as if she could see Bennett up there with you. Utterly bizarre! She is either a bloody good actress or a total psycho. Perhaps she's both. She looked like she was going to attack you just for being so close to her beloved Bennett. I still can't believe that someone like her could be so hot for a total wanker like him.' She paused as she realised that we were now standing at the graveside, next to Nigel Bennett and his weeping mother. 'No disrespect,' she added.

After the coffin had been placed in its deep dark hole and a few sad sods of earth had been tossed onto it by Bennett's family, we made our excuses and left, declining the family's kind offer of wine and sandwiches at the local Conservative Club. Olivia had been spirited away by her driver who had taken the sensible decision that, for her, the funeral was over. Natasha drove us slowly home through heavy traffic and under leaden skies, chattering incessantly about the events of the day. My head ached and my spirit was weary. I wanted to be a child again – to be able to curl up with my head on my mother's lap while she made everything all right. Most of all, I wanted this all to be over. For all the lies and deceit to end. For my life to return to the dull, routine ordinariness I had always enjoyed before.

# MILL HILL, NORTH LONDON

For a few days after the funeral, things were quiet. Every day I left the house early to avoid Natasha's questions about what I thought had happened in the church and why I seemed so jumpy. Every day I waited for the phone call telling me that Olivia had recovered from her shock sufficiently to tell Buddy – or her shrink or the press – the whole sorry tale. And every day I'd arrive home late from work, drink a glass or two of wine while sitting silently through whatever Natasha was watching on TV, then lie awake long into each interminable night, wondering what I would do and where I would go after the inevitable shit hit the inevitable fan.

Then we did get some news. One morning, after another night when I'd arrived home from work long after Natasha had gone to bed, she greeted me at breakfast with a big kiss, hardly able to contain herself, dying to tell me the latest developments in what she still referred to as the 'Bennett Affair'.

'Did you hear the terrible news about Olivia Finch?' she asked, handing me a cup of strong black coffee.

I felt the blood freeze in my veins. My mind filled with images of Olivia lying naked on the bathroom floor of a fancy hotel, her crumpled body surrounded by empty pill bottles, blood leaking from self-inflicted wounds, her eyes wide with grief and shock, tears frozen forever on that sweet, innocent face. 'No,' I said, 'what is it? What's happened? What's she done?'

'Well, what do Hollywood stars usually do when their lives and careers are in ruins?' Natasha asked.

'I don't know. What is it?' I repeated, the panic rising, strangling any attempt at rational thought. 'She hasn't done anything stupid, has she?

'Pretty stupid, yes,' Natasha said, then paused, deepening my feelings of impotence and concern, before adding with a certain amount of relish, 'she's only gone and joined the bloody Scientologists!' She brandished one of her glossy magazines in my direction. 'I read it in here. She's convinced now it wasn't Bennett who shagged her that night in New York.'

I had stopped breathing some time ago and was now as desperate for air as I was for Natasha to miss the guilt tattooed across my face. 'No?' I managed to ask without inhaling or exhaling.

'No! According to this, she reckons it was L. Ron Hubbard himself who "embraced" her in the hotel, then miraculously manifested himself at Bennett's funeral. That was why she had such a fit. When she looked at you and screamed, she actually thought she was looking at old Ronnie. Isn't that hilarious! Here, look at this. It's on pages eight to twenty-four but the best bits are from page sixteen onwards.'

I took the magazine from her and did as I was instructed, skimming through pages of froth about Olivia Finch's extraordinary rise and precipitous fall, all beautifully illustrated with photographs from every stage of her life and career. There she was as a baby, then as a strikingly pretty young girl at a talent contest, and so on through her early film roles, her romances, her engagements and her awards. The narrative ran out at page twenty with the remaining pages filled with more pictures, including some recent, grainy ones of Olivia walking around the walled gardens of some kind of clinic. I flicked through quickly to the end, then handed the magazine back to Natasha. 'Shame,' I said in reference to Olivia's terrible decline. Or perhaps I was talking to myself.

Natasha was still chuckling quietly to herself as she turned the pages and studied the remaining photographs. Then she interrupted me again. 'Hey Joe, look at this.'

'What?'

'Look at the picture on page twenty-three – the one of Olivia getting into the back of a limo.'

She passed the magazine back to me and I looked where she was pointing.

'What about it?'

'The caption says it was taken after the *Nothing Happened* premiere in New York. That's the night you were there, isn't it? The night she's supposed to have started her affair with Bennett?'

I grunted in what I hoped was a non-incriminating way, but the panic was rising as I scanned the picture. It showed

Olivia sitting in the back of a vaguely familiar car. The back door was open and a man in a dinner suit was clambering in beside her. He was bent over so you could only see his bottom half and a foreshortened version of his upper body. His head, atop his hunched shoulders, was just a dark amorphous, unidentifiable blob.

'And?' I said, relieved. I couldn't be convicted on this evidence.

'Don't you notice anything odd about it?'

'She looks a little worse for wear, I suppose,' I replied. 'But it was a pretty late night. I expect she was just tired.' I passed the magazine back to Natasha with studied nonchalance and turned back to my newspaper.

'I wasn't looking at her,' Natasha persisted, pointing at the picture. 'Look at the guy with her. Does that look like Bennett to you? It's an odd angle, but he looks too short and fat to be Bennett. He may have been an arse but, to be fair, he did look after himself.'

The magazine was shoved back in my direction as if we were two diners fighting over the bill. I looked again. He didn't look fat to me – and five feet eight is hardly short. I had to admit he didn't look much like Bennett. What concerned me was whether he looked like anyone else. I took a closer look. The head was fine – too well hidden to be identified. The body, too, could have belonged to anyone of average build. It was only when I looked way down low that I spotted the problem. There it was: below the turned-up cuff of the man's left trouser leg, revealed as he stepped up into the car – in glorious, 4 million-pixel digital Technicolor – was Mr Silly, Mr Sodding Silly on my 'Have a Sodding Silly Saturday' sodding sock.

'*Fuck*!' I thought. 'Well,' I said, 'perhaps it's not Bennett. Maybe they met up later. Or maybe they've got the caption wrong and this is a different night.' I paused, aware I was in danger of protesting too much. I needed to change the tone of the conversation. 'Or maybe it's Old Ronnie Hubbard,' I said, 'the dirty little devil.'

It doesn't seem funny now, but it worked then. Natasha laughed, closed the magazine and went off to the kitchen to prepare breakfast. I waited until I was sure she was fully occupied force-feeding Matthew his Weetabix, then took a black felt-tipped pen from Helen's Angelina Ballerina pencil case and carefully coloured over that stupid, incriminating sock on page twenty-three of her stupid bloody magazine and placed it back where Natasha had left it.

# CITY OF LONDON

I didn't get much work done that day. Everyone in the office was still shocked by Bennett's death and the story of his funeral dominated the coffee-machine conversations. People I'd never spoken to before bombarded me with questions about the whole curious business. I was glad to have four solid walls to hide behind. I could escape into my new office, lock the door, pull down the blinds and ask Polly to hold all my calls. If anyone asked, she would tell them I was working on a strategic reorganisation of the division.

Late that afternoon, as I skulked in my office, hiding away from what passed for reality in the outside world, I was wrestled from my torpor by the insistent ringing of my phone.

'Polly,' I said, failing to hide my irritation, 'I thought I said no calls. What is it?'

'Sorry to disturb you, Joe, but I think you'll want to take

this one,' she said. 'I've got Buddy Guttenberg's office for you. They say he needs to speak to you urgently.'

'They always think everything's urgent,' I replied like a sulking child, but took the call. Ten minutes later I replaced the phone in its cradle. 'Bloody Hell!' I said.

# MILL HILL, NORTH LONDON

I left work early that evening, keen to get home and tell
Natasha about the call. 'Hi, love,' I said, kissing her
lightly on the lips as I entered the living room. 'I've got
some really exciting news for you. You'll never guess what.'

'What? No, don't tell me,' Natasha said, taking my coat
from me and hanging it in the cloakroom. 'Bennett has
risen from the dead and taken over as head of the firm?'

'No,' I replied, 'even more amazing than that.'

'Go on then,' said Natasha, gently brushing Matthew
away as he tried to fly one of his planes between our legs,
'amaze me!'

'Buddy's offered me a job,' I said, watching my wife's face
closely to gauge her reaction, 'in LA. Executive Vice-
President of Production Finance. Half a million dollars a
year, plus bonus, healthcare, car. The whole nine yards, as
we'd say if we were living out there. It could be a new start
for us, a whole new way of life.'

Natasha's expression had remained pretty rigid as I'd been saying all this but now it reconfigured itself into a quizzical grimace. 'Why do we need a new start or a new life? What's wrong with what we've got here?'

'Nothing,' I replied, 'but wouldn't it be a fantastic opportunity. Think of all that sunshine, cruising along Sunset Strip in a top-of-the-range convertible, the kids going to a school like in *Beverly Hills 90210*. More money than we'd know how to spend in the shops on Rodeo Drive . . .'

'Drugs, knife crime, gangs, guns . . .'

'Not where we'd be living, love. We'd be in some fantastic villa high up in the Hollywood Hills, looking down on all that from our hot tub on the terrace. How would you like that, guys?' I said directly to the children. 'Living in America for a while? Swimming in our own pool every day after school?'

'Yay!' yelled Helen and Matthew simultaneously, already starting to sound like American kids.

'Don't bring them into it,' said Natasha, 'not yet. Not until we've had a proper chat about it. I'm sure I could be persuaded, but it's a hell of a move to think about. What about all our friends over here, and my mother?'

'We'd make new friends out there. And we could hire you a new mother. We could pay Meryl Streep to pop round once a fortnight and kvetch at us for a couple of hours. You wouldn't notice the difference after a while. And Buddy promised me he would personally spray us with cold water every day so we wouldn't miss the London weather.'

Natasha smiled and I sensed she might be starting to warm to the idea. 'I know,' I said, 'why don't I pop out and buy us a huge Chinese meal to celebrate. Even if we decide not to go, it's nice to be asked, isn't it?'

'OK, love,' said my wife, 'you do that. I'll tidy up in here. Are you OK if I chuck all these papers into the recycling?'

'Of course I am. And make the most of it – a couple of months from now, we'll have a maid to do all that for us!'

I left Natasha sorting through a pile of papers and magazines, deciding which ones were ready for pulping and which could decorate our living room for another couple of weeks. I drove the short distance to the Chinese takeaway and spent a small fortune ordering all of our favourites: half an aromatic crispy duck, sesame prawn toast, pancake rolls, prawn crackers and spare ribs for starters, followed by far too many main courses for the four of us to get through. As I waited for my order to be delivered, I imagined what I would say to Bill Davis when I handed in my notice. To lose one Head of Entertainment and Media might be unfortunate; losing two in a matter of months would definitely be considered careless. That would give him and that blood-sucking Welsh ghoul Dai Wainwright something to think about!

I collected my order and walked back to the car, whistling 'I'm a Yankee Doodle Dandy'. If I hadn't been carrying two overloaded plastic bagsful of monosodium glutamate, I would have attempted one of those hitch kicks that Jimmy Cagney used to do, clicking my heels together in mid-air to demonstrate my new-found happiness to the watching world. All the anxiety of the past few months had been lifted, leaving me feeling more content and at ease than I could remember.

Of course, moving to LA and working for Buddy carried

301

with it the risk that I might bump into Olivia – and even that, at some point, the whole sorry story might come out – but, having survived this long, that didn't seem too likely. Buddy had told me that, thanks to a potent combination of therapy and cod-religion, Olivia was recovering well from her traumatic experience at the funeral. He was pretty confident that she would soon be able to start working on the sequel to *Nothing Happened*. She never mentioned Joseph Bennett and considered that chapter of her life closed. LA was a big place and it wouldn't be too difficult to ensure that our paths never crossed. After all, she was talent and I was just a money-man. A backroom boy. An ordinary joe.

As I drove slowly home through the busy early-evening streets, I made myself a solemn vow: never again would I look at another woman – not even on the cinema screen. From that day forward, I pledged, my dreams and fantasies would feature only my wife: Natasha with her skirt blowing up around her waist as she stood on a subway ventilation grate; Natasha emerging from the surf in a skimpy leather bikini; Natasha floating out of control in her spacecraft as her clothes fell away from her.

To my amazement – it really was my lucky day – I found a parking space right in front of our house, carefully balanced the bags of food on my thigh as I pressed a button on the key fob to lock the car and walked down my front path, bursting with a renewed exuberance and joy. I still felt guilty about what had happened to Bennett – and to Olivia, too – but my priority now was to make sure that nobody else suffered because of my stupid, selfish actions. I had done something unforgivable and wrong and had had to dodge a fusillade of bullets, but now it felt like everything would work out for the best. Tomorrow would be another day. Life could still be wonderful. As wonderful as in the movies.

I rang the doorbell with my shoulder and waited for the door to open. I would let the comforting warmth of our meal thaw Natasha a little more before I returned to my campaign of persuasion, I decided. LA was famous for *its* Chinese food – just imagine the banquets we would enjoy over there!

The door opened and I looked into the eyes of my wife standing at the entrance to our home. Not the smiling, welcoming eyes I had been expecting, but red-rimmed, crying eyes – eyes filled with accusation, enmity and fear. I heard the snuffling of a distraught child and looked down to see Helen hugging one of her mother's legs while Matthew gripped the other, his hands wearing what looked at first glance like glove puppets but on closer inspection I realised were a pair of black socks. Black socks with a picture of Mr Silly and the motto 'Have a Silly Saturday' embroidered in red cotton upon them. Slowly, I looked back up, forcing myself to take Natasha's stare.

'You bastard,' said my wife, holding up a finger stained black with ink, 'you lousy, cheating bastard.'

# A HUGE THANK YOU . . .

. . . to everyone who has helped *Ordinary Joe* on the long journey from inside my head to into your hands – and that begins with you, Dear Reader, for doing me the honour of choosing to read my story when there are so many others you could have chosen. You would not be reading these words now but for the help and support, inspiration and perspiration of many, many people.

In the beginning were my parents, my brothers and sisters who put up with me when at times it must have been tempting to have me put down instead. So this is for you Sidney, Stephanie, Julie, Mike, Pete and Kate (and all my assorted nephews, nieces and in-laws). There is no greater fortune in life than to be born a Teckman.

This is also for my wonderful wife Anne who took on the mantle of principal carer in my adult years and kept me going when all I really wanted to do was stop, and still found time to raise our two amazing boys, Joseph and

Matthew. Without the three of you, this really wouldn't have been worth doing.

This novel first began to see the light of day at an Arvon Foundation course way back in 2007. Some of my earliest critiques and encouragement came from that group of Amazing Writers. My thanks to Anne, Kathy, Chris, Joel, Claire, Jan, Lisa and Charlene.

My first big breakthrough came when I was selected to attend the inaugural Curtis Brown Creative six-month novel-writing course. Many thanks to Anna Davis, Christopher Wakling, Rufus Purdy and all the CBC team for choosing me and for all your constructive, instructive advice. Thanks also for introducing me to the most extraordinary group of fellow writers, all of whom gave me invaluable feedback on the developing manuscript. I won't be truly fulfilled until I am reading the acknowledgements pages in your novels: Chris, Dan, Eleanor, Fran, Jacquie, Jayne, Karen, Lauren, Mariko, Olivia, Sally, Sam, Sara and Tim.

It is no small challenge to fight your way through an improperly formed, unedited, as yet unpublishable manuscript but many people did just that for me with earlier drafts of this work. Some of you even made it right through to the end! Your comments and enthusiasm gave me great confidence to carry on. I'm sorry that I don't have the space to mention you all individually but you know who you are and I really cannot thank you enough.

Many thanks also to David Parfitt and Ivan Mactaggart at Trademark Films who know a good story when they see one and saw one in *Ordinary Joe*. And to my great friend Steve Abbott who acted in *loco agencis* for me, offering much needed and always sage advice whenever it all became too complicated for me.

And finally, and in many ways foremostly, you would not be reading these words if it hadn't been for Katie Espiner and her fantastic team at Borough Press who took the courageous decision to pluck me from mid-life crisis obscurity and make my dream come true.

Thank you.

*Jon Teckman*
*July, 2015*